CALLANDER SQUARE

Anne Perry

FAWCETT CREST ● NEW YORK

CALLANDER SQUARE

This book contains the complete text of the original hardcover
edition.

Published by Fawcett Crest Books, a unit of CBS Publica-
tions, the Consumer Publishing Division of CBS Inc., by arrangement with St. Martin's Press, Inc.

ISBN: 0-449-24365-6

Printed in the United States of America

First Fawcett Crest printing: January 1981

10 9 8 7 6 5 4 3 2 1

ONE

The autumn air hung mild and faintly misty, and the grass in Callander Square was dappled yellow with fallen leaves in the late afternoon sun. In the small garden in the center of the square two men stood with spades, looking down into a shallow hole. The taller of them bent down and put his hands into the damp soil, searching. Gingerly he brought up the article he sought, a small, bloody bone.

The other breathed out noisily.

"What d'yer reckon it is, then? Too big to be a bird."

"Pet," the first replied. "Someone buried a dog, or the like."

The shorter man shook his head. "They didn't oughter do that." He looked disparagingly at the pale Georgian facades rearing up in severe elegance beyond the lacy birch leaves and the limes. "They got gardens for that sort of thing. They oughter have more respect."

"It musta bin a small dog," the taller man turned the bone over in his hand. "Maybe a cat."

"A cat! Go on. Gentlemen don't 'ave cats; and ladies don't go digging in gardens. Wouldn't know a spade if it up an' bit 'em."

"Must 'a' bin a servant. Cook, most like."

"Still didn't oughter do it," he shook his head to emphasize his point. "Like animals, I do. A pet what 'as done 'er service in the 'ouse oughter be buried proper: not where people's going to go and dig 'er up again, unknowing like."

"They mightn't 'a' thought we was going to dig 'ere. It's years since we put anything new in this bit. Wouldn't 'a' done now, except we got this bush give us."

"Well we'd better put it somewhere else: a bit over to the left p'raps. Leave the poor little thing in peace. It ain't right

5

to disturb the dead, even animals. Dare say someone cared for it. Kept someone's kitchen clean o' mice."

"Can't put it to the left, yer gawp! We'll kill the forsythia."

"You watch yer tongue! Put it to the right then."

"Can't. That rhode-thing grows like a house, it does. Got to put it 'ere."

"Then put the cat under the rhode-thing. Dig it up proper, and I'll do the burying."

"Right." He put his spade where he judged it would bring the body up in one piece and set his weight on it. The earth came up easily, soft with loam and leaf mold, and fell away. The two men stared.

"Oh Gawd Almighty!" The spade fell from his hands. "Oh Gawd save us!"

"What—what—is it?"

"It's not a cat. I—I think it's a baby."

"Oh Holy Mother. What do we do?"

"We'd better get the police."

"Yeah."

He let the spade down slowly, very gently, as if somehow even now it mattered.

"You going?" The other stared at him.

"No. No, I'll stay 'ere. You go and get a constable. And 'urry! It'll be dark soon."

"Yeah! Yeah!" He was galvanized into action, desperately relieved to have something to do, above all something that would take him away from the hole in the ground and the bloody little mess on the spade.

The constable was young and still new to his beat. The great fashionable squares overawed him with their beautiful carriages, their matched pairs of liveried footmen and armies of servants. He found himself tongue-tied when he was required to speak to them, the magisterial butlers, the irascible cooks, the handsome parlormaids. The bootboys, the scullery maids, and the tweenies were much more his class.

When he saw the hole in the ground and the gardeners' discovery he knew it was totally beyond him, and with horror and relief, told them to wait where they were, move nothing,

6

and ran as fast as his legs would carry him to the police station to hand the whole thing over to his inspector.

He burst into the office, abandoning his manners in the excitement.

"Mr. Pitt, sir, Mr. Pitt! There's been a dreadful thing, sir, a terrible thing!"

Pitt was standing by the window, a big man with long, curved nose and humorous mouth. He was plain to a degree, and quite incredibly untidy, but there was intelligence and wit in his face. He raised his eyebrows at the constable's precipitate entrance, and when he spoke his voice was beautiful.

"What sort of dreadful thing, McBeath?"

The constable gasped; he could not utter a coordinated sentence for his lack of breath.

"A body—sir. In Callander Square. Pitiful, sir—it is. They just found it now—the gardeners—dug it up. In the middle. Planting a tree, or something."

Pitt's face puckered in surprise.

"Callander Square? Are you sure? You haven't got lost again, have you?"

"Yes, sir. No, sir, right in the middle. Callander Square, sir. I'm positive. You'd better come and see."

"Buried?" Pitt frowned. "What sort of body?"

"A baby, sir." McBeath closed his eyes and suddenly he looked quite ill. "A very small baby, sir, like newborn, I think. Reminds me of my kid sister, when she was born."

Pitt breathed out very slowly, a sort of private sigh.

"Sergeant Batey!" he said loudly.

The door opened and a uniformed man looked in.

"Yes, sir?"

"Get an ambulance and Doctor Stillwell and come to Callander Square."

"Someone been attacked, sir?" His face brightened. "Robbed?"

"No. Probably only a domestic tragedy."

"A domestic tragedy?" McBeath's voice rose in outrage. "It's murder!"

Batey stared at him.

"Probably not," Pitt said calmly. "Probably some wretched

7

servant girl seduced, kept it to herself, and gave birth alone, and the child died. She'd bury it and tell no one, nurse her grief to herself, so she wouldn't be put out on the streets with no job, and no character to get another. God knows how many times it happens."

McBeath looked pale and pinched.

"Do you think so, sir?"

"I don't know," Pitt answered him, going toward the door. "But it wouldn't be the first time, nor the last. We'd better go and see."

It took Pitt the last half hour of daylight to look at the little body, poke round in the crumbly soil to see if there were anything else, to help identify it, and find the second, misshapen, cold little body. He sent the doctor and the ambulance away with them both, and a shaking, white-faced McBeath home to his rooms, then Batey and his men to post guard in the gardens. There was nothing else he could do that night until the doctor had given him some information: how old the babies had been, how long ago they had died, as near as could be estimated, and if possible what had been wrong with the second, deeper buried one to cause that misshapen skull. It was too much to hope they could tell now from what they had died.

He arrived at his own home in the dark and the fine, clinging dampness of fog. The yellow gaslights were welcoming, promising warmth not only to the body, but to the mind, and the raw, vulnerable feelings.

He stepped inside with an acute sense of pleasure that nearly two years of marriage had not mellowed. In the spring of 1881 he had been called to the horrifying case of the Cater Street hangman, the mass murderer of young women, who garroted them and left their swollen-faced bodies in the dark streets. In that dreadful circumstance he had met Charlotte Ellison. Of course at that time she had treated him with the dignified coolness any such well-bred young woman would use toward a policeman, who was rather lower in the social scale than a moderately good butler. But Charlotte was a girl of terrifying honesty, not only toward others, causing a social chaos; but toward herself also. She had acknowledged her

8

love for him, and found the courage to defy convention and accept him in marriage.

They were poor, startlingly so compared with the considerable comfort of her father's home, but with ingenuity and her usual forthrightness she had dispensed with most of the small status symbols without which her erstwhile friends would have considered themselves bereft. Occasionally when his feelings were raw on the matter, she joked that the relief from pretense was a pleasure to her; and perhaps it was at least half true.

Now she came from the small drawing room with its sparse, well-polished furniture and autumn flowers in a glass vase. Her dress was one she had brought with her, wine colored, a little out of fashion now, but her face glowed and the lamplight picked out all the warm mahogany tones in her hair.

He felt a quick surge of joy, almost of excitement, as he saw her and reached out immediately to touch her, to kiss her.

After a moment she pulled back, looking at him.

"What is it?" she asked with a lift of anxiety in her voice.

In the quick, enveloping warmth of meeting he had forgotten Callander Square. Now the memory returned. He would not tell her; heaven knew, after Cater Street there was little of horror that she could not cope with, but there was no need to distress her with this. She was quick to sympathy—the little bodies, whether crime or simple tragedy, would stir her imagination to all the pain, the isolation and fear, whatever lonely, terrible thoughts had possessed the mother.

"What is it?" she repeated.

He put his arm round her and turned her back to the drawing room, or perhaps parlor would have been a less pretentious name for it, in so small a house.

"A case," he replied, "in Callander Square. It will probably prove to be very little, but tedious in the proof. What have we for dinner? I've been outside and I'm hungry."

She did not press him again, and he spent a slow, sweet evening by the fire, watching her face as she bent in concentration over her sewing, a piece of linen worn beyond its

9

strength. Over the years there would be much patching and making do, many meals without meat, and when the children came, hand-me-down clothes; but it all seemed only a comfortable labor now. He found himself smiling.

In the morning it was different. He left early when the October mist still clung round the damp leaves and there was no wind. He went to the police station first, to see if Doctor Stillwell had anything to tell him.

Stillwell's dour face was even longer than usual. He looked at Pitt sourly, bringing with his presence an immediate reminder of death and human mutability.

Pitt felt the warmth slip away, the comfort he had woken with.

"Well?" he asked grimly.

"First one quite normal, as far as I can tell," Stillwell said quietly. "Which isn't very far. Been dead about six months I should judge, poor little thing. Can't tell you whether it was born dead, or died within a day or two. Nothing in the stomach." He sighed. "Can't even tell you if it died naturally or was killed. Suffocation would be easy, leave no marks. It was a girl, by the way."

Pitt took a deep breath.

"What about the other, the one lower down?"

"Been dead a lot longer, nearer two years, from what I can tell. Again, that's pretty much of a guess. And again, I don't know whether it was born dead, or died within a few days. But it was abnormal, I can tell you beyond doubt—"

"I could see that myself. What caused it?"

"Don't know. Congenital, not an injury in birth."

"Would there be something in the parents' history—?"

"Not necessarily. We don't know what causes these things. Children like that can be born to anyone, even in the best families; it's just that they more often manage to keep it quiet."

Pitt thought for a few moments. Could that be what it was, a matter of social embarrassment?

"What about the top one?" He looked up at Stillwell. "Was that one deformed as well, anything wrong with its brain?"

Stillwell shook his head.

10

"Not that I could see, but of course if it were going to become mentally defective, there would be no way of telling at that age. It was no more than a few days old at the most. It could even have been born dead," he frowned. "Although I don't think so. There wasn't anything I could see to cause death. Heart, lungs, and intestines seemed quite normal. But of course it was to some extent decomposed. I really don't know, Pitt. You'll just have to make your own inquiries, and see what you can find out."

"Thank you." There was nothing else to say. Pitt collected Batey and in silence they set out in the misty morning, the tree-lined streets smelling of rotting leaves and damp stone.

Callander Square was deserted; the sightseers such a discovery might have provoked elsewhere were abashed to invade its elegant pavements. There was no sign of life in the great houses except the whisk of a broom on an area step and the hollow sound of a footman stamping his boots. It was too early for errand boys; the cooks and parlormaids would barely have finished serving breakfast to the later risers.

Pitt went to the nearest house, up the steps, and knocked discreetly at the door, then stepped back.

Several minutes later it was opened by a well-built, darkly handsome footman. He looked at Pitt with heavy-lidded, supercilious eyes. Years of training had taught him to sum up a man even before he opened his mouth. He knew instantly that Pitt was a little better than a tradesman, but far from being a man of birth, let alone a gentleman.

"Yes, sir?" he inquired with a faint lift of his voice.

"Inspector Pitt, police." Pitt met his eye levelly. "I would like to speak to the mistress of the house."

The footman's face was impassive.

"I am not aware that we have suffered any burglaries. Perhaps you have come to the wrong house? This is the residence of General Balantyne and Lady Augusta Balantyne."

"Indeed. I did not know that. But it is the situation of the house that makes it of concern to me. May I come in?"

The footman hesitated. Pitt stood his ground.

"I'll see if Lady Augusta will see you," the footman conceded reluctantly. "You had better come in. You can wait in

11

the morning room. I shall discover if her ladyship has finished her breakfast."

It was a long, irritating half hour before the morning room door opened and Lady Augusta Balantyne came in. She was a handsome woman with bone china elegance of feature, and dressed in expensive and classic taste. She looked at Pitt without curiosity.

"Max says that you wish to see me, Mr.—er—"

"Pitt. Yes ma'am, if you please."

"What about, pray?"

Pitt looked at her. She was not a woman with whom to prevaricate. He plunged straight in.

"Yesterday evening two bodies were dug up in the gardens in the middle of the square—"

Lady Augusta's eyebrows rose in disbelief.

"In Callander Square? Don't be ridiculous! Bodies of what, Mr.—er?"

"Pitt," he repeated. "Babies, ma'am. The bodies of two newborn babies were found buried in the gardens. One was about six months ago, the other nearer to two years."

"Oh dear," she was visibly distressed. "How very tragic. I suppose some maidservant—To the best of my knowledge it is no one in my household, but of course I shall make inquiries, if you wish."

"I would prefer to do it myself, ma'am; with your permission." He tried to make it affirmative, as though he were assuring her agreement rather than asking her permission. "Naturally I shall be calling at all the houses in the square—"

"Of course. My offer was merely a matter of courtesy. If you discover anything that involves my household, naturally you will inform me." Again it was a statement and not a question. Authority sat on her easily, long a familiar garment, and she had no need to display it.

He smiled acknowledgment, but he did not commit himself in words.

She reached for the bell and rang it. The butler appeared.

"Hackett, Mr. Pitt is from the police. There have been two babies found in the gardens. He will be questioning the servants in all the houses. Will you please find him a quiet room where he can speak to any of the staff he wishes? And see that they make themselves available."

"Yes, my lady." Hackett looked at Pitt with distaste, but obeyed precisely.

"Thank you, Lady Augusta," Pitt inclined his head and followed the butler to a small room at the back which he supposed to be the housekeeper's sitting room. He obtained a complete list of the female staff, and the essentials of information about each one. He did no more than speak to them this time. Everyone showed shock, dismay, pity; and everyone equally denied all knowledge. It was exactly what he had expected.

He was in the hall, looking for either the butler or one of the footmen to say he was finished, for the time being, when he saw another young woman coming out of one of the doorways. There was no possibility she was a servant; far more suggestive of her position than her silk gown or her beautifully dressed and coiffed hair was the hint of swagger in her walk, the half smile on her full-lipped little mouth, the sureness, the suppressed excitement in her dark, fringed eyes.

"Goodness!" she said with mock surprise. "Who are you?" She raked him up and down with an amused, blue glance. "You can't be calling on one of the maids, at this hour! Have you come to see Father? Are you an old batman, or something?"

Only Charlotte had ever shaken Pitt's composure, and that was because he loved her. He looked back at this girl steadily.

"No, ma'am, I am from the police. I have been speaking to some of your servants."

"From the police!" her voice rose in delight. "How perfectly shocking. Whatever for?"

"Information." He smiled very slightly. "That is always what the police speak to people for."

"I have a suspicion you are laughing at me." Her eyes were bright. "Mr.—?"

"Inspector Pitt."

"Inspector Pitt," she repeated. "I am Christina Balantyne; but I suppose you knew that. What are you asking questions about? Has there been a crime?"

13

Pitt was saved from having to compose an answer at once civil and uncommunicative by the breakfast room door opening and a man coming out whom Pitt assumed to be General Balantyne. He was tall, nearly as tall as Pitt himself, but tighter knit, of stiffer bearing. His face was smooth-boned, lean, and aquiline. It was a striking head; too arrogant to be handsome, too strong of jaw and teeth.

"Christina!" he said sharply.

She turned.

"Yes, Papa."

"The policeman's business with the servants can hardly be of interest to you. Have you no letters to write, or sewing to do?" The question was academic; it was a dismissal. She accepted it with a straight back and stiff lip.

Pitt hid a smile and bowed his head fractionally.

"Thank you, sir," he said to the general after she had gone. "I was unsure how to answer her without distressing her with unpleasant facts." It was something less than the truth, but it served well for the moment.

The general grunted.

"Have you finished?"

"Yes, sir. I was looking for the butler to say so."

"Discover anything?" the general looked at him with quick, intelligent eyes.

"Not yet, but I have only just begun. Who lives next door?" He gestured toward the south side of the square.

"Reggie Southeron next to us," the general replied. "Then young Bolsover at the end on this side. Garson Campbell on the other; Leatitia Doran opposite Southeron; opposite us on the far side is vacant at the moment. Has been for a couple of years. Sir Robert Carlton on the far side, and an elderly fellow called Housmann, a complete recluse. Has no women in the house, hates them; all male staff."

"Thank you, sir, most helpful. I'll try Mr. Southeron next."

Balantyne took a sharp breath, then let it out. Pitt waited, but he did not add anything.

The Southeron house was busier—he heard the light laughter of children even before he had reached for the bell-pull. It was opened by one of the handsomest parlormaids he had ever seen.

14

"Yes, sir?" she said with perfect formality.

"Good morning, I am Inspector Pitt from the police; may I speak to either Mr. or Mrs. Southeron?"

She stepped back.

"If you would like to come in, sir, I'll inquire if they will see you."

He followed her into the hall, beautifully furnished, but less Spartan than the Balantynes'. There were baubles on the hangings, richly upholstered chairs, and even a doll sitting carelessly on a small side table. He watched the straight back of the parlormaid, and the becoming little twitch of her skirt as she walked. He smiled to himself; then hoped with a sudden acute stab of pity that she was not the one, that it was not the result of her seduction, her brief yielding to passion, buried out there under the trees.

She showed him into the morning room and left him. He heard a scampering of feet on the stairs—a tweeny maid, or a child of the house? There was probably little difference in age; some girls began their life in service at no more than eleven or twelve.

The door burst open and a thin, blue-eyed little face looked in. Her total composure proclaimed her immediately as a daughter of the house. Her hair was tied up in ringlets and her skin was scrubbed clean.

"Good morning," Pitt said solemnly.

"Good morning," she replied, letting the door swing open a little farther, her eyes still fixed on his face.

"You have a very elegant house," he said to her with courtesy, as if she had been an adult, and the house hers. "Are you the mistress?"

She giggled, then straightened her face with quick recollection of her position.

"No, I'm Chastity Southeron. I live here, since my Mama and Papa died. Papa was Uncle Reggie's brother. Who are you?"

"My name is Thomas Pitt, I'm an inspector of police."

She let out her breath in a long sigh.

"Has somebody stolen something?"

"Not as far as I know. Have you lost something?"

"No. But you can question me," she came into the room. "I might be able to tell you something." It was an offer.

He smiled.

"I'm sure you could tell me a great deal that is interesting, but I don't know what questions to ask, yet."

"Oh." She made as if to sit down, but the door opened again and Reginald Southeron came in. He was a wide man, fleshy-faced and comfortable.

"Chastity?" he said with good-humored exasperation. "Jemima will be looking for you. You should be at your lessons. Go upstairs this moment."

"Jemima is my governess," Chastity explained to Pitt. "I have to do lessons. Are you coming back?"

"Chastity!" Southeron repeated.

She dropped a tiny curtsey to Pitt and fled upstairs.

Southeron's attitude stiffened slightly, but the good humor did not leave him.

"Mary Ann says you are from the police." He sounded faintly disbelieving. "Is that so?"

"Yes, sir." Again there was no point in circumlocution, and Pitt explained his visit as simply as he could.

"Oh dear," Reggie Southeron sat down quickly, his rather florid face paling. "What an—a—" he changed his mind and began again. "What a shocking affair," he said with more composure. "How very distressing. I assure you I know nothing that could be of help to you."

"Naturally," Pitt agreed hypocritically. He looked at the man's wide mouth, sensuous jowls, and soft, well-manicured hands. No doubt he knew nothing of the bodies in the square, but if he knew nothing of their conception it might be more by good fortune than intent. "But I would like your permission to interview your staff," he asked.

"My staff?" The momentary discomposure returned.

"Belowstairs gossip is invaluable," Pitt said easily. "Even those who are in no way involved may know something, a word here or there."

"Of course. Yes, yes, I suppose so. Well, if you must. But I should be obliged if you would not upset them more than is absolutely necessary; so difficult to get good staff these days. I'm sure you understand—no—no—of course not—you

16

wouldn't." He was oblivious of patronage. "Very well. I suppose it is unavoidable. I'll get my butler to see to it." He hauled himself to his feet and went out without saying anything further.

Pitt spoke to all the staff one by one, informed the butler, and took his leave. It had occupied the best part of the morning and it was already time for lunch. In the afternoon he returned to the square. It was two o'clock when he knocked at the third door, which, according to General Balantyne, should be that of Dr. and Mrs. Frederick Bolsover. During lunch he had seen Stillwell again, and asked him if he knew of Bolsover professionally.

"Hardly in my category," Stillwell had pulled a face. "Probably makes more in a month than I do in a year. Must do, to live in Callander Square. Society doctor, comforting a lot of hypochondriac ladies who have nothing more interesting to do than contemplate their health. Nice practice, if you have the patience, and the manners, and from what I hear Bolsover has. Good family, good start, all the right connections."

"Good doctor?" Pitt had asked.

"No idea." Stillwell's eyebrows had gone up. "Does it matter?"

"Not in the least, I should think."

The Bolsovers' door was opened by a somewhat surprised parlormaid, small and pert, but in her own way almost as attractive as the last one. Of course, parlormaids were chosen for their looks. This one regarded Pitt with some dismay. He was not the sort of person admitted to the front door, and this was not the time of day for callers; he was at least an hour to an hour and a half early, and it was usually ladies who called for the afternoon social ritual.

"Yes, sir?" she said after a moment.

"Good afternoon. May I speak with Mrs. Bolsover, if she is at home. My name is Pitt; I am from the police."

"The police!"

"If I may?" He moved to step inside and she retreated nervously.

"Mrs. Bolsover is expecting callers," the maid said quickly. "I don't think—"

17

"It's important," Pitt insisted. "Please ask her."

The girl hesitated; he knew she was concerned in case he was still there when the lady callers arrived, thus embarrassing her mistress. After all, respectable people did not have the police in the house at all, let alone at the front door.

"The sooner you ask her, the more quickly I shall be able to finish my business," Pitt pointed out persuasively.

She saw his argument and scurried off to comply; anything to get him off the doorstep.

Sophie Bolsover was a pretty woman, not unlike her own parlormaid, had the girl been dieted a little, dressed in silk, and her hair curled and coiffed.

"Good afternoon," she said quickly. "Polly says you are from the police."

"Yes, ma'am." He respected her social embarrassment and explained his business as rapidly as possible, then asked her permission to speak to her servants as he had done in the other houses. It was granted hastily and he was almost physically bundled into the housekeeper's parlor to conduct his inquiries safely out of sight. He began with the parlormaid Polly, to leave her free for her afternoon duties as soon as the first caller should arrive.

He learned nothing but names and faces; he would store them all in his mind, consider them, rule out the impossibilities. Perhaps the sheer tension, the presence of the police in the house, would frighten someone into indiscretions, mistakes. Or perhaps they would never find out what sordid affair, or private tragedy of love and deceit, lay behind the small deaths.

The Campbells and the Dorans were, as General Balantyne had said, not in residence at the moment. He passed the vacant house, ascertained that the reclusive Housmann did indeed employ only menservants, and it was after four o'clock when he knocked at the last door—that of Sir Robert and Lady Carlton.

It was opened by a startled parlormaid.

"Yes, sir?"

"Inspector Pitt, from the police." He knew he was intruding, as it was the most inconvenient of all times to call, the time when the rigid etiquette of the social hierarchy was observed to the letter, the intricacies of rank, whether one called to visit, or merely left a card, whether calls were acknowledged, returned, who spoke to whom, and on what terms. To have the police at such a time was unforgettable. He endeavored to make his presence as inoffensive as possible. They could not have been taken by surprise. Backdoor gossip would long ago have reached them carrying his purpose, whom he had seen, what had been asked, probably even a minute description of him and an acute assessment of his precise social status.

The parlormaid took a deep breath.

"You had better come in," she stepped back, surveying him with anxiety and disapproval, as if he might have brought crime in with him like a disease. "Come through to the back, we'll find a place for you. The mistress can't see you, of course. She has callers. Lady Townshend," she added with pride. Pitt was ignorant of Lady Townshend's importance, but he endeavored to look suitably impressed. The parlormaid saw his expression and was mollified. "I'll get Mr. Johnson," she added. "He's the butler."

"Thank you." Pitt sat down where she pointed and she swept out.

At home Charlotte Pitt had attended to the ordering of her house, which took her no more than an hour, then had immediately dispatched her single housemaid to purchase a daily newspaper so that she might discover what it was that Pitt would not tell her. Previous to her marriage she had been forbidden by her father to read such things. Like most other men of breeding he believed them vulgar and totally unsuitable for women. After all, they carried little else but crime and scandal, and such political notions as were undesirable for the consideration of women, as well, of course, as intellectually beyond them. Charlotte had had to indulge her interest by bribery of the butler or with the connivance of her brother-in-law, Dominic Corde. She smiled now to think how she had loved Dominic in those days, when Sarah was still alive. The smile vanished. Sarah's death still hurt, and the passion for Dominic had long ago cooled to friendship. She had been shocked and dismayed to discover she was in

19

love with this awkward and impertinent policeman who had told her so disturbingly of a world she had never previously acknowledged, a world of petty crime and desperate, grinding poverty. Her own blind comfort had become offensive to her, her judgments had changed.

Of course her parents had been shaken when she had informed them she intended to marry a policeman, but they had accepted it with as good a grace as possible. After all, she was something of a liability on the marriage market, with her unacceptable frankness. She was handsome enough, in fact Pitt thought her beautiful, but she had not sufficient money to overcome her waywardness and her undisciplined tongue, devastating disadvantages in the eyes of any gentleman of her own station. Her grandmother had given up all hope and was dismally convinced poor Charlotte was destined to become an old maid. And there was the compensation of Emily having married a lord! And with the social stigma of a murder in the house, the Ellisons were no longer a family with whom one chose willingly to contract an alliance!

Pitt was a great deal firmer with Charlotte than she had expected; indeed, in spite of his being deeply and unashamedly in love with her, he was quite as insufferably bossy as all the other men she knew. She was amazed, to begin with, and even fought him a little, but in her heart she was quite glad of it. She had barely dared to admit it to herself, but she had been a little afraid that because of his devotion to her, and their previous relative social positions, he might have let her ride over him, bend his will to hers. She was secretly delighted to discover he had no intention of doing anything of the kind. Of course she had cried, and made an exhibition of both temper and hurt in their first quarrel. But she had gone to sleep with singing happiness inside her when he had come to her gently, taking her in his arms, but utterly and finally refusing to allow her her own way.

But he had never objected to her reading the newspapers, and as soon as the maid returned with the copy of today's she scrambled through it, fingers flying to find some reference to a crime in Callander Square. She did not find it the first time and had to search more diligently before she discovered a small piece, barely two inches long, stating simply that two bodies of babies had been found in the gardens, and a domestic tragedy among the maidservants was suspected.

She knew immediately why Pitt had concealed it from her. She herself was newly expecting their first child. The thought of some servant girl, alone, desperate not to lose her livelihood, deserted by a lover—the whole thing was appalling. She felt cold at the imagining of it. Yet when she put the paper down she was already determined not to drive it from her mind. Perhaps she would be able to help the girl, if she were thrown out. It was a possibility: not herself, of course, she had no position to offer. But Emily! Emily was rich—and she had a deep suspicion she was also just a little bored. It was two years since her marriage also, and she had by now met all George Ashworth's friends of any importance; she had been seen well dressed in all the fashionable places. Perhaps this would arouse her. Charlotte decided on the spot. This afternoon she would call upon Emily; early, so as not to collide with her more socially elite callers, and before Emily herself might be out.

Duly at two o'clock she presented herself at the front door of Emily's London house in Tavistock Square.

The parlormaid knew her and admitted her without asking explanation. She was shown into the withdrawing room where there was a fire lit already and barely a moment later Emily herself came in. She was already dressed for her afternoon visiting; she looked magnificent in pale apple green silk with dark brown velvet ribbons. It must have cost more than Charlotte would have spent on clothes in half a year. Her face was alight with pleasure. She kissed her sister delicately, but with genuine warmth.

"Goodness, if you're going to take up calling, Charlotte, I shall have to teach you what time to begin! It is not done to arrive before three at the very, very earliest. Ladies of rank, of course, later still."

"I haven't come calling," Charlotte said quickly. "I wouldn't think of it. I came to ask your help, if you can give it; and of course you are interested."

Emily's honey-colored eyebrows rose, but her eyes were bright.

"In what? Not a charity, please!"

21

Charlotte knew her sister too well to have come on such an errand.

"Of course not," she said sharply. "A crime—"

"Charlotte!"

"Not to commit, goose; to help, when it is solved."

Even Emily's new sophistication could not hide her excitement.

"Can't we solve it? Can't we help? If we—"

"It's not a nice crime, Emily, not a robbery or something clean," Charlotte said hastily.

"Well, what is it?" Emily did not look disconcerted. Charlotte had forgotten how composed she was, how easily she adapted to the unpleasantnesses of life. Indeed, from the day she had decided she would marry Lord George Ashworth, she had accepted frankly that he had faults and that she might never eradicate more than a few of them, but she made her decision and settled for the bargain as it was. She had never complained. Although in truth Charlotte did not know if she had any cause.

"Goodness, Charlotte," Emily prodded. "Is it so dreadful you cannot put tongue to it? I never before knew you at a loss for words."

"No. No, it is merely very sad. Two babies' bodies were dug up in the garden in the center of Callander Square."

Surprisingly, Emily was shaken.

"Babies?"

"Yes."

"But who would want to kill a baby? It's insane."

"A servant girl who was unmarried, of course."

Emily frowned.

"And you want to find out who it was? Why?"

"I don't want to find out who it was," Charlotte said impatiently. "But if they were born dead, as seems well possible, perhaps you might be able to find her another position, if she were dismissed—"

Emily stared at her, thoughts flashing in her face almost as transparently as they crossed her mind.

Charlotte waited.

"I know someone who lives in Callander Square," she said at last. "At least George does—Brandy Balantyne. His father

22

is a general, or something. I'm sure they live in Callander Square. He has a sister, Christina. I shall have George introduce us; it can be arranged, with a little thought. Then I shall call on her," her voice began to rise with excitement. There was a faint color in her cheeks and a set of determination about her head. "We shall discover the real truth. I can learn things the police never could, because I move in the right circles. They will speak to me. And you can speak to the servants; oh, the higher-up ones, of course—cook and governess, and the like. You won't tell them you are a policeman's wife, naturally. We shall begin immediately. As soon as George returns home I shall speak to him and he will arrange it!"

"Emily—"

"What? I thought you wanted my help. We cannot possibly know what is best to do if we do not know the truth. It is always best to know the truth, whether you then decide to dismiss it or to conceal it, or even to forget about it entirely. But if we do not know the truth to begin with, we can make the most unfortunate mistakes."

Charlotte looked at Emily's dancing eyes and every shred of common sense in her told her to refuse instantly.

"We shall have to be very discreet." Common sense suffered a quick defeat.

"Of course!" Emily was withering. "My dear Charlotte, I could not possibly have survived in society for two whole years if I had not learned to say everything but what I actually mean. I am the soul of discretion. We shall begin right away. Go home and discover whatever you can. I don't imagine you can be discreet, you never could; but at least don't volunteer our plans. Mr. Pitt may not approve."

That was an understatement of magnificence. Nevertheless, Charlotte stood up with every intention of obeying, a tingle of fear inside her, and a thin quiver of Emily's excitement.

TWO

The following day Pitt went back to Callander Square, hoping to interview the servants in the last two houses, but it was not until the early afternoon that they returned from their long weekends in the country. Consequently it was nearly three o'clock when he was shown by the Campbells' butler into the back parlor and, one by one, saw the rest of the servants. Of course they were expecting his questions—the news must have been virtually waiting for them on the doorstep in the shape of scullery maid, tweeny, or bootboy bursting with the events and their own rich interpretations of them.

Pitt learned nothing new, and he was ready to leave when he met the mistress of the house. The Honorable Garson Campbell was a younger son of a family of wealth and position, and he had maintained a lifestyle appropriate to it. Mariah Campbell was a pleasant looking woman in her late thirties, with broad, good-humored face and fine, hazel eyes. She had been busy unpacking and organizing her family, which she explained hastily, comprised a son, Albert, and two daughters, Victoria and Mary. She showed considerable distress on hearing of the purpose of his questions. Apparently the gossip had not reached her, and she begged that he would be discreet enough that the children might not come to hear of it.

"I assure you, ma'am, I should not dream of introducing such a subject to a child," he said honestly, although he forbore to say that if some child should mention the matter to him, he would not be averse to listening. He had usually found children much less affected by death than adults. And it was a rare child indeed that was not inveterately inquis-

25

itive, and would have extracted from the servants every last detail that was to be had, or even invented and embroidered upon.

"Thank you," she said courteously. "Children can be—hurt," she was looking out of the window, "and frightened. There is so much that is ugly. The least we can do is protect them from it as long as we are able."

Pitt was of a totally different opinion. He believed that the longer you hid from the truth the less able you were to cope with it when it finally broke through all the barriers, like a dammed river, and carried away the careful structure of your life with it. He opened his mouth to argue, to say that a little at a time bred some tolerance to pain, a balance; but remembered his place. Policemen did not give advice in the upbringing of children to ladies who lived in Callander Square. In fact, policemen did not philosophize at all.

"I'm afraid, ma'am, that they may well hear it from the servants," he said gently.

She frowned at him.

"I shall forewarn the servants," she answered. "Any servant who mentions such a thing will lose his or her position."

Pitt spared a thought for the unwitting maid who in a careless, garrulous moment might yield to childish insistence, or even petty blackmail, and thus lose home and job at one blow. Childhood would have given her no such protection from the unpleasant realities of life.

"Naturally," Pitt agreed sadly. "But there are other servants in the square, ma'am; and other children."

Instead of the anger he had expected, she merely looked suddenly tired.

"Of course, Mr.—Pitt, did you say? And children will tell each other such gruesome stories. Still, I'm sure you will not frighten anyone unnecessarily. Do you have children of your own?"

"Not yet, ma'am. My wife is expecting our first." He said it with a ridiculous sense of pride and waited for her approval.

"I hope everything goes well with her." There was no light in her face. "Is there anything else I can tell you?"

He was at a loss, deflated.

"No, thank you. I shall almost certainly have to return;
26

it may take us a long time to solve it, if we ever do. But that is all for today."

"Good afternoon, Mr. Pitt. Jenkins will show you to the door."

"Good afternoon, ma'am." He bowed very slightly and went out to the waiting butler and the front door into the leafy square.

The Doran house was utterly different from the other houses in the square. It was unbelievably cluttered with photographs, embroidery, flowers dried, cased in glass, pressed, growing in pots, and even some fresh and arranged in painted vases. There were also at least three birds in cages, all hung with fringes and bells.

The door was opened by a middle-aged parlormaid. This one was an exception to the generality: by no twist of the imagination could she have been chosen for her looks; except that when she opened her mouth her teeth were perfect, and her voice was as rich and smooth as Devon cream.

"We've been expecting you," she said calmly, with a faint southwestern distortion of the vowels. "Miss Laetitia and Miss Georgiana are taking tea. No doubt you will be wanting to speak to them first, as a matter of course." She did not seem to require an answer to that, and turned away, leaving him to close the door and follow her into the inner recesses.

Laetitia and Georgiana were indeed taking tea. Georgiana was displayed fragilely on a chaise longue, bony as a halfpenny rabbit, and dressed in delicious mauves and grays. Tea was balanced on a three-toed, piecrust table at her elbow. She looked at Pitt without displeasure.

"So you are the policeman? What an odd-looking creature you are, to be sure. Pray do not be vulgar with me. I am extremely delicate. I suffer."

"I am sorry to hear it." Pitt controlled his face with an effort. "I hope to disturb you very little."

"You have already disturbed me, but I shall put up with it in good grace, in the name of necessity. I am Georgiana Duff. This," she pointed to a slightly younger, better-upholstered version of herself in the other chair, "is my sister, Laetitia Doran. She is the one to have the misfortune, or the

27

ill-judgment, to own a house in such a disastrous place; so you had better address your remarks to her."

Pitt turned to Laetitia.

"Indeed, Mrs. Doran, my apologies again; but owing to the tragic discovery in the gardens, I am sure you understand it is necessary for us to question the servants, especially the younger, female servants, in all the houses that face onto the square."

Laetitia blinked.

"Of course," Georgiana said sharply. "Is that all you've come to say?"

"To ask your permission to speak to your servants," Pitt replied. Georgiana snorted. "You'll do it anyway!"

"I would prefer to do it with your permission, ma'am."

"Don't keep calling me 'ma'am.' I don't like it. And don't stand there towering over me. You make me feel quite giddy. Sit down, or I shall faint!"

Pitt sat down, stifling a smile.

"Thank you. Have I your permission to interview your servants?" he looked at Laetitia.

"Yes, yes I suppose so," she said uncomfortably. "Please endeavor not to upset them. It is so hard to replace a servant satisfactorily these days. And poor Georgiana must be properly looked after."

Pitt privately thought that "poor Georgiana" would see to it herself that, come hell or high water, she would be properly looked after.

"Of course," he stood up again and moved to the door before Georgiana had time to feel affected by his presence. "Have you had any servants dismissed in the last half year, young women who have left the house?"

"None," Laetitia said quickly. "We have been exactly as we are for years! Years and years!"

"You have no children, ma'am? Daughters who have married and taken a lady's maid with them?"

"None at all!"

"Thank you. I shan't need to disturb you again," he went out and closed the door softly.

He remained in the Doran house for two hours, but he learned nothing there either.

Charlotte was perfectly correct, Emily was beginning to find that the fashionable life lacked something, a certain bite, for which she was increasingly developing a taste. Beyond question, she enjoyed her life; it was the ideal mode of existence for her. When she and Charlotte were still at home in Cater Street with Mama and Papa, when poor Sarah was alive, Emily had known precisely what suited her. She had determined from very early in their acquaintance that she would marry Lord George Ashworth; and a very satisfactory arrangement it had proved. Of course George had his faults, but then what man did not? His overriding virtue was that he appreciated her, and was constantly both generous and civil; and he was undoubtedly handsome to look at, and witty when he chose. It would be pleasant if he would gamble a little less, it was a shocking waste of money. But if he flirted, he was eminently discreet about it, and he very seldom went out without inviting Emily also; and he did not nag her as to her occupations or the female society she kept. And that was a considerable point in his favor. Emily knew any number of wives who were forever being left at home while their husbands went to places wholly unsuitable for a woman of any decency at all, and yet criticized them for extravagance or for the afternoon parties they themselves put on.

But undeniably there was a certain lack, a purposelessness to her present round. Since she was Lady Ashworth, she had already done with relative ease all the social climbing she desired, at least for the moment. Charlotte's disgusting mystery might prove to be just the diversion she required, and it had the additional advantage of being genuinely helpful to someone, if the wretched girl were ever found!

And also, she was very fond of her sister. Of course Charlotte was socially impossible! It would never do to introduce her to the afternoons, the dinners, and the balls she herself attended; although on some of the more pompous occasions she had frequently found it passing through her mind to wonder what Charlotte might have said, had she been there. This affair would also give her an opportunity for them to do something together, which in itself would be pleasant.

When George returned, in time to change for dinner, she abandoned her dignity and scampered up the stairs after him. He turned at the top in surprise.

"What's the matter?"

"I want to meet Christina Balantyne," she said immediately.

"Tonight?" He was incredulous, a smile on his elegant mouth. "She's not all that amusing, I assure you!"

"I don't want to be amused. I want to be invited to her house, or at least to be able to call without obviously seeking her acquaintance."

"Whatever for?" His eyebrows went up over his dark eyes. "Is it Augusta you want to meet? Very grand, Augusta. Her father was a duke, and she's lived up to it all her life; not that it is any effort, I think."

It was not the reason, but it seemed an excellent explanation to adopt.

"Yes, I would. Please, George?" she smiled at him frankly.

"You'll be disappointed. You won't like her," he looked down with a faint frown.

"I don't care about liking her, I just want to be able to call!"

"Why?"

"George, I don't press you about your friends at White's, or Boodle's, or wherever it is; let me entertain myself by calling upon whom I please." She smiled at him with a mixture of charm, because she genuinely liked him, and honesty, because the pretense between them was wholly one of manners, and there was no real deception.

He patted her on the cheek and kissed her.

"It should be easy enough to look up Brandy Balantyne, and he's an amiable fellow. In fact he's the best of his family, by a long way. You'll be disappointed in the others, I warn you!"

"Maybe," she smiled seraphically, utterly satisfied. "But I wish to discover for myself."

It was three days before Emily's plans bore fruit and she was able to dress carefully in muted browns with gold trimmings and fur muff against the cold, and set out to call upon

30

Christina Balantyne. Her attire seemed to her precisely the right mixture of dignity and assurance, coupled with the quality of friendliness that a lady of title could afford to extend toward someone who was very nearly of her own social rank, but not quite. She had also taken the trouble to ascertain that Christina would be at home this afternoon: and that had required some delicate detective work through her lady's maid, who just happened to have scraped an acquaintance with the lady's maid of a certain Susanna Barclay, who was in the habit of calling at Callander Square herself. Indeed, there lay more in common between Emily and Mr. Pitt than Pitt would have imagined.

Emily duly bade her carriage with its footmen wait, and presented herself at the door of the Balantynes' house at quarter to four. It was opened by the parlormaid, as was the custom in the afternoon. Emily smiled charmingly, took her card from its ivory case, and held it out in an elegantly gloved little hand. She was proud of her hands.

The parlormaid took it, read it without appearing to, and returned the smile.

"If your ladyship would be pleased to come in, Lady Augusta and Miss Christina are receiving in the withdrawing room." It was an unusually voluble greeting, and could only be accounted for by the fact that Emily was a viscountess, and had not called before, therefore her visit in person, instead of merely leaving a card, was something of an honor; and a good parlormaid was as well versed in the niceties of social distinctions as her mistress.

She did not knock at the door, such would have been considered vulgar, but pushed it open and announced Emily.

"Lady Ashworth."

Emily was agog with curiosity, but naturally she concealed it with a magnificent dignity. She sailed into the room looking neither to right nor left, holding out her hand. There was a slight flutter among the half dozen or so ladies present, a natural interest quickly stifled by protocol. It was not done to display such an unsophisticated emotion.

Lady Augusta remained seated.

"How charming," she said with a slight lift in her voice. "Pray do sit down, Lady Ashworth. So gracious of you to call."

31

Emily sat down, arranging her skirt almost absently, but precisely to its best advantage.

"I'm sure we have many mutual friends," Emily said noncommittally. "It must be only chance that we have not met before."

"Indeed," Augusta would not commit herself either. "I know you are acquainted with my daughter, Christina." It was a statement. Emily looked across at the pretty face of Christina with its soft little chin and full lips. It was an unusual face; far more important than beauty, it had individuality, and considerable provocation, a face that men would no doubt find attractive. It promised both appetite and yielding. But then men were incredibly foolish where women were concerned. Emily could see at a glance the hardness in the balance of the pert nose and the curve of the lips. A taker, not a giver, Emily judged. She stored her decision, and turned to the next woman to whom Augusta was already directing her.

"Lady Carlton," Augusta was saying. "Sir Robert is in the government, you know, the Foreign Office."

Emily smiled across. This woman was entirely different, wide-mouthed, less pretty, warmer. But now her hands were knotted in her lap, and there were the finest of lines round her eyes and mouth. She was older than Christina, perhaps even in her middle thirties, and there was a nervousness, a tension underlying the pleasantness. She and Emily exchanged inclinations of the head and a polite recognition. Others were introduced and conversation began; first about the weather, which was exceptionally gentle for late October, then about fashion, and thence into the truly interesting area of gossip. Tea was served at four o'clock, brought in by the parlormaid and poured by Lady Augusta.

Emily contrived to engage herself with Christina and Euphemia Carlton. Without difficulty the subject of the bodies in the square was introduced.

"Quite shocking," Euphemia shivered. "Poor little souls." A bleak look passed over her face.

"I daresay they knew nothing about it," Christina answered realistically. "I understand they were newborn. In fact they may even have been born dead."

32

"They still had souls," Euphemia stared into the distance.

Emily felt a quick flicker of excitement, and a peculiar distress. Could this be it, so soon, so very easily? Was it guilt in Euphemia Carlton's face? Find out more about her. Why should she have done such a fearful thing? Indeed, why should any married woman of wealth and quality? As soon as possible she must ask Charlotte more about the babies. Had they been black, or of some other startling appearance that would betray infidelity?

"I assume you do not know about our little piece of horror," Christina was speaking again.

"I beg your pardon?" Emily turned an innocent face to her.

"Our horror," Christina repeated. "The bodies buried in the square."

"Only the few fragments you have mentioned," Emily lied without an atom of compunction. "Pray, if it does not distress you, oblige me with a little information." It was not, of course, that she imagined Christina knew anything that Charlotte had not already told her, indeed less; but she wished to see Euphemia's reaction to the retelling, and of course Christina's, if it were of any note.

"Little to tell," Christina began instantly. "The gardeners were digging to plant a tree, or some such, and discovered these dead bodies of babies. Naturally they sent for the police—"

"How do you know?" Emily inquired.

"My dear, from the servants, of course! Where does one ever learn anything that goes on, of any interest? And then the oddest policeman came round. Really, you never saw such a creature, all arms and legs and hair! I swear no barber ever took hand to it, far less comb or scissors. Or perhaps the working classes don't have barbers. And he was perfectly enormous!"

Emily smiled within herself at this view of Pitt, not wildly inaccurate. She would have recognized him from it.

"Imagine my surprise," Christina went on, "when he opened his mouth and spoke most civilly to me. Had I not seen him, I might have taken him for a gentleman."

"Surely he didn't question you?" Emily looked suitably

shocked, principally to exercise some emotion strong enough to override her amusement.

"Of course not! I merely chanced to see him in the hall. He has been questioning all the servants, all round the square. I imagine it must be some unfortunate girl who cannot control herself." She looked down for a moment, as if an embarrassment had caught her. Then she raised her head and the brilliance was back in her eyes. "Rather exciting, having detectives in the place. Of course Mother thinks it is all too macabre, and will lower the tone of the neighborhood. But I imagine people will understand. After all, everyone has servants. These problems are bound to occur. Ours is just a little more gruesome, that's all!"

Euphemia was pale, and it was obvious she did not wish to continue the subject. Emily rescued her.

"I'm sure they will," she agreed. "Lady Carlton, Lady Augusta said your husband is in the government. I imagine you must have to be most careful about your servants, only the most discreet."

Euphemia smiled.

"Sir Robert very seldom brings home work that is of a confidential nature; but of course it is important that servants are discreet as to conversations overheard at dinner, and so on."

"How exciting!" Emily feigned girlish delight, and pursued the subject until her tea was finished and it was the appropriate time to take her leave. She must make other calls, or it would appear she was too eager. A cultured woman of society never restricted herself to one visit. She would call on at least one other, and leave her card at two more.

She excused herself, her mind whirling to find some assured way of returning to Callander Square, if possible within the week.

"So charming," she murmured to Lady Augusta. "George has spoken so well of you, it was delightful to meet you," to remind her that George was a friend of Brandy Balantyne's and that they were of the same social circle.

"Most gracious of you," Augusta replied absently. "We are having a small entertainment this Friday afternoon. If you

34

have no previous engagement, perhaps you would care to call in?"

"How very pleasant," Emily said equally nonchalantly. "I believe I shall."

She swept out with a feeling of infinite satisfaction.

The following afternoon she put on a plain green dress, took a single unliveried footman, and went straight to Charlotte. It was far easier than waiting for Charlotte to come to her; for one thing, Charlotte did not have the use of a carriage, and had to resort to the hire of a hansom. The other reason, of course, was that she simply could not wait.

She burst in upon Charlotte, who was busy mending linen.

"What on earth are you doing?" she demanded. "Put it down, and listen to me!"

Charlotte held the linen in her hand.

"I thought ladies did not call before three? It is hardly a quarter past two," she said with a smile.

Emily snatched the linen and threw it on the sofa.

"I have the most exciting news!" she said urgently. "I have been to the Balantynes' and I have made the acquaintance of Christina and Lady Augusta; and infinitely more interesting, of a Lady Euphemia Carlton, who is peculiarly discomfited by talk of the babies in the square! I truly believe she knows something about it. She is laboring under some burden, I will swear to that! Charlotte, do you think I have solved it already?"

Charlotte looked at her seriously.

"Is Lady Carlton not married?"

"Of course she is married!" Emily said impatiently. "But perhaps she is having an affair. Perhaps the children, the babies, would have betrayed it! Were they of any unusual appearance, such as a dark skin, or red hair, or the like?" Emily drew breath and rushed on before Charlotte had time to consider the question and reply. "Her husband is in the government. Perhaps it is a foreign lover, a Greek or an Indian or something. Maybe there are secrets involved. Charlotte, what do you think? She is very handsome, you know; not beautiful, but warm. She looks as if she might well fall in love and behave quite irresponsibly."

Charlotte looked back at her, thought deep in her face.

"I shall have to ask, but I doubt Thomas will tell me—"

"Oh, don't be so feeble!" Emily said exasperatedly. "Don't tell me you can't persuade him! The man is besotted on you. Invent some reason! I need to know, else why should she do it? A woman does not kill her own children, or even bury the stillborn, without some overpowering reason."

"Of course not," Charlotte agreed reasonably. "But Thomas will not imagine I ask out of idle curiosity. He is not as amiable as George, you know; nor anything like as innocent," she added.

Emily had never thought of George Ashworth as innocent; but on consideration she realized what Charlotte meant; only perhaps it was not so much lack of guile as lack of concern. He considered he knew what Emily would do in any given situation, and had explicit trust in her good sense. Pitt, on the other hand, had far more perception than to trust anything so erratic as Charlotte's good sense.

"Nevertheless, you will try," she persisted.

Charlotte smiled, her thoughts inward.

"Of course. I have always expressed an interest in his work. I shall endeavor to help him." Her smile broadened. "With a woman's point of view, which of course he cannot get from his policemen."

Emily gave a sigh of relief that left Charlotte laughing.

By the time Emily arrived in Callander Square on Friday afternoon she had heard from Charlotte the rather disappointing news that there was nothing remarkable about the appearance of the second baby, but a deformity of the head of the first one, the one buried the deeper. But her heart had lifted when Charlotte pointed out that since the unfortunate bodies had been in the earth for some time, it was impossible to tell if at birth they might indeed have had skin or hair of an unusual color. Emily had not considered the point of putrefaction, and the thought of it distressed her unexpectedly. Of course, the flesh would not remain. In fact, Charlotte pointed out that, according to Pitt, it was only the clay nature of the soil that had preserved them so far. It was an extremely disagreeable consideration.

She had dismissed it from her mind when she presented herself at the Balantynes' door. She was admitted immediately and was shown from the hall into the great reception room where a small crowd had already gathered, of both men and women. An enormous gleaming grand piano stood in the center, its legs decently masked. At a glance Emily saw Christina, Euphemia Carlton, Lady Augusta, and several others she knew from her own social round. She also recognized Brandy Balantyne, tall, slender, dark like his mother and sister, but with an easier face, outward looking. He turned as Emily entered and his face lit in a smile.

"Lady Ashworth, how delightful," he came forward to welcome her, ushering her in. "Do you know Alan Ross? No. Alan's misfortune."

"Mr. Ross," she acknowledged him with grace. He bowed a little formally. He was in his thirties, slight of build but with a strong, delicate face of unusual intensity.

"Lady Ashworth, I am honored," he offered no further compliment, and she was rather pleased. Flattery could become a bore. It was, after all, no more than a formula in the mouth of most men, as automatic as "good morning" or "goodbye."

They fell to discussing some innocuous subject, none of them paying more than cursory attention. Emily let her eyes stray to Euphemia Carlton. She was piqued to see that today the woman looked uncommonly well, indeed it would hardly be an exaggeration to say she glowed. Could the tension and the guilt Emily had seen before have been no more than an indisposition? Emily dismissed the thought. It was too early to tell.

She accepted a delicate refreshment from a crisp-aproned maid. There was a footman over by the door—a handsome man, in a heavy-lidded, sensuous sort of way. Emily had seen the same features on dandies and spendthrifts leaving George's clubs, the big winners and losers. That man would have been one of them, had his birth been kinder to him. Now he stood against the wall of a general's house, dressed in livery and waiting on ladies and the few gentlemen who had nothing better to do with this particular afternoon. She saw Christina Balantyne walk past him, laughing, as obliv-

37

ious of his humanity as if he had been a piece of furniture, a carving to hold flowers.

The entertainment began, first a rendition of a waltz by Chopin, more precise than lyrical; then a rather wavering contralto sang three ballades. Emily forced a look of rapt attention on her face, and let her mind wander.

She had not been introduced to Sophie Bolsover, but she had overheard her name in a neighboring conversation, and knew that she also lived in Callander Square. Now Emily looked sideways at her, partly from interest, partly because it was easier to keep her face straight when not looking directly into the contralto's earnest eyes. Sophie Bolsover was a type she had become familiar with over the last couple of years; still very young, pretty enough by nature for art successfully to concentrate on her good features and mask the poor ones. She was born of a good family with enough money to insure a satisfactory marriage. She had never had to fear being left an old maid, dependent; she had not had to fight the way ahead of numerous sisters in a female-ridden house. All this Emily knew from the calm, rather shallow assurance in her face.

As soon as the songs were finished and suitably applauded, Emily made a point of seeking her acquaintance. Emily was charming, skilled, and quite ruthless in such social arts. Within five minutes she was conversing with Sophie about fashion, mutual acquaintances, and speculation as to who might marry whom. Emily guided the considerations toward those resident in the square, beginning with a compliment toward Christina.

"So beautiful," Sophie agreed with a smile.

Emily would have quarreled with the choice of words; Christina was fashionable, appealing, to men certainly, but not beautiful.

"Indeed," she said confidentially. "No doubt she will be able to take her pick of offers."

"I thought at one time she might have married Mr. Ross," Sophie inclined her head very slightly toward Alan Ross, who was talking earnestly to Euphemia Carlton. "But of course he has never got over poor Helena," Sophie went on.

Emily's ear sharpened.

"Helena?" she inquired with a masterly attempt at indifference. "Did some tragedy befall her?"

"She is never spoken of," Sophie said somewhat inconsequentially.

Emily's interest grew even keener.

"My dear, how fascinating! By whom is she never spoken of?"

"Why Laetitia Doran, of course." Sophie opened her eyes wide. "Helena was Laetitia's only child. Georgiana did not live with her then, naturally."

"She came—afterward?" Emily pieced it together.

"Yes, to console her."

"For what?"

"What? Why, when Helena ran away. Eloped—so they say. What an irresponsible and foolish thing to do! And such a shame to her mother."

"With whom did she elope? Why did she not marry him? Good gracious, was he a servant, or something?"

"Who knows? Nobody ever saw him!"

"What? You cannot mean it?" Emily was incredulous. "Was he so appalling she dared not—oh my gracious! He wasn't already married, was he?"

Sophie paled.

"Oh dear, I do hope not. How perfectly dreadful! No, I shouldn't think so. She was very beautiful, Helena, you know. She could have had her choice among—oh, I don't know how many men. Poor Mr. Ross was quite stricken when she went away."

"Did he know about it?"

"Of course. She left a letter saying she had run off. And of course those of us with any sense knew perfectly well she had an admirer. Women know that sort of thing. I remember I thought it rather romantic, at the time. I never dreamed it would end so awfully."

"I don't see that it is so very dreadful," Emily replied with a little frown, "if she ran off and married him somewhere else. Perhaps he was someone her mother did not approve of, but who loved her. A trifle silly, I agree; especially if he did not have any money; but not entirely fatal. Romantic loves are a little impractical, when it comes to day to day living, paying the cook and the dressmaker and so on. But if one has good sense, it can be quite bearable. One of my sisters married a considerable degree beneath her, and seems to be disgustingly happy on it. But she is an unusual creature, I will be the first to grant."

"Is she really happy?" Sophie raised her eyebrows in interested surprise.

"Oh yes," Emily assured her. "But you and I would find it quite dreadful. Perhaps Helena is like her, but feared her mother's objections, so simply took the easiest way out."

Sophie's face brightened.

"What a delicious thought! Perhaps she is in Italy, married to a fisherman, or a gondolier, or something."

"Do you have many gondoliers calling in Callander Square?" Emily asked politely.

Sophie stifled a rich giggle, and then looked about her in dismay at her own social gaffe—the spontaneous laughter, not the idiotic question.

"How deliciously refreshing you are, Lady Ashworth," Sophie said through the fingers over her mouth. "I'm sure I've never met anyone so witty."

Emily felt a withering reply to that rise to her lips, but she merely smiled.

"Poor Mr. Ross," she said noncommittally. "He must have been very devoted to her. Was it long ago?"

"Oh, it must be well over a year, perhaps closer to two years."

Emily's heart sank. Helena Doran had sounded like an excellent possibility as a suspect. With Sophie's answer she receded into profound unlikelihood. She looked instinctively across the room at Euphemia. There was a man with her whom Emily had not seen before, a man of considerable distinction, perhaps fifty-five or sixty years old.

"Who is that most elegant gentleman with Lady Carlton?" she asked.

Sophie's eyes followed hers.

"Oh, that's Sir Robert! Did you not know?"

"No," Emily shook her head slightly. He must be at least twenty years older than his wife—a most interesting fact. "I think I should be a little in awe of so grand a husband," she said carefully. "He looks so very—important. He is in the government, is he not?"

"Yes, indeed. You know, I believe I should also. How perceptive you are. You put so excellently into words exactly what was in my mind, had I but known it."

Emily was hot on the scent.

"I should not think him a great deal of fun," she pursued.

"No, indeed." Sophie looked her up and down and moved a little closer. Emily knew a confidence was coming and her blood tingled with excitement. She smiled encouragingly.

"She is very," Sophie hesitated, "attracted—to Brandy Balantyne. So charming, Brandy. I swear if I were not simply devoted to Freddie, I should be quite in love with him myself!"

Emily took a deep breath, her heart beating in her throat.

"You mean," she said in wonder, "she is having an affair with Brandy?"

Sophie held up her finger to her lips, but her eyes were dancing. "And she is expecting!" she added. "About the third month!"

THREE

It was three days before Emily could visit Charlotte and report to her on the Friday afternoon party and deliver her astounding news. The weekend was quite out of the question, not only because George had arranged for them several engagements: a day at the races on Saturday, and then dinner with friends, and on Sunday a society wedding in the mid-afternoon and the inevitable celebration afterward; but also, of course, because Pitt would be at home. Having reached the rank of inspector, he was not required to work at such times unless he were pursuing a most urgent case. The deaths of two babies, probably illegitimate and some servant girl's, would not fall in that category.

Emily was in no way ashamed of what she was doing, but she preferred that Pitt should remain unaware of it, at least for the time being.

However, by Monday morning she could contain herself no longer, and took the unprecedented step of calling for her carriage at ten o'clock and having herself driven directly to Charlotte's house.

Charlotte was both incredulous and amused. She opened the door herself, in a plain stuff dress and apron.

"Emily! What in goodness' name are you doing here?" There was no need to ask if some disaster had brought her, her face was glowing with excitement; indeed Charlotte could not remember having seen such a look of satisfaction on her face since Emily had announced that she was going to marry George Ashworth: not that he had known it at the time, of course.

"I have the most devastating news!" Emily said, almost

43

willing Charlotte out of the way so she could enter. "You will hardly believe it when I tell you."

Charlotte summed up the nature of her news immediately.

"Detecting agrees with you more than I expected," she said with wide eyes. "Perhaps *you* should have married Thomas, not I!"

Emily stared at her with withering reluctance, and then dismay. It was quite a moment or two before she realized Charlotte was teasing her.

"Why, Charlotte—you—" she could think of no word that both described her feelings, and was fit for the tongue of the lady she felt herself to be.

Charlotte laughed.

"Come in, tell me what you have detected, before you burst!"

Emily had intended to drop her clues one by one, to extend the story to its utmost tension, but she could not bear it herself.

"Euphemia Carlton is having an affair!" she said proudly. She waited for Charlotte's amazement.

Charlotte gratified her, widening her eyes and letting the duster fall from her hand.

"There!" Emily shone with satisfaction. "Pitt hasn't found that out, has he? The affair is with Brandy Balantyne, and that isn't all!" She hesitated, for effect.

Charlotte sat down.

"Well?" she inquired.

Emily sat beside her.

"She is expecting! The third month!"

Charlotte was genuinely impressed, and she was perfectly sure Pitt did not know any of this, whether it was actually relevant or not.

"How do you know?" she asked. It seemed the oddest information to have come by on so short an acquaintance.

"Sophie Bolsover told me. She is a silly, harmless creature, and does not seem to have the least notion of its meaning."

"Or else she knows it has no meaning," Charlotte did not wish to burst the bubble of Emily's excitement, but the truth always came to her mouth as soon as it occurred to her mind, and she had not yet managed much skill in controlling it.

Besides, it was kinder in this instance not to let the supposition grow without examination.

"How could she possibly know such a thing?" Emily demanded. "If Euphemia is having an affair with Brandy Balantyne, the child will be his! And another thing I haven't told you—I saw Sir Robert Carlton. He is quite old. Very grand and distinguished, but fearfully grim looking. And his hair is fair and his eyes quite light. Brandy is very dark; his hair is black and his eyes hazel, dark-colored."

Charlotte remained unimpressed.

"Euphemia is fair!" Emily exploded with exasperation. "Her hair is very handsome, red gold! If the child's hair is black, there will be the most fearful scandal! No wonder she is frightened." She blinked. "Thank goodness George is dark and I am fair. "Whatever my child should be like, it will raise no comment," she said quite casually, merely a thought in passing. Emily was practical, above all things.

Charlotte accepted it as such.

"That really is very important," she said seriously. "About Euphemia and Brandy Balantyne, I mean."

Emily beamed with satisfaction. She was more pragmatic and more assured than Charlotte, and yet there was something in Charlotte, perhaps an inner certainty of her own beliefs, that made Charlotte's praise peculiarly valuable to her.

"Shall you tell Mr. Pitt?" she asked.

"I think I must! Is there any reason why I should not?"

"No, of course not. Why else should I tell you? My dear, you know better than to imagine I should trust you with a secret!"

Charlotte was hurt, and it showed in her face.

"Not that you would tell it," Emily said quickly. "But you would never lie, not successfully. You would betray that you knew something, by your very discomfort, and then have to swear silence. The whole thing would be awful, and grow to be far more important than the secret itself."

Charlotte stared at her.

"I lie very well," Emily added. "I think that makes for a good detective, especially if you are not of the police, and therefore cannot be direct in your interest. As soon as I discover something further, I shall tell you."

Charlotte thought for a moment or two, and then spoke carefully.

"Perhaps you had better see if you can find out how long this affair has been going on. But Emily—please be careful! Do not be carried away with your successes. If they discover what you are doing, you may become very disliked." She took a deep breath. "More than disliked. As you say, there would be a dreadful scandal. Sir Robert is in the government. If Euphemia was prepared at best to bury her own dead children without Christian rites, or, at worst, actually to kill them herself to protect her reputation, she will not easily let you expose her now!"

Emily had not considered any personal danger before, indeed it had never entered her head that any part of the business would affect her at all. Now she was suddenly cold. The story had suddenly become reality.

Charlotte saw her face pale, her hands clench involuntarily. She smiled and put her fingers over Emily's.

"Just be careful," she warned. "Detection is not just an exercise of the mind, you know. People are real, and love and hate are dangerous."

When Pitt returned in the evening Charlotte met him almost at the door. Emily's news had been simmering inside her all day, and with the sound of Pitt's step on the pavement, it had finally come to the boil. She caught hold of his lapels and kissed him quickly.

"Emily came this morning!" she said the instant she let go. "She has discovered something tremendous. Come in and I shall tell you." It was almost an order, and she freed herself from his grasp and swept into the parlor, standing in the middle to watch his expression as she delivered the broadside.

He came in, his extraordinary face crumpled a little in apprehension.

"Emily has found out that Euphemia Carlton is having an affair with young Brandon Balantyne!" she said dramatically. "And that she is expecting a child!"

If she had wished to shock him, she was fully satisfied.

His face went blank as he absorbed the information; then clouded a little with doubt.

"Are you sure she is not—" his eyebrows arched. "—indulging in gossip, a bit of scandalizing?"

"Of course she is indulging in gossip!" she said exasperatedly. "How else does one get information? It is for you to determine if it is true. That is why she came to me, so that I could tell you. It shouldn't be difficult—" she stopped, as he was laughing at her. "What amuses you?" she demanded.

"You do, my dear. Where did Emily come by this invaluable piece of—gossip?" He moved over to the fire and sat down.

She followed him and knelt on the floor in front of him, commanding his attention.

"From Sophie Bolsover, who seemed to be quite unaware of its importance. And that is not all. Apparently Sir Robert is much older than Euphemia, and very grand and grim. And he has fair hair."

"Fair hair?" Pitt repeated, looking at her; but his eyes were sharper now. Her heart bumped with excitement. She knew she had woken his interest.

"Yes!"

"I take it Brandon Balantyne is dark?"

"Very. You see?"

"Of course I see. Euphemia has the most beautiful red-gold hair and very fair skin. You would not know, but naturally, Emily will have told you!"

She smiled in great satisfaction.

He touched her cheek gently with his fingers, finding a loose strand of her hair; but his face was unusually stern.

"Charlotte, you must warn Emily to be careful. People in society care very much about their reputations; they matter to them more than we can understand. They may take it very ill if Emily meddles—"

"I know," she assured him quickly, "I told her. But she will try to learn how long the affair has been going on, if it was already begun when the babies died."

"No. Leave it for me to do. You must call on her tomorrow. Warn her again." His hand fell and he gripped her shoulder as she stiffened with quick apprehension. "They are not likely

47

to think her anything more than a nosy woman," he went on, "with nothing better to amuse herself than gossip, but if Robert Carlton is powerful—"

"Sir Robert?" she was surprised, for a moment uncomprehending.

"Of course Robert, my dear. If he has been thrice cuckolded, he will not want the world to know of it! To be the subject of scandal is one thing, to be laughed at, quite another. Emily would tell you that!"

"I never thought of it." Suddenly she was really unhappy. She could see Emily's newfound glory eclipsed in a single, sweeping move. How idiotic they had been, playing at detectives. "I'll call on her tomorrow morning. If she doesn't listen to me, I shall tell George. He will make her."

He gave her a small smile which she could not read.

"But the information is useful?" she pressed, harking back to her triumph.

"Oh extremely!" He was genuine in his appreciation. "It is even possible it will lead to the answer. The problem now is how shall I discover the duration of this affair, and if she has given birth to any other children?" He scowled in thought, growing fiercer as the answer receded.

"That's easy," Charlotte stood up, as her feet were getting pins and needles. "Speak to her lady's maid—"

"Lady's maids are extremely loyal," he answered, "as well as needing to keep their employment! She is not likely to tell me her mistress is having an affair and has had two babies who have since disappeared!"

She turned at the table, wriggling her foot to wake it up.

"Of course not!" she agreed with disdain. "Not on purpose! Find out what size dress she takes, if she has lately increased her size, and if she did so two years ago and six months ago. Find out if the seams have been let out on her bodices. If I could look at them, I should soon tell you!"

Pitt smiled broadly.

"Is that not detection?" she demanded hotly. "And discover if she has visited the country." She frowned. "Although since the bodies were buried in Callander Square, that is not likely." Her face brightened again. "Discover if she has been ill, feeling squeamish or faint. Then if she has a good or bad

48

appetite. If she has overeaten and put on weight, you are answered! Especially if she has had fancies for certain foods she does not normally care for. Look to the clothes yourself, and don't ask the lady's maid about the appetite and the fainting, or she will know well enough what you are thinking. Ask the kitchen maid about the food, and a parlormaid or someone about her health."

He was still smiling.

She looked at him, then began to doubt herself. The advice had seemed excellent to her as she gave it.

"Is that not the right way?" she blinked.

"Most professional," he agreed. "It makes me wonder how we have managed to solve crimes at all without women on the force."

"I think you are laughing at me!"

"Most certainly. But I still think the advice is excellent, and I shall take it."

"Oh good," she relaxed and gave him a dazzling smile. "I should like to think I was helping."

He burst out in spontaneous laughter.

The following morning Charlotte did as she had been bidden, and called upon Emily. She warned her very solemnly about the vengeance she might bring upon herself, and even upon George, if she stirred up gossip, however unwittingly, about Euphemia Carlton.

Emily heard her out with a calm, obedient expression, and duly swore to abandon the matter, and do no more than pursue her normal social round. Charlotte thanked her, and left with an unreasonable feeling that she had somehow failed. For one thing, it had been far too easy. She had seen no fear in Emily's eyes to account for such sudden capitulation, but she could hardly ask for more than one promise to the same effect. She went home and gave the parlor a furious spring cleaning, although it was the first week in November, and beginning to rain.

Pitt returned to Callander Square, and at quarter past ten knocked on the Carltons' door and asked if he might speak to the servants again. He was shown into the housekeeper's sitting room, and the parlormaid was sent for.

"Come in." Pitt sat down in one of the great chairs, so as not to tower over the girl. "Sit down. I hope this business has not distressed you too much."

She looked at him with some awe.

"No, thank you, sir." Then she thought better of it. "Well, I mean, yes, it is dreadful, isn't it? I'm sure I don't know who it can be!"

"And your mistress? I imagine it may have upset her also?"

"Not more than what pity you'd expect," she replied. "Very well, she is. I never seen her look so well."

"Not upset her appetite? Does, with some people, you know; ladies of a delicate disposition."

"Lady Carlton ain't delicate, sir, fit as an 'orse, she is, if you'll pardon the h'expression. None of your fainting and vapors for her—at least—"

He raised his eyebrows in interested sympathy.

"Well, she did come over a bit queer a couple of times, but I reckon that's her condition, if you take me. O Lor'," she put her fingers to her mouth and stared at him with round eyes. "You got that out o' me!"

"No, no," he said gently. "Besides, I am concerned with the past, not the future." He hid his annoyance. Now it would not be possible to get any further information from the girl without her immediately knowing what he was seeking. Better speak to the others straight away, before she spread the alarm, even inadvertently.

He went upstairs to see the lady's maid, past the objections of the bristling housekeeper, because he wished to see the dresses himself; although he had, as yet, no idea what excuse he might use for his interest.

He found the lady's maid brushing a riding habit and sponging the skirt where the autumn mud had splashed it. She dropped it in some alarm when she saw him.

"Don't disturb yourself, ma'am" he said as he walked over and picked it up, feeling it between his fingers appreciatively, not yet passing it back to her. "An excellent piece of stuff." He flipped it over so that the waist was in his grasp. "And well-tailored, too." He felt quickly at the seams. Nothing. He glanced at the waistband where Charlotte had told him to

50

look. He found it immediately, an extension to the band, a piece let in. He gave it back to the maid, quite casually, smiling at her. "I like to see a well-dressed lady. Gives everyone pleasure."

"Oh, this is last year's," she said quickly. "Quite old, in fact. Lady Euphemia has far better than this!"

"Indeed? I should like to see better than this," he let a note of polite disbelief fall into his voice. "It's a very fine cloth."

She went over to an enormous wardrobe and threw it open. There was a gleam of light on the purples and fuschias and lambent greens of silk.

"How very beautiful," he said quite genuinely. He went over and touched the soft, shining stuff with his fingers, for a moment forgetting his purpose. There was an amber gown, almost corn gold where the light fell on it, and deep fire russet in the shadows. It must have looked magnificent on Euphemia Carlton, but he saw it on Charlotte. He felt a sharp stab of pain because he could not buy such things for her. He forgot the maid, and Callander Square, and his mind whirled wildly for some idea, some other occupation where he might be able to earn that sort of money.

"Lovely things, aren't they?" There was a note of wistfulness in the woman's voice too. He was jerked back to reality. He looked at her pinched figure in its dark stuff dress and white apron.

"Yes," he agreed, "yes, very." Rapidly he searched for the waist seams, the sides where letting out would be done. "I expect they take a lot of looking after." He found nothing yet. "You must be very skilled with a needle."

She smiled at the compliment.

"Not many men as thinks of that. Yes, I does a lot of work, but she looks a rare sight when I send 'er out of 'ere, if I say that as shouldn't. I've never sent 'er out less than perfect."

Pitt seized his chance and looked openly at the minute stitching. The waist had definitely been let out, a couple of inches or more.

"You're quite an artist," he said, and meant at least part of it. What must it be like for a woman to put all her labor and her love into making another woman beautiful? Then to sit at home and watch her leave for parties and balls, to dance all night and be admired while she stayed upstairs, waiting to receive the clothes back again, press them, mend them for the next time?

"You have every right to be proud," he said. He let the silk fall and closed the wardrobe doors.

She blushed with pleasure.

"Thank you, I'm sure," she stammered.

He must ask her something, lest she think afterward and become suspicious. His mind searched for some likely question.

"Does your mistress ever give away any of her old clothes, to deserving servant girls, or the like?" He knew the answer—no mistress wishes to see a servant wearing the style and quality of garment she herself wore, no matter how old, or how deserving the girl.

"Oh no, sir! Lady Euphemia sends them all to the country, to some cousin or other, who don't know what's fashionable and what's not, and very glad of them she is."

"I see. Thank you," he smiled reassuringly at her and took his departure to the kitchen.

Neither the cook nor the kitchen maids yielded anything conclusive, but it seemed Euphemia had indulged in sudden bouts of eating every so often, put on weight, and then dieted again. They attributed it to a healthy appetite, a love of sweet things, and then a re-emergence of vanity and the dictates of fashion. There was nothing to prove them either right or wrong. He thanked them and left the house, filling in time through the afternoon until he could call on Sir Robert Carlton and Lady Euphemia herself, and expect to find them at home.

He returned a little after six. He knew it was inconvenient, but there is no convenient time for the sort of question to which he sought an answer.

The footman received him coolly and showed him into the library. It was several minutes before the door opened and Sir Robert Carlton came in, closing it gently behind him. He was a little above average height, slender, stiff. His face was, as Charlotte had said, extremely distinguished, but the mildness of his expression robbed it of arrogance.

"I understand you wish to see me?" he said quietly. His voice was clear and precise, and contained a slight lift of surprise.

"Yes, sir," Pitt replied. "If you please. I apologize for calling at this hour, but I wished to be sure of finding you in." Carlton waited politely and he continued. "I'm afraid I have reason to believe that the mother of the babies found in the square may be a member of your household—" He stopped, ready for outrage, denials. Instead there was only a tightening of the skin across Carlton's high cheeks, as if he anticipated pain. Pitt wondered quickly if either he already knew, or at least suspected his wife. Was it possible he had even personally accepted it, long since fought his private battle?

"I'm sorry," Carlton said quietly. "Poor woman."

Pitt stared at him.

Carlton turned his face to look at Pitt. There was anxiety and compassion in his eyes. It was something he did not understand, but struggling to imagine, and for which he was deeply sorry. Pitt felt a surge of anger against Euphemia, and against young Brandon Balantyne, whom he had not yet met. Carlton was speaking again.

"Have you any idea who it is, Mr. Pitt? Or what will happen to her?"

"That rather depends on the circumstances, Sir Robert. If the children were born dead, there may be no criminal prosecution. But she will lose her character, and unless she is extremely fortunate, her position, and be without reference to obtain another."

"And if they were not born dead?"

"Then there will be a charge of murder."

"I see. I suppose that is inevitable. And the wretched woman will be hanged."

Pitt realized too late that he should not have committed himself; he should have left it in doubt. Perhaps in that single carelessness he had forfeited Carlton's help.

"That is only an opinion," he tried to withdraw. "There may be some mitigating circumstances, of course—" He could think of many, for himself; but none that would appeal to the lords justices.

53

"You said, someone in the house," Carlton continued as if he had not spoken. "I take it you do not as yet know whom?"

"No, sir. I thought perhaps Lady Carlton, knowing the servants better, might be able to assist me."

"I suppose it is necessary to bring her into this?"

"I regret so."

"Very well," Carlton reached for the bell cord and pulled it. When the footman appeared he gave instructions that Euphemia should be asked to come. They waited in silence until she arrived. She closed the door behind her and turned to them. Her face was smooth and utterly guileless, even when she saw Pitt. If she had any guilt, then she was either one of those rare creatures who genuinely see no interest but their own, or was the most accomplished actress.

"My dear, Inspector Pitt believes that the mother of these unfortunate children may be someone in our house," Carlton said courteously. "I regret it is necessary that you should endeavor to assist him."

Her face paled a little.

"Oh dear, I'm so sorry. Of course it can really make no difference, but I hate to think of it being someone I know. Are you sure, Inspector?" She turned to look at him. She was a most attractive woman, there was a warmth about her more appealing than beauty.

"No, ma'am, but I have cause to believe it."

"For what reason?" she asked.

Pitt took a deep breath and plunged in.

"It would seem that someone in this house is having an affair, a love affair." He watched her face. For a moment she remained perfectly serene, merely interested: then there was a slight tightening of the hands on the plum-colored silk of her dress. A faint color spread up her throat. Pitt glanced across at Carlton, but he appeared detached, unobservant.

"Indeed?" she said after the slightest hesitation.

He went on.

"There is a strong possibility that as a result of the attachment, she may have become with child."

The color deepened painfully in her face. She turned away so that the shadow fell across her.

"I see."

Carlton still seemed unaware of anything but the concern of a mistress for her maids.

"Perhaps you had better make inquiries, my dear. Is that what you wish, Inspector?"

"If Lady Carlton feels she might discover something." Pitt looked at her, deliberately choosing his words so that she should understand his meaning, in spite of his apparent casualness.

Euphemia kept her face from the light.

"What is it that you wish to know, Mr. Pitt?"

"How long the—attachment—has existed," he said quietly.

She took a deep breath.

"It may not be," she struggled for precisely the right expression and failed, "of the nature, or the—the emotions that you suppose."

"The emotions are not our concern, my dear," Carlton said quietly. "And the nature of it can hardly be in question, since there have been two dead children found in the square."

She swiveled round to stare at them, horror in her face, eyes wide.

"You cannot suppose—I mean—you cannot leap to judge that because someone is—has an attachment, that they are responsible for those—deaths! There may be any number of people in the square who have some relationship or other— some—"

"There is a world of difference between a mild flirtation and an affair that produces two children, Euphemia." Carlton still did not lose his courtesy, his air of judiciousness, almost indifference. "We are not speaking of a mere admiration."

"Of course not!" she said sharply, then as his high face smoothed a little in surprise, she regained control of herself with an effort. Pitt, standing beside her, saw the muscles in her throat contract, the material of her dress strain as she held her breath in. He wondered if Carlton were as oblivious of her turmoil as he appeared. They seemed an ill-matched couple in more than years. Was she a young woman trapped by ambitious or impecunious parents in a marriage of convenience—their convenience? It flickered to his mind to wonder what Charlotte would have thought, even what she might have done, had it been she. He determined to meet young Brandon Balantyne as soon as possible.

"I will discover what I can, Mr. Pitt," Euphemia looked directly at him, meeting his eyes with a direct, golden amber glaze. "But if anyone in my house has an attachment of such a standing, I know nothing of it."

"Thank you, ma'am," he said softly. He knew what she was trying to say, that she had understood him, and that she was denying the length of her own involvement, but he could not afford to believe her, unsubstantiated. He excused himself and left with the same feeling of sadness he had felt innumerable times before when he first glimpsed the truth of a tragedy that had turned into a crime.

Emily had no intention whatsoever of obeying Charlotte's instructions, except insofar as she would exercise a little more caution than she had hitherto. She would no longer directly question anyone, although in truth, Sophie Bolsover had hardly required it. Instead she would cultivate friendships; and with such an end in view she again called at Callander Square, this time specifically to see Christina. She had acquired a piece of information regarding a dressmaker, which she knew would be of interest to Christina, and took the liberty of calling in the morning when she would not run into the social ritual of the afternoon.

The door was answered by the footman Max.

"Good morning, Lady Ashworth," he said, showing only the slightest surprise. His dark eyes flickered down her habit appreciatively, then up again to her face. She stared back at him coldly.

"Good morning. Is Miss Balantyne at home?"

"Yes, my lady. If you care to come in, I will tell her you are here." He backed away, pulling the door wider. She followed him into the hall, and then into the morning room where there was already a fire burning.

"Can I bring you anything, ma'am?" he asked.

"No, thank you," she replied, deliberately not looking at him.

He smiled very slightly, inclined his head, and left her alone.

She had been waiting about ten minutes and was beginning to become a little impatient when finally Christina came in. Emily turned to greet her, and was surprised to see her looking quite casual, almost disheveled. Her hair was less than perfectly done, there were dark wisps lopsidedly on her neck, and she looked unbecomingly pale.

"My dear, have I caught you at an inconvenient time?" Emily had nearly asked if she were unwell, then realized that to suggest someone looked ill was less than flattering, and she did not wish to jeopardize Christina's somewhat tenuous friendship so soon.

"I confess," Christina put her hand on the back of the chair and held it firmly, "I do not feel in the best of health this morning. Most unusual, for me."

"Pray sit down," Emily went toward her, taking her hand. "I do most sincerely hope it is but a passing indisposition, a slight chill, perhaps? After all, the change in the weather can so easily cause such things." She was doubtful in her mind as she said it. Christina was an extremely healthy girl and she showed none of the signs of a chill, no rasping in the throat, no running nose or feverishness.

Christina slid into the chair. She looked uncommonly pale and there were the faintest of beads of perspiration on her skin.

"Perhaps a little tisane?" Emily suggested. "I'll call the footman."

Christina protested and shook her head, but Emily had already rung the bell. She stood by it, and when Max appeared she spoke over Christina's head to him.

"Miss Balantyne is feeling a little unwell. Will you please have cook brew her a tisane, and send it up?"

The man's heavy eyes looked across at Christina and Emily caught the glance. He looked away quickly and retreated to obey.

"I am sorry to have found you so," Emily said with the best mixture of cheerfulness and sympathy she could manage. "I only came to tell you the name of the dressmaker you were inquiring for. I managed to persuade her to consider us both, although she is in the most absolute demand. She has such skill in cutting she can make even the ugliest creatures

57

look graceful," she smiled at Christina's white face. "And meticulous at finishing off, no threads or half-stitched buttons. And she is so clever at designing she can hide a few extra inches so one's own mother would not know one had put on weight."

Christina blushed suddenly and deeply.

"What on earth are you suggesting? I am not putting on weight," she crossed her hands over her stomach.

Emily's mind raced.

"You're lucky," she said lightly. "I fear I always do in the winter." It was a complete fabrication. "It happens without fail," she went on. "It must be all the hot puddings and things. And I have a dreadful weakness for chocolate sauce."

"If you will excuse me," Christina climbed to her feet, still clutching her hands in front of herself. "I think I had better go upstairs. The mention of food has made me feel quite sick. I would be obliged if you would not tell Max. Drink the tisane yourself, if you wish."

"Oh my dear!" Emily caught hold of her. "I'm so sorry. Let me help you, you are in no condition to be by yourself. I shall assist you at least to your rooms, and your maid can wait upon you. Shall I have someone call for the doctor?"

"No!" Christina was fierce, her eyes blazing. "I am perfectly well. It is nothing of any import. Perhaps something I have eaten does not entirely agree with me. Pray do not mention the matter. I would take it as a true sign of your friendship if you were to treat the whole incident in complete confidence," she put out a cold little hand and grabbed Emily hard.

"Of course," Emily reassured her. "I shall not mention it. One does not wish one's indispositions discussed about the place. The matter is quite private."

"Thank you."

"Now you must come upstairs," Emily guided her across the hall and up the wide staircase till they met her lady's maid on the upstairs landing, who took charge of Christina.

Emily had come down again and reached as far as the hall when she was nearly brushed aside by a tall man, broad-shouldered and wide-chested, who swept by her.

"Perkins!" he shouted angrily. "Perkins, damn it!"

58

Emily stood stock still.

He swung round and saw her. He opened his mouth as if to shout again, then realized she was not the errant Perkins. His face was striking, with a great deal of bone. Now he colored faintly at having made an exhibition of himself. He raised his head still higher.

"Good morning, ma'am. May I be of some assistance? For whom were you looking?"

"General Balantyne?" she asked with magnificent composure.

"At your service," he said stiffly, his temper barely beneath the surface.

Emily smiled with devastating charm.

"Emily Ashworth," she extended her hand. "I came to see Miss Balantyne, but she is a trifle indisposed this morning, so I shall take my leave. Have you lost a butler? I believe I saw him depart in that direction," she pointed vaguely behind her. It was an invention, but she wished to appear helpful, and if possible even to engage him in some slight conversation.

"No. Housemaid. Damn woman always moving my papers. Actually I can't remember if her name is Perkins or not, but Augusta always calls downstairs housemaids Perkins, whatever they call themselves."

"Papers?" The beginning of an utterly brilliant idea was forming in Emily's mind. "Are you engaged upon writing something?"

"A family history, ma'am. The Balantynes have fought in all the great battles of the nation from the last two hundred years or so."

Emily breathed out, trying with all her considerable acting skill to invest her bearing with interest. Actually warfare bored her to tears; but she must make some intelligent remark.

"How very important," she replied. "The history of our men of war is the history of our race." She was proud of that, it was an excellent observation.

He looked at her narrowly.

"You are the first woman I have met to consider it so."

"From my sister," she said quickly. "My sister has always

59

had an interest in such things. I learned from her of its great importance. One does not realize—but I keep you from your work. If I cannot help, I must at least not hinder. You should have someone to assist you, keep your papers in order, someone who understands such things to dust and care for your study, and perhaps take notes, should you not? Or maybe you have?"

"If I had, ma'am, I should not now be searching for some housemaid to see what she has done with them!"

"Do you think such a person might be of service to you?" She put her utmost effort into appearing quite casual.

"To find a woman who had any sense of military history would not only be extremely fortunate, ma'am, but even more would it be unlikely."

"My sister is most competent, sir," she assured him, "and as I have said, has a longstanding interest in things of a military nature. My father, naturally, did not approve, so she has not been able to indulge it as her nature inclined. However, I am sure there would be no disapproval if she were to spend a little time being of assistance to someone such as yourself." Of course she had no intention of telling him Charlotte was married to a policeman.

He stared at her. A lesser woman than Emily might well have quailed before him.

"Indeed. Well, if it meets with your father's approval, I daresay it might prove of assistance to me. I pray you, raise the matter to him, and see if she is agreeable. If she is, she may call upon me, and we shall arrange some terms satisfactory to us both. I am obliged to you—Miss—" he had forgotten her name.

"Ashworth," Emily smiled again. "Lady Ashworth."

"Lady Ashworth," he bowed very slightly. "Good day to you, ma'am."

Emily dropped a tiny curtsey and hurried out in an ecstasy of delight.

She climbed straight into the carriage and commanded the driver to take her post haste to Charlotte's house. It mattered not a pin what time of the morning it was; she must deliver herself of her plans, and fully instruct Charlotte in her future part in them.

60

She had totally forgotten Charlotte's warning to her, and her promise.

"I have been to Callander Square this morning!" she said the instant Charlotte opened the door. She swept past her and into the parlor, swinging round to face her sister. "I have learned the most incredible things! For a start, Christina Balantyne is indisposed, nausea at this time in the morning! And she nearly bit my head off when I suggested she might put on weight. She begged me to say nothing of it to anyone! Implored me! What do you think of it, Charlotte? True or not, whatever the fact, I can see well enough what it is she fears! It can be only one thing. And she would not permit me to call a doctor."

Charlotte was pale. She stood just inside the door, her eyes wide.

"Emily, you promised!"

Emily had no idea what she meant.

"You promised!" Charlotte said fiercely. "What do you imagine the Balantynes will do if they discover you know such a thing? From what you said of Lady Augusta, she will hardly sit by and allow you to ruin Christina! Have you no sense at all? I shall tell George myself, and perhaps he will be able to prevent you from being so idiotic!"

Emily waved her aside.

"Oh for goodness' sake, Charlotte; do you imagine I don't know how to conduct myself socially? I have climbed far higher than you ever will. Mostly, of course, because you won't exert yourself. But do you imagine that because you won't keep your opinions to yourself that I cannot, if I wish? I can lie so that Mr. Pitt would not know it, and certainly not Augusta Balantyne. I have no intention of ruining either myself, or George.

"Now please pay attention to what I have been telling you about Christina! I have no idea who the man may be; but while I was there an opportunity arose, and I had the most brilliant idea. Naturally I seized upon it immediately. General Balantyne is writing a military history of his family, of which he seems to be extraordinarily proud. He needs some help to keep himself organized, take notes, and so forth." She stopped for a moment to draw breath, her eyes on Charlotte.

For the first time she actually considered the possibility that Charlotte might refuse.

"Well?" Charlotte said with a slight frown. "I cannot see what General Balantyne's military memoirs have to do with Christina's fears."

"Why, they are the perfect answer!" Emily banged her hand on her skirt in frustration at Charlotte's obtuseness. "I have volunteered that you will go and help him with his papers! You are the ideal person. You even like military matters—you can remember who fought whom, in which battles, while most of us cannot even recall why, and certainly don't care. You must go and—"

Charlotte's face had fallen in incredulity.

"Emily, you must have lost your senses! I cannot possibly go and—and work for General Balantyne! It would be preposterous!" But even as she was saying it, her voice was slowing down, the outrage slipping out of it. Emily knew that in spite of her words, she had not at all dismissed the idea, in fact she was, in framing its very ridiculousness to herself, turning over in her mind the faint possibility of accepting it.

"Thomas would never permit it," Charlotte said carefully.

"Why not?"

"It would be—unseemly."

"Why? You do not need to take any payment for it, if it is beneath his dignity for you to do so. All he needs to know is that you are helping a friend, and at the same time pursuing your own interest. And who knows what you may discover? You will actually be in the house, day by day!"

Charlotte opened her mouth to protest again, but her eyes were looking beyond Emily, into the distance of her imagination, and there was a deep light in them. Emily knew she had won, and there was no time for decorating the victory.

"I shall call for you tomorrow morning at half past nine. Wear your best dark dress, that wine one, it is new enough, and the color becomes you—"

"I am not going in order to engage his attentions, Emily!" Charlotte made a last, automatic protest.

"Don't be obtuse, Charlotte. Every woman, if she succeeds at anything, does so by engaging some man's attentions. Anyway, whatever your purpose is, it can hardly hurt!"

"Emily, you are a thoroughly conniving creature."

"So are you, you are just afraid to admit it to yourself."
She stood up. "I must go. I have other calls to make. Please
be ready at half past nine in the morning. Tell Pitt what you
please." She blinked. "By the way, naturally I did not tell
General Balantyne you were married to a policeman, much
less the officer investigating the affair in the gardens. I said
you were my sister, so you had better be Miss Ellison again."
She swept out before Charlotte could register any protest,
although in fact Charlotte was too entertained with the idea
to seek objections, and was already busy considering the most
judicious explanation to offer Pitt, and how best she might
satisfy General Balantyne as to her competence.

The following morning as Charlotte was surveying herself
in the mirror, adjusting her dress for the tenth time and
making sure yet again that her hair was both tidy and at the
same time shown to its best advantage, Augusta Balantyne
was staring across the breakfast table at her husband.

"Do I understand you correctly, Brandon, that you have
engaged some young woman of indeterminate background
and restricted means to come into this house and assist you
in these family memoirs you are—" her voice froze, "occupied
with?"

"No, you do not understand me, Augusta," he replied over
his cup. "Lady Ashworth, whom I gather to be a friend of
yours, recommended her sister to me as a woman of intelligence and propriety, who would be willing to put my papers
in order and take some notes, as I may dictate them. You
will not be required to entertain her socially: though why
the matter should concern you, I don't know. She could not
possibly be either plainer or more foolish than some of the
women you have in here."

"Sometimes, Brandon, I think you say such things entirely
to provoke me. One cannot order one's acquaintance on the
basis of good looks, or, unfortunately, of intelligence."

"I think they would be criteria quite as satisfactory as
either birth or money," he opined.

"Don't be naive," she snapped. "You know perfectly well
63

what is of value in society and what is not. I hope you do not intend this young woman to eat in the dining room?"

He raised his eyebrows in surprise.

"I had not considered her eating at all. But now that you mention it, perhaps cook had better prepare her something and she can eat in the library, as the governess used to."

"The governess ate in the schoolroom."

"The difference is academic." He stood up. "Have Max show her into the library when she comes. You know, I dislike that man. A spell in the army would do him good."

"He is an excellent footman, and a 'spell in the army' would ruin him. Please do not meddle with the governing of the household servants. That is what we employ Masters for; besides, you know nothing about it."

He gave her a sour look and went out of the door, shutting it sharply behind him.

Augusta made it her business to be in the hallway at ten o'clock when Charlotte arrived promptly. She saw Max open the door and watched with interest, and an odd mixture of superiority and reluctant approval as Charlotte was shown in. She had expected a dowdy dress and a pinched, submissive face: instead she saw rich wine-colored skirts, a little outdated in fashion, but still flattering; and a face anything but submissive. Indeed, it was one of the most flagrant and willful faces she had ever seen, yet having at the same time a surprising gentleness in the mouth and the soft curve of cheek and throat. Definitely not a woman she wished in her house, not a woman she could like, or understand; not a woman who would be easily governed by the rules of society by which Augusta had lived all her life, had fought and won all her many intricate battles.

She sailed forward in her most frigid manner.

"Good morning, Miss—er?" she raised her brows in inquiry.

Charlotte met her eyes squarely.

"Miss Ellison, Lady Augusta," she lied without a thought.

"Indeed." Dislike hardened in her; she smiled barely, "I believe my husband is expecting you." She glanced at Max who obediently went to the library door and opened it. "I understand you have come to be of some clerical assistance to him." Best to let her know immediately her standing in the house.

"Miss Ellison." Max's heavy-lidded eyes followed Charlotte in, lingering on her shoulders and her waist.

The door closed behind her and Charlotte stood still, waiting for the general to look up. She was no longer trembling inside; Lady Augusta's patronage had turned her fear into anger.

General Balantyne sat behind an enormous desk. She saw the handsome head, the lean bones of the face. Her interest was immediate. In her imagination she saw the long battle line of history stretch out behind him: Crimea, Waterloo, Corunna, Plassey, Malplaquet...

He looked up. The bland courtesy washed out of his face and he stared at her. She stared back.

"How do you do, Miss—"

"How do you do, General Balantyne. My sister, Lady Ashworth, considered I might be of some service to you. I hope that may be so."

"Yes." He stood up, blinking, still staring at her, frowning a little. "She said you had some interest in military affairs. I am setting in some order the history of my family, which has served with distinction in every great battle since the time of the Duke of Marlborough."

Thoughts as to how she should answer flashed through Charlotte's mind.

"You must be very proud," she said honestly. "It is a good thing you should record it accurately for people to know; especially those in the future, when the men who can remember our great battles are gone."

He said nothing, but his shoulders straightened as he considered her, and there was a very small smile at the edges of his mouth.

In the rest of the house the usual business of the morning was conducting itself, housemaids and upstairs maids and ladies' maids were all furiously occupied. Augusta was supervising because she was expecting guests of great social importance for dinner, and also because she had nothing else to do. At half past ten she could not find the tweeny. The wretched girl had left a distinct rime of dust on the frames of the pictures on the landing—it showed gray on Augusta's finger—and the child was nowhere to be seen.

Augusta had long known the favorite bolt hole of idle servants, between the stillroom and the butler's pantry, and she now repaired to it with some determination. If the girl was loitering among the footmen or bootboys, she would give her a criticism that would not lightly be forgotten.

At the stillroom door she stopped, conscious that there was someone in the small room beyond. There was a whispered voice, she could not hear the words, nor even if they were spoken by a man or a woman; then the rusle of—surely not silk—on a maid?

She pushed the door open soundlessly and saw black-suited arms cradling a taffeta bodice, and over the slender shoulder the sloe-eyed, sensuous face of Max, his lips on the white neck. She knew the neck, knew the elegant coils of dark hair. It was Christina.

Please, dear heaven, they had neither of them seen her! She could not look anyone in the face at this moment. Her heart rose cold in her chest, beating painfully. She backed away from the door. Her daughter, giggling, in the arms of a footman! Horror froze her normally agile brain. Icy, paralyzing minutes passed before she could even begin to think what to do about such a monstrous thing, how to nullify it, obliterate it from existence. It would take work, skill: but it must be done! Otherwise Christina would be ruined. What man of birth in his right mind would marry her after this, if it were known?

FOUR

Reggie Southeron sat in the library in his house and stared out at the leafless trees in Callander Square. The gray November sky scudded past above them and the first heavy gusts of rain clattered on the glass. He had a schooner of brandy on the small table beside him and the decanter winked comfortably in the firelight. Under any other circumstances he would have been entirely happy, but this miserable business in the gardens was causing him a nagging anxiety. Of course he had no idea who might be responsible—any one of a score! There was little else of entertainment in a servant's life, and everyone knew that most of the girls, especially those who came up from the country to improve themselves, were not averse to a little fun: at least everyone who kept an establishment of any standard. But it was possible that someone like the police, who were, after all, no better than tradesmen or servants themselves, held quite a different view. Some police, the local ones in the country, for example, knew how to be discreet; but it was a different case with the London men who were used to dealing with the criminal classes in general, and in all probability had no concept of social rank or refinement.

And it was this that was worrying Reggie. Like most men, in his opinion, he availed himself of the odd pleasure with a handsome parlormaid. After all, what healthy man, woken in his bed in the morning by a young, clear-skinned, well-rounded wench bending over him, would not be tempted? And if she was willing, as they invariably were, why resist? His wife, Adelina, was well enough, and she had borne him three children, although unfortunately the boy had died. But she had taken no enjoyment in it; she suffered his advances with fortitude and did what she had been taught was her duty. Parlormaids enjoyed it, laughed, responded in a fashion that would have been unthinkable in a woman of quality.

Naturally one did not marry parlormaids. Everyone knew of such arrangements, but one conducted oneself discreetly. One did not wish to be the subject of gossip, nor to embarrass one's wife. What was presumed and what was actually known were two entirely different things.

But as he had already realized, the police might fail to understand how these things were conducted to the satisfaction of all concerned. It would be very difficult if this Pitt fellow were to discover Reggie's present taste for the parlormaid, Mary Ann. He might misconstrue it entirely. The girl was uncommonly handsome, quite the best looking Reggie could recall: and she had been in service in Callander Square for three years.

Great heavens! It wasn't possible that she—actually—? Reggie broke out in a cold sweat, in spite of the fire. He took a rapid swig at the brandy and poured himself another. For pity's sake, calm down, man! Remember the trim waist, the saucy bottom. She had not been with child in this house! Surely he could not be so unobservant as not to have noticed? She was a big girl. Would she have changed shape so obviously? He had to admit, he had been very spasmodic in his attentions. Sometimes he had been away for weeks at a time—but this was ridiculous! Someone would have noticed! He was worrying for nothing.

It was only a matter of making sure that the police did not leap to any foolish and entirely unwarranted conclusions. How intelligent was this chap, Pitt? Was he a man of the world? Some of the working classes could be appallingly narrow-minded: quite distressingly vulgar in their speech and eating, not to mention dress, but positive prudes when it came to personal liberty. It could be very trying having to deal with them. Pity the man in this case could not have been a gentleman, who would have understood; indeed, would not even have needed an explanation.

Better to forestall the whole business by seeing the others in the square who might be affected, and come to some understanding. Between them they ought to be able to keep this police fellow out of harm's way, discreetly.

He had made up his mind to this, and was feeling considerably easier, when there was a knock on the door. He was surprised. Servants did not usually knock. If they had something to do, they simply came in and did it.

"Come in," he answered, swiveling to face the entrance.

The door opened and the governess, Jemima, stood there.

Reggie sat up with a smile. Handsome girl, Jemima, though a bit on the thin side. He liked a rounder bosom, plumper shoulders; but there was a definite charm about her, a spirit in the way she held her head, a delicacy of bone. He had frequently been on the point of putting his arm round her in response to the inviting femininity of her slender back; but she had always moved away, or someone else had appeared.

Now she stood in front of him, looking levelly at him.

"Yes, Jemima?" he said cheerfully.

"Mrs. Southeron said I should speak to you concerning Miss Faith's music, sir. Miss Faith wishes to learn the violin, instead of the piano—"

"Well, let her, by all means. You are competent in the violin, aren't you?" Why on earth did Adelina send him such trivial matters?

"Yes, Mr. Southeron. But since Miss Chastity already plays the violin, that will give us two violins and a cello. There is very little music written for such a trio."

"Oh, yes. I see. Well, perhaps Chastity would like to learn the piano?"

"No, she wouldn't," Jemima smiled. She had a charming smile, it went all the way to her eyes. She would have made a good parlormaid, had she been a little sturdier.

"Send her to me, I'll change her mind," Reggie leaned farther back in his chair and slid his feet toward the fire.

"Yes, sir," Jemima turned and walked to the door. She had a nice walk, straight-backed, head high. She was one of those country girls with a swinging step. She made him think of open skies and clean, windy shores: things he liked to contemplate from a winter armchair, or see in a good painting. She was a pleasing creature, Jemima.

It was quite five minutes before Chastity arrived.

"Come in," Reggie smiled and sat up a little.

She obeyed, solemn-faced, her hair tied back making her eyes look unusually wide.

"Sit down," Reggie offered, pointing to the chair opposite him.

Instead of perching on the edge, like the other children, she snuggled far back in the deep corner, like a cat, with her feet tucked under her. She still managed to look prim. She waited for him to speak.

"Would you like to learn to play the piano, Chastity?" he asked.

"No, thank you, Uncle Reggie."

"Playing the piano is a most useful art. You can sing at the same time. You cannot sing at the same time as playing the violin," he pointed out.

She lifted her chin very slightly and stared back at him.

"I cannot sing anyway," she said with blank honesty. "No matter what I played." She hesitated, looking at him with thought. "Faith can. She sings very well."

The argument defeated him, and he could see from the look in her bright, frank eyes that she knew it.

"Why doesn't Faith play the cello?" she pressed home her advantage. "Then Patience could learn the piano. She can sing, too."

He looked at her with a jaundiced eye.

"And if I tell you to play the piano?"

"I shall be no good at it," she said decidedly. "And then we shall have no trio, and that would be a shame."

He narrowed his eyes and poured himself another brandy, admiring the rich color of it shining like smoky topaz in the firelight.

"That would be a pity," Chastity was still regarding him with measured consideration. "Because Aunt Adelina likes us to play for her guests sometimes, at her afternoon parties."

He gave up. He was about to try another tack, to wit, bribery, when the footman opened the door and announced Inspector Pitt.

Reggie swore under his breath. He had not yet considered

70

his defense. Chastity snuggled still farther into the recesses of the chair. He looked at her.

"You may go, Chastity. We will discuss the matter another time."

"But that's the policeman with the untidy hair, Uncle Reggie and I like him."

"What?" he was startled.

"I like him. Mayn't I stay and talk to him? I might be able to tell him something!"

"No, you may not. There is absolutely nothing you could possibly know that would be of any use to him. Now go upstairs and have your tea. It must be tea time. It's getting dark."

She climbed out of the chair reluctantly and meandered to the door where Pitt was standing holding it open for her. She stopped, craning her head to look up at him.

"Good afternoon, Miss Southeron," he said solemnly.

She dropped a small curtsey and the corner of her mouth flickered reluctantly into a smile.

"Good afternoon, sir."

She seemed disposed to linger and Reggie spoke to her sharply. With a look of hurt dignity she swept out, which was an accomplishment, since she was wearing a short skirt and pinafore. Pitt closed the door.

"I apologize," Reggie said affably. "The child is a menace." He looked at Pitt's face and his quaint, rather untidy attire. He made an instant decision to assume an air of frankness, and try to enlist the man as an ally, or at least a confidant. "Children so easily misunderstand," he went on with a smile. "As indeed do a lot of people. Still, I expect as a man of experience, you've seen a lot of life, and you know truth from error when you see it. Have a glass of brandy?" Pity to use the best brandy on a policeman who probably would not know it from the stuff they sold at alehouses. But it might be a good investment in the long event.

Pitt hesitated, made a rapid decision, and accepted.

"Sit down," Reggie offered expansively. "Wretched business. Don't envy you. Must be damned hard to sift the truth from all the inventions."

Pitt smiled slowly, taking the brandy from him.

71

"Maids bound to spin a few stories," Reggie continued. "Natural thing. Read too many penny novels, too much imagination. Never realize the damage it can do."

Pitt raised his eyebrows inquiringly and sipped at the brandy.

Reggie decided to press home the point while the fellow seemed so agreeable. Better to set him straight in advance of any gossip he might hear belowstairs, where he would undoubtedly go in time.

"Easy to understand," he elaborated in an attempt at jocularity without obvious condescension. "Poor creatures haven't a lot of excitement, I suppose. A man of intelligence would be bored to death. Bound to embroider the truth a little, eh?"

"Could be mischievous," Pitt agreed, his clear eyes smiling back at Reggie.

Nice fellow, Reggie thought. Should not be too difficult to steer him into dismissing any unpleasant tales he might hear.

"Quite," he agreed. "I can see that you understand. Must have run into it before, I daresay. Had this kind of thing happened often?"

Pitt took another sip of his brandy.

"Not quite like this. Not in a square of this—quality."

"No—no, I suppose not. Thank goodness, eh? Still, I expect you've run across servant girls who've got themselves into trouble before now, eh, what?" he laughed.

Pitt looked blandly back at him; for a man with so remarkably expressive a face, he now conveyed almost nothing.

"All sorts of people with problems," he agreed.

"Ah, but you know what sort of trouble I mean." Reggie wondered for an instant if the man were foolish. Perhaps he had better be more explicit. "Babies must be some servant girl's who got herself with child and the fellow wouldn't marry her; or perhaps she didn't even know who he was, eh?"

Pitt opened his eyes a little wider.

"Any girls of that sort of character in your establishment, sir?"

"Good God, no!" Reggie stiffened indignantly, then realized with a flash of anger that he had just defeated his own

72

purpose. "I mean, not that I know of, of course. But it only takes one mistake! Perhaps a girl who entertains romantic notions, thinks to better herself, or—oh, well!" he broke off, not quite sure what to suggest next.

"You think that such a girl might—" Pitt chose just the right phrase "—put her daydreams into words, and inadvertently cause mischief?"

"Quite!" Reggie pounced on it. At last the fellow seemed to have grasped the point. "Exactly! You take my meaning to a nicety. Could be embarrassing, don't you see?"

"Oh very," Pitt agreed. "Very difficult to disprove, too," he smiled guilelessly and Reggie felt sharply uncomfortable. There was a very ugly truth in it.

"There must be laws against that sort of—irresponsibility!" he said hotly. "A decent person must be able to protect himself!"

"Oh, there are," Pitt affirmed smoothly. "Slander, and all that. Always take it to court."

"Court! Don't be preposterous, man! Whoever heard of a man taking his servant girl to court because she said he slept with her! You'd be the laughingstock of society!"

"Probably because in many cases it would be true," Pitt looked at the bronze-colored brandy in his glass. "And no one would believe you were one of the innocent; nor, I suppose, would they greatly care."

Reggie felt the sweat break out on his body and turn cold.

"There must be a law, a way, something to prevent it! It's monstrous! You can't ruin a man just like that!" he snapped his fingers furiously and the soft flesh refused to click. "Damn!" he swore in frustration.

"I agree," Pitt swallowed the last of his brandy and set the glass down. "One must be very careful indeed when one uses another's good name. The damage done can be incalculable, and there can be financial redress, but there is no undoing it."

Reggie gathered control of himself, at least on the surface.

"I shall certainly dismiss without reference or character any servant I find speaking loosely or spreading malicious gossip," he said with absolute decision.

"Without a character," Pitt repeated, and there was a bit-

73

terness in his face Reggie was at a loss to understand. Peculiar fellow. Bit unreliable.

"Certainly," Reggie agreed. "Man or woman who behaves like that is a menace, not fit to employ. Still, suppose you know that. Must have run into slander before, eh? After all, it is a crime, and crime is your livelihood, what?"

Pitt did not argue. Instead he asked permission to speak to the servants again, and when it was granted, took his leave. It did not occur to Reggie until the evening, long after Pitt had gone, to wonder what Pitt had wanted to see him for in the first place. Perhaps the blighter just saw the brandy and the fire and fancied a few minutes' relaxation. The working classes were often the same, give them a chance to idle and they'd take it with both hands. Still, couldn't blame them entirely. Their life was gray enough. He would have done the same.

After dinner the thought bothered him still more. What had the wretched fellow come about? Was it possible he had already heard some gossip? Got to kill this thing before it got underway. That sort of accusation, in the wrong quarters, could make him look ridiculous, a figure of jest. To take a toss with one's parlormaid was perfectly accepted, probably half of London did it; but to have it a subject of talk was quite another thing. Discretion and good taste were the cornerstones of a gentleman's conduct. There were certain functions which everyone knew about and no one discussed. Relieving one's appetites with the servants was one of them. To do so was normal, part of the natural man: to be supposed to do so was not worthy of comment; but to be known to do so from other sources than one's own innuendos was to be a figure of ribaldry and contempt. It was worse than that, it was bad taste.

Better nip this thing in the bud. It was a pleasant enough evening, for late November. He decided to walk across the corner of the square and see Freddie Bolsover. Good fellow, Freddie; man of sense. Still, suppose doctors usually were; knew the facts of things, the inner man, no dressing it up, what?

He found Freddie sitting in his withdrawing room listening to Sophie play the piano. He stood up quickly, smiling when Reggie came in. He was a tall, slender young man with fair face, good features in a well-bred way. He complemented Sophie nicely.

"Reggie, nice to see you. Nothing wrong, I hope. You look well enough."

"Oh fine, fine," Reggie grasped his hand for a moment, then let it go. "Evening, Sophie, my dear," he kissed her high up the arm, squeezing it a little. Handsome piece, in her own way, nice hair, better than Adelina's, although her body was a bit bony round the shoulders, not enough bosom for Reggie's taste. "How about you?" he added as an afterthought.

"Oh, very well," Sophie answered and Freddie nodded agreement.

"Got a bit of a problem in another area, old fellow." Reggie glanced very slightly at Sophie to indicate it was a masculine affair and she should be politely dismissed.

Freddie obliged, and Sophie took herself off on some made-up errand.

Freddie sat down again, extending his feet toward the fire. It was a beautiful room; and Reggie happened to know, because Adelina had told him, that all the furniture and draperies were new, and of the latest fashion. He accepted the port Freddie offered him. That was jolly good too, damned old.

"Well?" Freddie inquired.

Reggie frowned, trying to frame his thoughts without betraying himself too far. Freddie was a good chap; but no point in telling him anything he did not need to know.

"Had that police fellow nosing around again?" he asked, looking up.

Freddie's fair eyebrows rose in surprise.

"Don't really know. Suppose he's bound to question the servants, and so forth. Haven't seen him myself, but then there's nothing I could tell him anyway. Don't follow the romantic affairs of the servants' hall!" he smiled.

"Course not," Reggie agreed. "No one does. But has it occurred to you the damage they could cause by a bit of mischievous gossip in the wrong place? I've spoken to this police chap. Civil enough, but not a gentleman, of course. Bound to have working class ideas. Wouldn't have servants in his own house, beyond a woman for the heavy stuff—" he stopped, not sure if Freddie was following him.

"Damage?" Freddie looked puzzled. "You mean if they said something stupid to this fellow, lied, and so forth?"

"That," Reggie agreed, "or—oh come on, Freddie! Most of us have pinched a few bottoms now and then, kissed a good-looking maid, spot of fun, what?"

Recollection flashed in Freddie's face.

"Oh, of course. You're worried about Dolly? That was her name, wasn't it?"

Reggie felt acutely uncomfortable. He had hoped Freddie might have forgotten that. Dolly was dead and the whole thing was in the past now. Of course it had been very sad. The poor girl should never have gone to a back-street abortionist. He would have provided for her, found her some place in the country where no one would have known her; a long way from Callander Square, naturally. There was no call for her to have panicked in that way. It could hardly be said to be his fault! Still, he could have wished Freddie had forgotten it. He had had to call Freddie at the time. The girl had died in Reggie's house, and there was no time to call a regular doctor; Freddie had been nearest. Freddie had been alone with her for a while before she died. He had no idea what she might have babbled to him then. Please heaven he had not believed any of it.

"Yes," he said, recalling himself. Freddie was still waiting for his reply. "Yes, Dolly. But that couldn't have anything to do with this. It was over years ago, poor girl. She's been dead four years by now. But you know servants, they romanticize. If that fellow gets to question them some silly girl could be indiscreet. Might say I had a fancy for her. Police could read more into it than there was."

"Oh quite," Freddie agreed. "Can't expect chaps like that to understand."

"Wouldn't do any of us any good," Reggie went on. "Scandal, and so on. Give the square a bad name: we'd all suffer. Rubs off. Mud sticks, you know?"

"Oh quite," Freddie's face clouded as he realized precisely what Reggie meant, and the disadvantages to all of them. "Yes."

76

Reggie wondered whether Freddie had thought of the harm to his burgeoning professional career, which depended so much on a reputation for uprightness and discretion. Would it be necessary to put it in words for him? He prodded delicately.

"Trouble is, everybody that matters knows everybody else. Damn women, spend all afternoon talking—"

"Yes," Freddie's pleasant face screwed up. "Yes. Better to prevent it happening in the first place. Little care, save a lot of talk and they'll be without a position. Perhaps it would be a good idea to prime the butler, and see that he is with any female servant questioned by this Pitt fellow in the future."

Relief flooded through Reggie.

"What a damned good idea, Freddie old chap. That's the answer. I'll have a word with Dobson, see that none of the women is—" he smiled a little, "harassed, what? Thanks Freddie, you're a decent fellow."

"Not at all," Freddie smiled up at him from the back of his chair. "Have some more port?"

Reggie settled down and filled his glass.

The following evening he thought it would be a good idea to further consolidate the position by having a discreet word with Garson Campbell as well. After all, Campbell was a man of the world, man of affairs, knew how to conduct things. It was a bitter night, sleeting hard, and several times he looked out of the window at the turbulent darkness, the wet, thrashing leaves, and pavement glistening in the gaslight, then back at the fire and thought that tomorrow would do well enough. Then he remembered that tomorrow that wretched policeman might come sneaking round the servants' halls again, and goodness knows what could be said, and too late to do anything about it by then.

With a last reluctant look at the comfort of his chair, he drank two fingers of brandy, collected his coat from the footman, and set out. It was less than two hundred yards, but by the time he reached the shelter of Campbell's doorway he was already shivering, perhaps more from the expectation in his mind of cold than from the actuality.

The Campbells' footman opened the door and Reggie

stepped in smartly, easing his coat off his shoulders almost before the man could get to it to take it from him.

"Mr. Campbell in?" Reggie asked.

"I'll inquire, sir." It was a stock answer. Of course the man would know whether Campbell was in or out, it was whether he wished to see Reggie that he had to discover. He was shown into the morning room where there were still the embers of a fire, and he stood with his back to it, warming his legs, until the footman returned and told him Campbell would see him.

He was received in the main withdrawing room. Campbell was standing by a blaze that burned halfway up the chimney; he was a heavy-chested man with rather a long nose, not ill-looking, but yet certainly not handsome. Such charm as he had lay in a dignity of bearing and a fastidiousness both of manner and of person.

"Evening, Reggie," he said cordially. "Must be urgent to get you away from your fireside on a night like this. What is it, run out of port?"

"Sack a butler who'd let me do that," Reggie replied, joining him over by the fire. "Filthy night. Hate winter in London, 'cept it's a damn sight worse in the country. Civilized men should go to France, or somewhere. 'Cept the French are a lot of barbarians, what? Don't know how to behave. Paris the weather's as bad as here, and the south there's nothing to do!"

"Ever thought of hibernating?" Campbell raised his eyebrows sardonically.

Reggie wondered vaguely if he were being laughed at; but it did not worry him. Campbell had a habit of jeering slightly at most things. It was part of his manner. Who knew why? People cultivated manners for a variety of reasons, and Reggie was hard to offend.

"Frequently," he said with a smile. "Unfortunately things tend to need prodding and probing every so often, y'know. Like this wretched business of the bodies in the square; filthy mess."

"Quite," Campbell agreed. "But hardly our concern. Nothing we can do about it, except be more careful about servants in the future. Always give the girl some sort of help, I suppose, if it turns out the child was born dead. Find her a place in the country, where no one would know about it. That what you want? I've loads of relatives who could be prevailed upon."

"Not quite," Reggie sidled closer to the fire. Why on earth couldn't the miserable fellow offer him a drink? He glanced at Campbell's wry face, and found the blue eyes on him. Damn fellow knew he wanted a drink, and was deliberately not offering one. Nasty sense of humor, the honorable Garson Campbell.

"Oh?" Campbell was waiting.

"Bit anxious about the police," Reggie avoided his stare and assumed an attitude of concentration, as if he knew something Campbell did not. "Nosing around the servants' halls, you know. Don't know quite how responsible these police are. Ordinary sort of chap, working class, naturally. Could start a lot of silly gossip, without realizing the harm it could do. Freddie agrees with me."

Campbell turned his head to look at him more closely.

"Freddie?"

"Saw him yesterday," Reggie said casually. "Pointed out what a nuisance it could be, for all of us, if the square got the reputation for loose behavior, immoral servants, general bad taste, and so on. Not good, you know. Don't want to be the butt of a lot of gossip, even if it's all supposition."

Campbell's mouth turned down at the corners.

"Take your point," he said with a slight rasp. "Could be difficult. Even if people don't believe it, they'll pass it on. Find ourselves snubbed in clubs, laughed at." His face darkened fiercely. "Bloody damned nuisance! Some idiotic girl who—" his anger died out as suddenly. "Way of the world. Poor little bitch. Still, what did you come to me about, except to commiserate?"

Reggie drew a deep breath.

"Commiseration's not much use—"

"None at all," Campbell agreed.

"Better to prevent it before it happens."

Campbell's face betrayed interest for the first time.

"What are you suggesting, Reggie?"

"A discreet word, with the butler or housekeeper, to speak

79

to the rest of the servants. See that one or the other of them is present every time this police fellow interviews any of them. Get them to make sure nothing—foolish—is said. Natural enough, what? Not to let a young servant be bullied. Got to protect them, eh?"

Campbell smiled with harsh amusement.

"Why, Reggie, I never suspected you of such subtlety—or such common sense."

"Then you'll do it?"

"My dear idiot, my household is already aware that loose talk would cost them their livelihoods: but I admit it would be an added protection to make sure a butler or housekeeper is present if this, what's-his-name—Pitt—comes back again. Personally I think they'll probably drop it after a reasonable show of trying. After all, to whom does it really matter if some servant girl has two children stillborn? It's hardly worth raising hell in an area like this. He'll know that he'll find out nothing that matters, and offend a lot of people who could make life damned difficult for him, if he gives them cause. Don't get yourself upset, Reggie. They'll run around to give the impression of intent, then quietly let it die. Do you want a glass of port?"

Reggie took a moment for the idea to seep through him with its relief: then he realized Campbell had offered him the port at last.

"Yes," he accepted graciously. "Thank you, very civil of you."

"Not at all," Campbell smiled to himself and walked away to the side table to fetch the decanter.

Augusta had noticed Christina's indisposition; and at first she had thought nothing of it, beyond a natural sympathy. It was easy enough to eat or drink something which did not agree with one. Then on the appalling discovery of Christina in the arms of the wretched footman, Max, the incident came back to her mind with rather more anxiety. When the indisposition occurred again a week later, and she heard from the lady's maid that Christina was to remain in her bed for the morning, she felt something considerably more like alarm.

She did not wish General Balantyne to know anything

80

about it—he would be entirely useless if indeed there were such a crisis as her worst fears framed, and if there were not, there was no purpose in alarming him. They were at the breakfast table when she was informed, and after a moment's silent panic, she thanked the woman civilly and bade her return to Christina and care for her, then she requested the general to pass her the orange conserve to spread upon her toast.

"Pity," the general said quietly, passing across the jar. "Poor girl. Hope it's nothing serious. Want to send for the doctor? Always ask Freddie to slip over, if she doesn't want a fuss."

"Nothing he can do for a chill on the stomach," she replied smoothly. Heavens above, the last thing she wanted now was a doctor! "Charming as he is, he can't change the weather. Lots of pestilence of one sort or another in the autumn. I shall have cook make her an herbal tea. That will do as much good as anything. No doubt it will cure itself in a day or two."

He looked at her with slight surprise, but rather than argue, continued with his deviled kidneys, bacon, eggs, and toast.

When she had finished her meal, so as not to appear in a hurry and give the matter undue importance, she excused herself and went upstairs. If there were no reason for alarm, so much the better, but if her worst fears were valid—and she remembered with a cold shiver through her flesh the familiarity of that touch in the stillroom pantry, the ease with which the hands had caressed the silk bodice under the breasts—and it was indeed true, then she must think now what to do about it. If there were any hope at all of saving the situation, it lay in immediate action. Every additional day would make it harder.

And if she did not succeed—a lesser woman would have flinched even from the thought, but even her enemies, and she had several, would never have denied that Augusta had courage—there lay ahead for Christina little but endless unhappiness. To have an illegitimate child was a sin never completely forgiven by the society in which Christina moved, in which she had been brought up, and in which were all her friends, indeed the society which would enable her to have

81

the only life for which she was fitted. It might be possible, with care and money dispersed in appropriate places, to create some fiction to take her away from London for the necessary period of time, have the child brought up on the country estate, adopted by some good serving woman. It would take skill, but it was not impossible: it had surely been done by others! Christina was not the first, nor would she be the last in this predicament.

If only that were all!

But there was Max: an ambitious and ruthless man. Of course she had realized from the day she had employed him that he was intent, above all things, on bettering himself. And she had thought that that would make him an excellent footman. Ambitious men were good employees; and so he had proved, in respect of his job; he was always immaculate, always punctual, always more than civil; indeed she had received many compliments as to his quality. But she blamed herself now for not realizing that his ambition would lead him to use any means that offered to advance himself, even to lying with his employer's daughter. She did not delude herself for a moment that there was any affection involved— on either side. And she should also have known her daughter better, she should have seen the weakness in her, and protected her from it. What else were mothers for?

Max had forged himself a weapon. If he chose to use it, to spread gossip, gently, like slow poison, Christina would be ruined. No man of her own class would marry her, no matter what her dowry. There was always a surfeit of personable young women in the marriage market, and Christina possessed no special advantage; at least none that would outweigh the reputation of a trollop. To be high-spirited was one thing, to be a whore and to have borne a child to a footman was quite another. The only world she knew, or could cope with, would be as closed to her as the Bank of England.

Max must be silenced: not by bribery of any sort. Give in to him even once, and they would be hostage to him for the rest of their lives. It must be a counterthreat of equal magnitude. Not only for Christina's sake, but for the whole family, for the general, and for young Brandy, as well as herself. If Brandy should fall in love, or even find agreeable some well-connected girl, what parents would allow their daughter to marry into a family whose blood bred such as Christina?

She was on the landing with her hand raised to Christina's door when the worst thought of all came to her. She nearly fainted from the sheer horror of it. Max had been in their employ for six years. She sincerely believed that if such an appalling thing had happened before she would have known it—but what if she had not? And would the police believe it? Could they even afford to? Unless she was very much mistaken, that young man Pitt was of uncommon intelligence. He would pursue the matter, question Christina, perhaps even discover that it was Max, and draw from him all the sordid truth. What would he believe of the bodies in the square then? What did she herself believe?

She let her hand fall to the wood, and before Christina replied, she pushed the door open.

Christina was lying on the bed, looking pale and peaked, her features unusually sharp, her dark hair spread on the pillow around her.

Augusta felt a moment's pity for her, then it passed and she forced her attention to preventing the far worse pain that threatened.

"Sick?" she asked simply.

Christina nodded her head.

Augusta came in and shut the door. There was no point in mincing words. She sat on the end of the bed and looked at her daughter.

"Is it an illness you have caught from Max?" she said, looking at Christina's eyes.

Christina tried to look away, and failed. She was used to getting her own way, to charming or dominating everyone, but never since childhood had she succeeded with her mother.

"What—what do you mean, Mama?" she said stiltedly.

"There is no point in prevaricating, Christina. If you are with child, there is a great deal we have to do. I have no wish to frighten you unnecessarily, but I don't think you have realized the seriousness of our predicament, if it is so."

Christina opened her mouth, and closed it again.

Augusta waited.

"I don't know," Christina said very quietly. There was a

83

shiver in her voice and she was having to struggle hard not to cry. It was only pride that prevented her, and the knowledge that her mother would not have cried.

Augusta asked the question she dreaded, but she would shirk nothing. She needed to know.

"Is this the first time?"

Christina stared, eyes enormous with indignant disbelief, and then horror as she realized what Augusta meant, what she was thinking. Her face was as bleached as the sheet.

"Oh, Mother! You can't think I would—oh no!"

"Good. I did not think you would. But it is not what I think that matters, it is what the police think, or have enough cause to consider that they raise the possibility—"

"Mother—!"

"I shall deal with it. You will not see Max again. Until I have secured his silence, you will remain in bed. You have a chill. Is that understood?"

"Yes, Mama," she was too shocked and too frightened to argue. "Do you think—the police—I mean—?"

"I intend that they shall not know anything to think one way or the other. And you will do exactly as I tell you, to that end."

Christina nodded silently, and Augusta looked at her pale face, remembering how she had felt for the first few weeks when she had been with child, with Christina herself. What a lifetime ago that seemed. Brandy had been a small boy, still in skirts: and his father had been younger, his face less lean, his body a few pounds slimmer, but just as straight, shoulders as broad and stiff. How could a man change so little? His voice, his manners, even his thoughts seemed all the same.

"It will pass," she said gently. "It will not be more than a few weeks, then you will feel better. I shall have cook make you a beef tea."

"Thank you, Mama," Christina whispered, and closed her eyes.

Augusta racked her brains and her imagination for a way to make sure of Max's silence, without at the same time giving him a weapon for future use. But by the following morning she had achieved no more than the elimination of all the impossibilities, and was left with little else. She was in an ill temper to receive him when Pitt arrived at a quarter past ten.

When she first learned that it was Max who had shown him in, a moment of panic seized her, then she realized that Max's ambition would never allow him to waste his valuable knowledge by giving it to Pitt, who would pay him nothing for it, instead of first offering it to Augusta, who might pay him in all sorts of ways, only beginning with money, and progressing through advancement to heaven knew what avaricious heights.

She found Pitt in the morning room, warming his hands in front of the fire. It was another bitter day, a hard east wind driving needles of sleet in from the North Sea, and she could hardly blame any living creature for availing itself of any warmth at all, yet she resented this policeman in front of her fire. He did not move because he had not heard her enter.

"Good morning, Mr. Pitt," she said coldly. "What is it this time?"

He was startled, and he took a moment to compose himself before he turned to face her.

"Good morning, ma'am. I'm afraid we have not yet discovered the truth regarding the bodies in the square—"

"Do you seriously imagine, Mr. Pitt, that you ever will?" She raised her eyebrows in disbelief.

"Perhaps not, ma'am; but I must try a great deal harder before I give up."

"Indeed. It seems like a waste of public money to me."

"It was perhaps a waste of human life, which is infinitely more precious."

"We also seem to have infinitely more of it," she said dryly. "But of I presume you have to do your duty, as you see it. What is it you imagine I can do that will help you?"

"Give me your permission to speak to your staff again, ma'am; and perhaps to Miss Christina Balantyne. She may have observed some behavior, some small sign that you have been too busy to note."

Augusta felt her stomach tighten. Was it conceivable he

85

had already heard something? Could Max have been so—no, surely not! Max was, above all, ambitious. He wanted his advantage to use, not to squander.

"I'm sorry, you may speak to the servants, of course; although I must insist that you do not distress them unnecessarily, and I shall have some responsible person with you, to that end; but I regret my daughter is unwell and confined to her bed. Naturally she cannot see anyone."

"Oh dear," his expressive face composed itself into lines of sympathy. She had no idea whether he meant it or not. "I do hope it is only a passing indisposition."

"We believe so," she replied. "The season of the year, no doubt. It is inclined to affect one. Now which of the servants do you wish to see? The female ones, I presume?"

"If you please."

She reached for the bell.

"I shall have the butler assist you."

"I should prefer to speak to them alone. His presence might inhibit them, make them feel less free to—"

"No doubt. But for their protection, the butler will remain with you. I will not have young girls who are my responsibility intimidated, even unwittingly, into saying things which they may afterward regret. Perhaps you do not realize how young and how ignorant some of them are; most suggestible, and easily led."

"Lady Augusta—"

"Those are the conditions on which you may speak with them, Mr. Pitt. Quite reasonable, I believe."

There was no further argument he could offer without betraying foreknowledge of some particular guilt, and she defied him at this point to do so.

"Ma'am," he acquiesced with a slight smile in recognition of her superior tactics. Had he been a gentleman, she might even have liked him, for a moment.

She felt no such sentiment toward Charlotte Ellison when she arrived shortly before midday to assist the general with his papers. Miss Ellison was a young woman she could not warm to—there was an element of emotion about her, of unpredictability, which was dangerous. One could not plan for it because it fell within none of the rules. And yet she seemed harmless enough. She came and went silently and was certainly both civil and, at least to all appearances, well-bred enough. But why should any young woman desire to help a middle-aged general sort out papers pertaining to battles and regiments, instead of seeking herself a husband? It was a question to which, at a less preoccupied time, she would have sought an answer.

As it was she contented herself with asking Brandon over luncheon what manner of creature she was, and if she gave satisfaction as to her clerical ability.

"Yes," he said with slight surprise, "she appears to be of uncommon intelligence, for a woman."

"You mean of uncommon interest in those things which interest you—for a woman," Augusta replied with some asperity.

"Is that not more or less what I said?"

"No, it is not. Most women have perfectly good intelligence for the things which matter, such as the conduct of one's daily life; but do not desire to apply themselves to the dissection of battles that concerned other people in other countries and at other times. I consider such an interest quite eccentric, and most unnatural in a young woman of decent upbringing."

"Nonsense," he said briskly. "Anyone of intelligence ought to appreciate the great history of our nation. We are the greatest military nation in the world; we have spread our civilization to every land and clime God made. We have created an empire and a peace that is the envy and the blessing of the world. Every woman of British blood should be proud of that."

"Proud of it, of course," she agreed testily, reaching for the anchovy pâté, "but not concerned with the details!"

He took the last piece of toast and did not bother to reply.

It was after that conversation that Augusta turned her thoughts uninterruptedly to the matter of Max's silence; and at last came up with a satisfactory answer. It was in the quiet hour previous to dinner that she decided to tackle the practical application of it. She went to the small withdrawing room where she would be undisturbed, and sent for Max to attend her.

She felt an overwhelming, almost suffocating dislike of him when he came in. He looked completely bland, as if he expected to discuss some small domestic affair with her. She had never noticed before how insolent his eyes were, how veiled. She must keep the most perfect control of herself.

"Good evening, Max," she said coolly.

"Good evening, my lady."

"There is no purpose to be served by our prevaricating. I have sent for you to discuss a matter which I intend shall be dealt with, if not to our mutual advantage, at least not to the disadvantage of either of us. Whether that turns out to be so, depends on you."

"Yes, my lady?" his face betrayed nothing.

"You have been foolish enough to engage yourself in a liaison with my daughter. You will cease immediately to pay her any attentions whatsoever. You will leave my employ and take up a post in Scotland, which I shall arrange for you and for which I will provide you with references—"

"I have no wish to work in Scotland, my lady." He stood square in front of her, his eyes burning with slow amusement.

"Probably not. But that is of no concern to me. I have relations in Stirlingshire who will oblige me by finding you a place. The alternative is prison, which I believe is even colder and more barbarous than Scotland."

"Prison, my lady?" he raised surprised eyebrows. "To lie with a lady of quality, especially if that lady is more than willing, I may add, may be indiscreet, even socially offensive to some, but it is not a crime. And even if it were, I doubt you would wish to charge me with it." There seemed a distinct sneer on his mouth.

"No, of course not. But stealing silver from one's employer is a crime." She met his eyes equally unflinchingly.

His face froze for an instant, understanding dawning in his eyes.

"I have not stolen any silver, my lady."

"No. But if silver were to be missing, and it were to be found in your belongings, you would find it uncommonly difficult to prove that you had not."

"That is blackmail."

"How perceptive of you. I thought you would take the point quite easily."

"If I were to be charged with such a thing, I should naturally, in my own defense, give the reason for your accusation," he watched her carefully, waiting for the slightest sign of weakness.

She gave him nothing.

"Possibly," she said coolly. "But that would be foolish, because you would then find yourself charged with slander as well. And who do you imagine would be believed—Lady Augusta Balantyne, dealing with a dishonest servant with ideas above his station, or the servant, bearing a grudge for having been discovered? Come, Max, you are, above all, not stupid."

He stared at her with malignant hate swelling in his sensuous face.

She did not look down, but stared back at him with equal and undeviating steadiness.

FIVE

General Balantyne was very satisfied with the way his memoirs were coming along. The military history of his family really was remarkable, and the more he put his papers in order, the more outstanding he perceived it to be. There was a heritage of discipline and sacrifice of which anyone might be proud. But far more than that, there was an urgency, an excitement to it more real than the petty domesiticity and the polite fictions of his daily life in Callander Square. The early winter rain drenched the gray cobbles outside, but his imagination felt the rain of Quatre Bras and Waterloo nearly seventy years ago, where his grandfather had lost an arm and a leg struggling through the mud of Belgian fields behind the Iron Duke; scarlet coats and blues, the charge of the Scots Grays, the end of an empire and the beginning of a new age.

The heat from the fire in the grate scorched his legs and he felt in it the blistering sun of India, thought of Tippoo Sultan, the Black Hole of Calcutta, where his great-grandfather had perished. He knew the heat himself. The spear wound on his thigh was not yet totally healed from the Zulu Wars, only three years ago. It still ached in the cold to remind him. Perhaps that would be his last battle, as the nightmare of the Crimea had been his first. He was still frightened far back in the recesses of his memory by the dreadful cold and the slaughter at Sebastopol, the dead lying all over the place, bodies wasted with cholera, blown apart by shot, frozen to death in grotesque positions, some huddled like children asleep. And the horses! God knew how many horses dead, poor beasts. Foolish that the horses should worry him so much.

He had been eighteen at Balaclava. He had come up with a message from his own commander for Lord Cardigan in time to see that unspeakable charge. He remembered the wind in his face, the smell of blood, gunpowder, and the torn-up earth as six hundred and seventy-three men and horses galloped against the entrenched guns of the entire Russian position. He had sat his horse beside the craggy old men, bemused in the uproar, angry, while below them in the valley two hundred and fifty men and six hundred horses obeyed their orders and were slaughtered. His father was in the Eleventh Hussars, and was one of those who did not stagger back.

His uncle had been in the Ninety-third Highlanders, and held the "thin red line," five hundred and fifty men between thirty thousand Russians and Balaclava itself. Like so many he had died where he stood. It had been he, Brandon, who had sat in the bitter cold of a trench to write to his mother to tell her her husband and her brother were dead. He could still feel now the agony of trying to find the words. Then he had gone on to fight at Inkerman, and the fall of Sebastopol. It had seemed then as if the whole tide of Asia were sweeping over them with the fetch of half the earth behind it.

Surely those not yet born would hear in their hearts the guns of these battles and feel the pride and the pain, the confusions—and the sweep of history? Could he be so inarticulate as to have lived it himself, and pass on nothing of the taste in the mouth, the beat of the blood, the tears afterward?

The young woman, Miss Ellison, seemed competent, and pleasant enough. Although perhaps "pleasant" was not the word. She was too definite in her attitudes and opinions to be entirely agreeable to him. But she was intelligent, that was beyond question. He was relieved of the necessity of having to explain anything more than once, in fact on occasion he had found she had seized the point before he had finished with a first instruction, which he had found faintly annoying. And yet she meant no harm, and she certainly gave herself no airs. Indeed, she appeared to be more than happy to eat in the servants' hall, rather than put cook to the trouble of setting her a separate tray.

More than once she had actually made suggestions as to how he might proceed, which he had difficulty in accepting with grace. But he was obliged to admit that her ideas were quite good, in fact he had not actually thought of anything better himself. As he was sitting in the library now, he considered what he would write next, and what Miss Ellison might judge of it.

He was irritated to be interrupted by Max at the door to say that Mr. Southeron was in the morning room, wishing to see him, and was he at home?

He hesitated. The last thing he wanted was to be bothered with Reggie Southeron right now, but Reggie was a neighbor, and as such had to be tolerated. Not to do so would provoke reactions that would be endless, and cause all sorts of minor discomforts.

Max was waiting silently. His immaculate figure and calm smile annoyed him as much as the request he made. Wish Augusta would get rid of him and find someone else.

"Yes, of course," he said tartly. "And you'd better bring something to drink—the Madeira, not the best."

"No, sir," Max withdrew, and a moment later Reggie came in, large, affable, clothes already settled in comfortable creases, although he could not have had them on for more than a couple of hours.

"Morning, Brandon," Reggie said cheerfully, eyes glancing round the room, noting the fire, the comfortable, deep leather chairs, looking for the decanter and glasses.

"Good morning, Reggie," Balantyne replied. "What brings you visiting on a Saturday morning?"

"Been meaning to see you for a while, actually." Reggie sat down in the chair nearest the fire. "Not had a decent opportunity before; always something else going on, what? Place like a beehive lately."

Balantyne had not, to this point, been paying more than nominal attention to him, but now he began to hear a note of strain in Reggie's voice, and that in spite of his bonhomie, he had come about something specific that caused him an anxiety he was needing to share. Max would be back with the Madeira in a moment, and there was no point in approaching anything serious until he had gone.

"I gather you've been busy," he said conversationally.

"Not me, really," Reggie replied. "Those wretched police

93

fellows, all over the damn place. Pitt, what's-his-name, creeping around the servants' halls, upsetting everything. Damnation, how I hate upheavals in the house. Servants all in a twitter. Great heavens, man, you must know how difficult it is to get decent servants and train them to the way you want them, to know your own tastes, and how to cater to them. Takes long enough. And then some damned fool thing like this has to happen, and before you know where you are, they're all unsettled. It's hard enough at any time to keep a good servant. Get ideas of bettering themselves. Fancy working for a duke or an earl, or something. Take an idea for foreign travel. Think they're badly done by if they don't get to spend the season in London, summer in the country, and the worst of the winter in the south of France! Wretched creatures take offense at the oddest things and before you know it they're off! Deuce knows why, half the time; no loyalty. But doesn't take a fool to know they'll all go if this damned fellow Pitt goes on asking questions about their private lives and their morals, interfering and making suggestions." His voice trailed off in exasperation as he anticipated a bleak winter of training new and unsatisfactory servants, cold rooms, burnt meals, unpressed clothes.

Balantyne did not think the eventuality in the least likely, although admittedly he did not especially value his creature comforts; but he did value his peace of mind. The domestic conflict such a crisis would provoke was truly appalling to contemplate. He did not like Reggie very much, they were as different as men could be; but he was sorry for the man's obvious fears, unfounded though they might prove to be.

"Shouldn't worry about it," he said casually. Max came in with the decanter and glasses, set them down, and departed, closing the door silently. Reggie helped himself without being asked.

"Wouldn't you?" Reggie demanded with a mixture of anxiety and offense.

"Not very likely." Balantyne declined the Madeira. He did not like the stuff, and it was too early in the day. "No good servant is going to hand in notice because she's asked a few questions, unless she's already got another place to go to.

And he's pretty civil, this fellow Pitt. None of my household has complained."

"For God's sake, man! Would you know if they had?" Reggie lost his temper at last. "Augusta runs your house like a regiment. Most efficient creature I've ever met. She wouldn't tell you if the whole lot were in revolt! She'd deal with it, and you'd still get your dinner in time."

Balantyne resented the implication that he was a useless appendage to his own household, but he reminded himself that the man was frightened, although he had no idea why; and he made an allowance for him.

"It is not very likely anyone will give notice now," he said calmly. "It would suggest guilt to the police, and no doubt make things harder for them than remaining here and carrying on in a normal manner."

Oddly enough, even this, with its impeccable logic, did not noticeably soothe Reggie. He sat rumpled, deep in the armchair, and glowered at his glass.

"Bad business, though," he said gloomily. "Don't suppose for a moment they'll ever find out who did it. Waste of time. All they'll do is stir up a lot of speculation and gossip." He looked up. "Could do us a lot of harm, you know, Brandon. Not good to have the police hanging around. People think there must be something wrong."

Balantyne could see his point, but there was nothing they could do about it, and he was inclined to think that Reggie was exaggerating.

"I'll lay you odds Carlton would agree," Reggie said quickly, a lift in his voice. "'Above suspicion,' you know, 'Caesar's wife,' and all that. Foreigners are inclined to be funny. Got to keep an immaculate reputation."

What he said was probably true. Balantyne frowned, looking at Reggie through narrowed eyes. Reggie had poured himself another glass, and unless Balantyne was mistaken, it was not his second, or even his third today. What was he really frightened of?

"What does he say?" Reggie pressed.

"Haven't spoken to him," Balantyne replied honestly.

"Might be a good idea if you did," Reggie tried to smile,

and ended with a grimace that was more like bared teeth. "Would myself but I don't know him as well as you do. Influential man. He might be able to make the police see sense. They'll never find out who the woman was, not a chance in hell. Probably some servant girl who's moved away by now. Wouldn't want to hang around, would she?"

"The police will have thought of that," Balantyne answered. "We haven't dismissed any servants or had them leave in the last couple of years; have you?" Suddenly recollection came to him in a blinding understanding. It seemed stunningly obvious now. "How long ago since Dolly died?" he said baldly.

The blood drained from Reggie's face till Balantyne thought he was going to faint. His skin looked sweaty gray.

"Was that your child that killed her, Reggie?" he asked.

Reggie's mouth opened, like a fish, and closed again silently. He could not find a lie that would be of any use.

"I thought that was more than two years ago," Balantyne went on.

"It was!" Reggie found his tongue at last, his lips stiff. "It was! Four years. Couldn't possibly have anything to do with it! But you know what people are, give a dog a bad name. They'll think because—" he foundered in the lie, and took another glass of Madeira.

There was no need to press him about the present; the truth was too obvious, the reason he wanted the police out of the square, away from talkative servants. Poor fool!

"I expect they'll give up of their own accord soon," Balantyne said with a pity he resented feeling. "But I'll see what Carlton feels, when I get an opportunity. Don't suppose that Pitt chap wants to spend more time than he has to up a blind alley. No good for his career."

"No," Reggie cheered up visibly. "Don't suppose we need to point that out to him." His words were a little blurred. "But speak to Carlton all the same. He must know people; few words in the right places, could get it closed a bit sooner. Save a lot of nasty gossip; some public money too. Whole thing's a waste of time." He stood up a little shakily. "Thanks, old man. Thought you'd understand."

Christina did not appear for luncheon, and Brandy was

96

spending a week in the country with friends. He found himself alone at the table with Augusta.

"Christina still not better?" he said with a touch of anxiety. "Why hasn't she seen a doctor? Get Freddie to look at her, if Meredith can't come."

"Not necessary," Augusta replied, reaching for cold salmon. "It's only a chill. Cook prepared her a tray. Have some of the salmon. It's one Brandy caught last weekend in Cumberland. Very good, don't you think?"

He took some and tasted it.

"Excellent. Are you sure it's nothing worse? She's been in bed for a long time."

"Quite sure. A spell in bed will do her no harm. She's been overdoing it lately. Too many parties. Which reminds me, have you remembered we are dining with the Campbells this evening?"

He had not remembered. Still, it could have been worse. Garson Campbell was an interesting fellow, dry humor, if a little cynical; and Mariah was a more than usually sensible woman. Hardly ever heard her indulge in gossip or the endless flirtations that so many women seemed to engage their emotions with.

"Was that Reggie Southeron here this morning?" Augusta asked.

"Yes."

"What did he want, on a Saturday morning?"

"Nothing really. In a bit of a lather about the police upsetting the servants with a lot of questions and insinuations."

"Upsetting the servants?" she said incredulously.

He looked at her across the salmon.

"Yes. Why not?"

"Don't be ridiculous, Brandon. Reggie never gave a hoot about the servants, his own or anybody else's. What did he intend you should do about it anyway?"

He smiled in spite of himself.

"What makes you think he intended me to do anything about it?"

"He didn't come here to drink your Madeira. You always give him the worst, and he knows it. What did he want?"

"He suggested I should speak to Robert Carlton to see if

he can persuade the police to let the thing lie. They'll probably never discover the truth, anyway, all they can achieve is to waste their time, and stir up a lot of gossip. He could be right."

"He is right," she agreed tartly. "But I doubt that is why he is concerned. And I would be surprised if that odd young man—Pitt, I think his name is—will let it die until he has explored a good deal further than he has so far. But you can try, by all means, if you wish. Don't let Reggie make a fool of himself. It will rub off on all of us. Apart from the embarrassment to Adelina, poor creature."

"Why should Reggie make a fool of himself?" He had no intention of telling her about Dolly. It was not a matter for a decent woman to know of.

Augusta sighed.

"Sometimes, Brandon, I wonder if you affect to be obtuse merely to annoy me. Reggie wishes to keep the police from questioning his own servants too closely, which you must know quite as well as I do."

"I don't know what you are talking about." He did not wish to have to explain to her something which would both shock and distress her. She would find it sordid; as indeed perhaps it was, but a common human failing which women were apt, since the offense was against them, to view differently, and without the compassion a man might feel.

Augusta snorted and pushed away her empty plate. The pudding was brought in and served. When they were alone again she looked at him coolly.

"Then perhaps I had better tell you, before you unwittingly say something clumsy and embarrass us all. Reggie sleeps with all his parlormaids, so no doubt he is afraid the police will discover it, and be less than discreet about it. They may even think he has wandered farther afield."

He was stunned. She was speaking about it as if it hardly mattered!

"How on earth do you know?" he said hoarsely.

"My dear Brandon, everybody knows. One doesn't discuss it, of course; but one knows."

"Adelina?"

"Of course she knows. Do you take her for a fool?"

"Doesn't she—mind?"

"I've no idea. One doesn't ask, and naturally she doesn't mention it."

He was stunned. He could think of no reply adequate to his confusion. He had always known that women's minds and emotions worked on lines not comprehensible to men, but never before had it been so forcibly brought home to him.

Augusta was still looking at him.

"I wish there were some way it could be kept from that policeman, for Adelina's sake," she went on, "but I have not so far thought of any. That is why it might be a good idea for you to approach Robert Carlton to see if he can get the investigation shelved. It can hardly serve any purpose now, even in the unlikely event of their discovering which poor girl was responsible."

"There is the small matter of justice," he said indignantly, his feelings stunned once again. How on earth could she speak of it as if it were all irrelevant, as if they had not been human babies, now dead, possibly murdered?

"Really, Brandon, sometimes I despair of you," she said as she passed him the caramel sauce. "You are the most impractical man I ever knew. Why are soldiers such dreamers? You would think with the command of armies in their charge they would at least be practical, if nothing else, wouldn't you?" she sighed. "But then I suppose war is really the most idiotic of all pursuits, so perhaps not."

He stared at her as if she were a totally alien creature, as if she had changed shape from the known to the unknown in front of him.

"Naturally you don't understand war," he dismissed the last subject. "But even if justice is too abstract a concept for you, surely as a woman, who has borne children herself, you are moved to compassion?"

She put down her spoon and fork and leaned a little forward.

"The children are dead; whether they were born dead or died afterward, they are beyond our help now. The mother will have been through deeper hell than you can imagine, or probably than I can either. Whatever manner of woman she was, she will have paid for it in grief in this life, and will

99

answer to God for it in the next. What else is it you want from her? Her example will not prevent it happening again, I assure you, as long as there are both men and women in the world.

"Yes, your idea of justice is far too abstract for me. It is a word that sounds sonorous and pleasing to you; but you have no idea what it means from day to day; you have satisfied your ideals, and someone else is left to live it through.

"This thing is better buried. It is a pity those men ever went to plant their tree. If you can persuade Robert Carlton to exert a little influence and have the police leave well enough alone, it will be the best day's work you have done in a long time.

"Now if you intend to eat that pudding you had better do so before it gets cold, or it will give you indigestion. I am going upstairs to see how Christina is," and she stood up and walked out, leaving him staring after her, speechless.

Balantyne worked on his military papers in the afternoon, because they were something he was sure of; perhaps in time Augusta would explain herself, or else the matter would fall into recess of memory and cease to be important.

It was early evening, and already dark and turning very cold when Max announced Robert Carlton. Balantyne had always liked Carlton, he was a man whose quiet confidence and dignity appealed to him, the best type of Englishman, who followed the military into all the corners of the empire to govern and teach civilization where it was hitherto unknown. They were two partners to the same cause, and he felt they had an instinctive understanding, an inbred sense of duty and justice.

This evening he was especially pleased to see him because the mass of papers palled on him. It was more difficult without Miss Ellison to assist him, and in truth, gave him less than the usual satisfaction. He stood up with a smile, his hand out.

"'Evening, Robert, come in and warm yourself. Best fire in the house. Have a sherry, or whisky if you like? It must be about that time," he glanced at the brass carriage clock on the mantelpiece. How he hated the ormolu one in the withdrawing room and the fat cherubs round it; it did not even keep correct time!

"No, thank you, not yet."

Balantyne looked at him in surprise, then saw his face clearly for the first time. There were gray lines under his eyes and a flat, bare look about his whole aspect. Augusta would have been subtle, but he was incapable of it.

"For heaven's sake, man, have one, you look as if you need it! What's the matter?"

Carlton stood by the fire, unsure how to begin, and Balantyne realized he had embarrassed him by noticing a private distress he was not yet able to put into words. He was in turn embarrassed by his own clumsiness. Why could he not be warmer, more instinctive? He knew how to act in a crisis, but so often not what to say.

The silence hung between them, growing worse.

It was Carlton who resolved it.

"I'm sorry. Yes, I would like a whisky. I'm a little upset this evening—" he stopped, still looking not at Balantyne but at the fire. "Am I holding you up from changing to dine?"

"No, no. Plenty of time. Going to the Campbells."

"Oh yes, of course. So are we. Forgot."

Balantyne poured two whiskys from the decanter on the sideboard and passed him one. Surely Carlton wanted to discuss whatever it was? Was that not why he had come?

"Anything wrong in particular?" he asked.

"Had that police chap, Pitt, round again."

Balantyne opened his mouth to ask if the servants were upset, then realized that such a domestic disturbance would hardly cause the distress he thought he saw. He remained silent, waiting for Carlton to frame whatever it was that lay so close under the surface.

It was a few minutes before it came, but this silence was one of patience.

"I think they suspect Euphemia," Carlton said at last.

Balantyne was stunned. He could think of nothing coherent to say. How could they possibly suspect Euphemia Carlton? It was preposterous. He must have misunderstood: especially since the more he thought about it, the more he honestly believed it was most likely to be some indulgence

101

of Reggie's, and Reggie knew it, which was why he was in such a sweat.

He suddenly remembered that Reggie had wanted him to get Carlton to have the investigation suppressed! It was ludicrous.

"They can't," he said flatly. "It doesn't make any sense at all, and Pitt's an ordinary sort of chap, but he's not a fool. They wouldn't let him be an inspector if he made wild charges like that. You must have misunderstood something. Apart from anything else, Euphemia could have no reason!"

Carlton still looked into the fire, keeping his face away.

"Yes, she has, Brandon. She has a lover."

From many men that would have meant little, as long as it were not publicly known, but to Carlton it was a sacrilege against his home, his most private person. Balantyne understood that much, although he could not feel the same inner injury to purity and pride himself. If Augusta had betrayed him, he would have been above all surprised; and yes, angry too; but not wounded except on the surface.

"I'm sorry," he said simply.

"Thank you," Carlton accepted it with the same politeness he might have received a compliment or a glass of wine, but Balantyne could see the pain in his drawn face. "You see," Carlton went on, "they think she might have got rid of the children, in case the—made her—her situation obvious."

"Yes, of course. But surely, you would have known? I mean—a woman you live with—your wife! If she had been with child—?"

"I do not ask a—a—great deal of Euphemia," Carlton said awkwardly, his shoulders stiff, his face turned away. "I am considerably older than she is—I do not—like to—" he could not find words to finish, but his meaning was obvious.

Balantyne had never been so delicate about feelings, least of all Augusta's, and suddenly he saw himself as a boor. He was ashamed for himself, and for Carlton he was inexplicably hurt. How could Euphemia, with a man so sensitive to her, loving her so deeply, have behaved like this? But neither his anger nor his disgust would be of any ease to Carlton now.

"I'm sorry," he said again. "Do you know who?"

"No. it is all very—discreet still. The police say as little as they can."

"Do you know if she—cares for him?"

"No, I don't."

"You haven't asked her?"

Carlton turned and sheer surprise, for a moment, superseded the pain in his face.

"Of course not. I couldn't—speak—to her of it. It would be—" he held out his hands helplessly.

"No." Balantyne had no idea why he agreed. He was agreeing for Carlton, not for himself—he would have had a blazing row about it—but he could see that this quiet man, with whom he had thought he had so much in common, was utterly different. "I'm awfully sorry, Robert. I wish I knew what to say."

For the first time Carlton smiled very faintly.

"Thank you, Brandon. There really isn't anything to say. I don't know why I bothered you with it, except that I felt like speaking to someone."

"Yes," Balantyne suddenly found his awkwardness again. "Yes, yes, of course. I—er—"

Carlton drank the last of his whisky and put the glass down.

"Better get back home. Must be toward dinner time. Got to change. Give my regards to Augusta. Good night, and thank you."

"Good night—" he let out his breath again. There was nothing to say.

He thought several times of mentioning the subject to Augusta, but somehow could not bring himself to do it. It seemed a private matter, between men. For another woman to have known would have compounded the injury.

It was still at the back of his mind when Miss Ellison arrived on Monday morning to continue with the papers. He was surprisingly pleased to see her, perhaps because she was outside the family, and knew nothing of Callander Square or its wounds. Added to which she was cheerful, without being in the least coquettish. As he grew older he found coquettish women increasingly offensive.

"Good morning, Miss Ellison," he smiled without thinking. She was a pleasing creature, not conventionally beautiful, and yet there was a richness about her, the wealth of mahogany-colored hair, the clear skin, and the intelligence in her eyes. For a woman, she talked remarkably little nonsense; funny, she was probably not more than four or five years older than Christina, who seldom spoke of anything but gossip or fashion, and who might marry whom.

He realized with a start that she was waiting for him to instruct her as to what he wished her to do.

"I have a box of letters here," he fished it out, "from my grandfather. Would you please sort them out, those that refer to military matters from those that are purely personal."

"Certainly," she took the box. "Would you like them categorized?"

"Categorized?" he was still not concentrating.

"Yes. Those from the Peninsular War, those written before Quatre Bras and after Waterloo, and those from the military hospital and during the hundred days? Do you not think they would be interesting also?"

"Yes. Yes, please, that would be excellent." He watched her remove them and go to sit at the far side of the room, by the fire, her head bent over the old paper and the faded, youthful handwriting. He saw in her, for a moment, his grandmother as she must have read those letters, sitting in an England at war with the Emperor, a young wife with infant children. He had no idea what she had looked like. Had she the same long curve of cheek, slender throat, so very feminine, and the tiny wisps of hair soft on the nape of the neck?

He shook himself strongly. The thought was ridiculous: she was merely a young woman who had an interest in old letters, and was competent to sort them.

Charlotte, on the other hand, was quite unconscious of the general. She forgot him as soon as she read the first sentence in the round, faded writing. Her imagination took her to lands she had never seen, and she tried to feel with the young soldier the emotions he described, his terror of the pressed men in the ranks, which he knew he must hide, his friendship for the surgeon, his awe at meeting the Iron Duke himself.

There was humor in them, and unconscious pathos sometimes, and a lot of things he did not say about cold and
hunger, aching legs, wounds, and fear, long monotony and
sudden confusion of action.

She went down to luncheon in a dream, and the afternoon
slipped by before she thought of time. It was dark when she
got home, and less than a half hour later Emily arrived at
the door, her coach horses stamping in the frost outside, their
breath adding to the early fog.

"Well?" she demanded as soon as she was through the
door.

Charlotte was still in Spain and the Peninsular War. She
stared at Emily blankly.

Emily shut the door behind her and took a deep breath.

"What have you found out at the Balantynes'?" she said
patiently. "You have been there, I presume?"

"Oh yes, of course," Charlotte realized with a wave of guilt
that she had done nothing to justify Emily's trust in her, over
the six days she had already been in Callander Square.
"Many times," she added. "I am coming to know some of the
servants quite well."

"Never mind the servants!" Emily said quickly. "What
about Christina? Is she with child? And whether she is or
not, why does she think that she is? Who is the father? And
why does she not marry him, instead of allowing this ridiculous situation? Is he already married, or promised to someone else?" Her eyes widened. "Oh! Of course, he is unsuitable!
It is a love match!" Then her face fell again. "No, it isn't. Not
Christina." She sighed. "Oh Charlotte! Haven't you found out
anything at all?" Her expression crumpled in disappointment
till Charlotte felt genuinely sorry for her, and even more
strongly that she had let her down.

"I really will try tomorrow. But Christina has been in bed
ever since I got there. They say she has a chill, but they
haven't called the doctor—"

"Who are 'they'?" Emily asked, her interest quickening
again.

"The servants, of course. Good gracious, Lady Augusta
doesn't speak to me, except to be civil, and the general never
talks of anything but his papers. But servants are very in-

105

quisitive, you know. They would not do anything they would be obliged to admit to as gossip, but if it can be disguised as anything else, they will tell you everything they know, and most of what they merely surmise."

"Well?" Emily said eagerly. "What do they surmise? For pity's sake, tell me, before I explode!"

"They think that the police will never discover the truth, and will not really exert themselves greatly to try, because whoever is guilty, it will doubtless involve a gentleman, and therefore they will not be able to prosecute anyway! Which I would like to think is nonsense, but I fear they may speak with a bitterness of experience."

"Which gentleman?" Emily could hardly contain herself, and her words came out in exasperation between closed teeth.

"There are as many ideas on that as there are servants to propose them," Charlotte replied honestly. "Indeed, there have been some most heated exchanges. One of the housemaids is sure it cannot be young Brandon Balantyne, because he has never made an advance toward her, although the cook tells me he has assuredly been given the opportunity! Another housemaid is perfectly certain that it is him, for precisely the same reason! He has not made an advance toward her either, therefore he must have some dreadful secret—"

"Of course! Euphemia Carlton!" But Emily's answer lacked any satisfaction. "Somehow I am reluctant to think that it is she, perhaps because I liked her. I fear I am not cut out for detection. But it will soon be appropriate for me to call again, without appearing to be too pushy in the acquaintance." She sighed again. "But Charlotte, you really will have to do better! You are not trying! How can you possibly consider a war that was over in 1814 to be more interesting than a murder that is going on this very minute?"

"1815," Charlotte corrected automatically, "and we don't know that it is murder."

"Oh, don't be so pernickety! What does it matter as to the niceties? It is certainly the most terrific scandal! Which is more than you can say for your wretched wars! Do pull yourself together, please, and apply your mind properly!"

"I will, I promise. I will do my very best to see Christina

myself, and if possible at least to begin to discover why she does not marry her lover, and who he is, if I can."

"Thank you," Emily assumed an air of patient generosity, as one who has decided to overlook an offense. "You might even get the opportunity to speak with other servants in the square. Of course, if you do, you will avail yourself of it!"

It was on Charlotte's tongue to tell her younger sister not to be bossy, when she took into account Emily's passion for the matter, and the possibility of her boredom with the point-lessness of her own social round, and instead merely agreed to do her best, and leave no chance unexplored.

When Pitt arrived a moment later, Emily was just leaving, a broad, anticipatory smile on her face.

"She looks like a cat who has spied the canary out of its cage," Pitt observed when the door was closed.

"She is very well," Charlotte said noncommittally.

"Beyond doubt," he agreed. "A cat in excellent health. Who is to be the unfortunate canary this time?"

"That is unfair." She was very reluctant to let him know anything about it, because as yet he knew only that she was assisting General Balantyne in some clerical work, in which she herself had a longstanding interest that her father had not let her indulge. He had no idea that she was, or planned to be, concerning herself in the Callander Square affair; still less that Emily had ignored her promise to let the matter drop. "She was only indulging in a little speculative gossip," she finished. That should satisfy him as likely enough, with-out in any way giving him to believe an untruth.

"About whom?" he asked.

"Pardon?"

"Come, Charlotte," he put his hand on her shoulder and turned her to face him. The warmth and the strength of him still thrilled her. She raised her eyes to look at him, in part quite genuinely because she loved him, and wished him to know it, and only in small part to distract him from his question.

A moment or two later he let go of her.

"Charlotte, what is Emily doing in Callander Square?" he repeated. "And even more important, what are you doing—apart from sorting papers for General Balantyne?"

She considered lying, but as Emily had said, she was no good at it. Instead she made a strategic withdrawal.

"Emily has not been calling at Callander Square lately. To do so too often would be obvious, and so defeat the purpose. She asked me if I had learned anything about Christina Balantyne. Of course I have not. She is in bed with a chill, and I haven't even met her. Emily persuaded me that I should endeavor at least to find out who her lover is, and why she does not marry him, instead of taking to her bed."

"Charlotte?" he frowned, and there was a mixture of amusement and apprehension in his eyes.

She felt totally innocent.

"Yes?"

"What makes you suppose Christina has a lover?"

"Oh," she realized she had given herself away. Pitt was waiting and there was no evading him now without lying, which she could not do. "Emily found out," she admitted. "and she told me; Christina is afraid she may be with child. That naturally must mean that she has a lover."

He stared at her, and she had no idea what thoughts were in his mind. His eyes grew wider and his eyebrows climbed higher. He had the clearest, most penetrating eyes she had ever seen; she felt as if the very inside of his mind reached out into her. Then just as suddenly his mood changed.

"How very enterprising of Emily!" There was a lift of admiration in his voice, and she thought of amusement, also. "That explains why Lady Augusta would not let me see her," he went on. "That is a most interesting question; why not simply marry, albeit a little hastily?" The interest faded from his expression. "Charlotte, you must tell General Balantyne you cannot assist him any more."

She was horrified.

"Oh no! I can't possibly do that! I am less than half way through—"

"Charlotte. If they have something to hide—"

"There's no danger!" she said quickly. "I haven't asked any questions! I merely listen to the servants at meal times. I'm not like Emily, I shall be very discreet—"

He laughed outright.

"My dear, you are nothing like Emily; she is a model of

108

discretion compared with you. You are to make your apologies, say you are unwell, or your mother is—"

"No! What can they do to me? I have no social position to lose: and they don't even think of me as a person! They won't suspect anything! I'll just listen, I promise." Another thought flashed into her mind, and she played her trump card. "If I leave now, they may indeed wonder why, and take the trouble to discover who I am!" She knew enough not to remind him of any danger to his own career; it would be the last way to deter him. "The best way," she went on, "is to continue normally, and then they will think nothing of it." She smiled sweetly, in the last moment, sure of herself.

He hesitated, weighing his decision.

"Will you give me your promise you will not ask questions?" he said finally.

She wondered whether she could keep it. She plunged.

"Yes. I'll only listen. I give you my word," she reached up and kissed him, but he still regarded her carefully, assuring himself that she indeed intended her promise.

It was a promise that was increasingly difficult for Charlotte to keep, as the very next day presented her with boundless opportunities to ask questions, discreetly and without seeming anything more than normally sympathetic. And of course she had her promise to Emily to keep as well. The chance to do something about the latter arose at luncheon when the lady's maid was harassed beyond endurance by a multitude of tasks and Charlotte offered to take up Christina's tray, to save the poor woman from at least one small chore.

"Oh, you don't have to do that, miss," but the girl's face brightened hopefully.

"Nonsense," Charlotte swooped in and took the tray from under her nose. "It will be no trouble, and my luncheon is too hot to eat at the minute."

"Oh, thank you, miss. Don't let her ladyship catch you!"

"Don't fear," the bootboy said cheerfully, "She's at luncheon 'erself. Won't leave the table, till the general 'as eaten 'is pudding 'ot. Gives 'im indigestion wicked it does, if 'e eats it cold, then 'is temper's something awful."

Charlotte thanked him and hastened upstairs before anything could dissuade them, and had to stop a tweeny on the landing to ask her where Christina's bedroom was.

She knocked on Christina's door, and a moment later was inside. It was not so very unlike what her own room at Cater Street had been; a little larger, a little more expensively furnished perhaps. For a moment her girlhood came back to her; it was a sweet memory, but she was content that it was only a memory. She had a happiness now quite different from anything she had dreamed of then, but also it was deeper, with dimensions she had not guessed. She looked at Christina sitting up in the bed, her dark hair piled round her shoulders, her pretty little face now wide with surprise. What kind of happiness did she dream of, and with whom? A girl's dreams could be so innocent, and so ignorant.

"Who are you?" Christina said a little petulantly.

"Charlotte Ellison," she only just remembered the "Ellison" in time. "I'm helping General Balantyne with some clerical work, and as your lady's maid was trying to do three jobs at once, I brought your luncheon for you. I do hope you are feeling better." She looked at her as she said it, trying to disguise the careful assessment in her eyes as simple courtesy. Christina looked perfectly well, to all outward appearances. Certainly she had a fine color, her eyes were clear, and there was no puffiness in her nose and cheeks, such as one gets with a chill.

"Yes, thank you," Christina replied coolly, then recollected herself and her situation. "I feel better today, but unfortunately it comes and goes."

"I am sorry," Charlotte set the tray down gently. "I daresay it is the weather."

"I daresay. It was good of you to bring the tray up. There is nothing more I need, thank you, you may leave."

Charlotte felt her face tighten; to be patronized had always woken her temper faster than anything else. She had to make a considerable effort to control herself.

"Thank you," she said stiffly. "I do hope you will be recovered soon. It is wretched to be in bed, one misses so much. It is quite distressing in society how quickly one gets left

110

behind!" And with the satisfaction of her parting shot, she sailed out, closing the door with a final click.

Downstairs she cooled, realizing Emily would have charmed, dissimulated, controlled herself, and kept a friend. Instead Charlotte had now assuredly made an enemy. But then she was perfectly sure she could never like Christina, so perhaps she had merely accomplished at once what she would inevitably have achieved in time.

In the midafternoon it was totally different. She was asked as a favor, because the parlormaid was a little faint, if she would run an errand next door to the Southerons'. She accepted with alacrity, another excellent opportunity, and no sooner was she in the Southerons' kitchen than she met Jemima Waggoner, the governess. She took an immediate liking to her, sensing in her a frankness like her own, and even perhaps feelings that propriety and her dependent situation forbade her expressing. She imagined such things in the wide gray eyes, and a touch of humor in the mouth.

"Would you care for tea, Miss Ellison?" Jemima offered. "It is about that time, and we were preparing to have ours. You would be most welcome."

"Thank you, indeed it would be refreshing," Charlotte accepted instantly. The general would have to wait. No doubt he would also stop for tea. If he offered her more on her return, she would have to accept it, even if she were virtually awash. But it was unlikely, he seldom thought of such things; he was singleminded and too absorbed in the dust of battle to think of cups of tea.

A few moments later she found herself alone in the governess's room with Jemima, sipping tea and eating sandwiches.

"Are you really helping General Balantyne with his war histories?" Jemima asked. "I can never be sure if gossip is true or not."

"No one can," Charlotte agreed quickly. "Unless one had begun it oneself, and even then one cannot recognize it after a week! But this is perfectly true."

"Do you enjoy it?" Jemima asked as if she expected an affirmative answer.

"Oh yes, I do. It is most interesting, especially the old
111

letters. The letters from the soldiers are so different. We can hardly imagine! But the letters from wives and sweethearts—how little we have changed, all the same concerns, loves, illnesses, children, a little scandal." She was stretching the truth a little, but she wanted to get back to Callander Square, and she felt that Jemima was not one to gossip easily.

"I suppose scandal doesn't change," Jemima said thoughtfully, looking down at the tea swirling gently in her cup where she had stirred it. "It is always speculation about someone else's follies, or misdemeanors."

Charlotte opened her mouth to press the point, to say something about Callander Square, and found she did not wish to. Jemima had framed her own thoughts; it was all other people's sins and misfortunes perpetuated, exaggerated, and relished.

She said as much, and saw the quick sympathy in the other girl's eyes, and felt a warmth toward her. She found herself smiling back.

"How many children do you teach?" she asked instead.

"Most of the time, just the three girls here, but three times a week Victoria and Mary Campbell come over. Do you know the Campbells? They live over on the other corner of the square." She pulled a little face with wry humor. "I don't care for Mr. Campbell very much. He's very witty sometimes, but there always seems to be a sort of hopelessness underneath it, as if he is only pretending to be amused and he knows the whole thing is futile in the end. I find it depressing, and a little frightening," she looked at Charlotte to see if she understood.

"Cynicism frightens me too," Charlotte agreed. "One can fight against so many things, but one cannot argue people into hope. What about Mrs. Campbell, is she like that also?"

"Oh no, she is quite different: quiet and competent. Actually she is about the best mother I have worked for, she neither spoils the children nor is she indifferent or overly strict. I think she is a very strong woman." This last opinion was given with some thought.

They spoke for a few more minutes about other people in the square, a little about the Balantynes and Charlotte's work. Charlotte discovered that Jemima had met young

Brandon Balantyne on two or three occasions, and from the very delicate color in her fair skin, gathered that she found him attractive, although of course she would not say so. It was not for governesses to have opinions about the sons of generals and the grandsons of dukes.

They had finished their tea when the door burst open and quite the handsomest parlormaid Charlotte had seen came in, her face bright with anger, her uniform disarrayed.

"One day I'm going to slap him good and proper, so help me I am!" she said furiously. "I shall forget myself, I swear!" Then she realized Charlotte was not of the household. "Oh, I'm sorry, miss. I didn't see you there. Beg your pardon."

"That's quite all right," Charlotte said easily. She forgot her promise to Pitt. "Has someone been taking liberties?"

"Liberties! I should say."

"Mary Ann," Jemima broke the slight awkwardness. "This is Miss Ellison, who is helping General Balantyne next door with his papers."

Mary Ann inclined her head politely; as an employee Charlotte did not rate a curtsey. "I suppose you've had your tea," she said with a glance at the pot. "I expect they'll have some in the kitchen," she went out again, twitching her skirt behind her, still not satisfied with its replacement.

"Perhaps it would be a good idea if she did slap him, nice and hard," Charlotte said when the door was closed again. "One cannot make one's position too clear."

"Slap him?" Jemima laughed, turning down the corners of her mouth with a little gesture. "Mr. Southeron is very good-natured, but he would not take kindly to a parlormaid who slapped his face."

"Mr. Southeron!" Charlotte tried to hide her surprise, and triumph. Now she had really pertinent news to tell Emily, and she had asked no questions; at least only one, and that had been accidental.

She could see that Jemima regretted having spoken so freely.

"I should not have said that," she was a little abashed. "I only surmise, from what I have overheard. I should not leap to conclusions. Perhaps Mary Ann is exaggerating?"

"She is certainly angry about something," Charlotte said

113

carefully. "But perhaps we should not speculate too far as to what it might be. I trust you have never been—?" she left it hanging delicately.

To her surprise Jemima suppressed a laugh.

"Well, once or twice I've thought he was about to, but I moved out of the way. He did look a bit annoyed. But once you allow any familiarity, you cannot go back, you have abandoned your position, so to speak." She lifted her eyebrows slightly, to question Charlotte if she understood what she meant.

"Oh yes," Charlotte agreed; and although she was only guessing, she felt a sharp sympathy with this girl who was obliged to work and to live in other people's houses, and dare not risk offending them.

She remained a little longer, and then excused herself and returned to General Balantyne, who surprised her by pacing the library floor waiting for her. At first she thought he was going to berate her for her absence, but his temper evaporated and he seemed content to resume work with no more than a short complaint.

Pitt was late home that evening and Charlotte had no chance to tell him what she had learned, and the following morning he was out early. She arrived at Callander Square ready for her duties. Again an opportunity presented itself for an errand elsewhere in the square, and she seized it eagerly. Thus at quarter to two she found herself standing in the Dorans' crowded withdrawing room with a bunch of dry winter flowers in her hand, facing Miss Georgiana.

Georgiana was swathed in smoke-gray chiffon and artificial flowers. She lay on the chaise longue with one arm resting on the back. She was so bony and pale that, but for the brilliant eyes, she would have reminded Charlotte of an artistic corpse laid out in shroud and flowers, the Lady of Shallott, perhaps, twenty years after! The thought made her want to giggle, and she maintained her composure only with the greatest effort. She could feel the laughter boiling up inside her: her sense of the ludicrous had always been unreliable.

Georgiana looked at her narrowly.

"Who did you say you were?"

"Charlotte Ellison, Mrs. Duff. Lady Augusta wished me to bring you these. I believe they are said to be excellent for the house, a very delicate perfume," she proffered them to the clawlike little hand, winking with jewels.

"Nonsense," Georgiana put them to her nose. "They smell like dust. Still, it was civil of Augusta to send them; no doubt she thinks they will suit Laetitia, and I daresay she is right."

Charlotte could not help glancing at the velvet and plush roses that decorated the couch, the cushions, and Georgiana herself.

Georgiana's diamond-sharp little eyes caught her.

"Quite different," she said simply. "I love beauty. I am very sensitive. I suffer, you know, and it helps to have flowers."

"I'm sure it must," Charlotte could think of nothing sensible to say to such a remark. She stood awkwardly in the center of the room, unsure whether to remain, or to excuse herself.

Georgiana was regarding her with curiosity.

"You don't look like a maid. What did you say you were?"

"I am helping General Balantyne with his war memoirs."

"Disgusting. What does a young woman like you want with war memoirs? Money, I suppose?"

"I find them very interesting," Charlotte did not feel obliged to prevaricate or hide her feelings. "I think it becomes us all to know the history of our country, and the nature of the sacrifices that have been made."

Georgiana's eyes narrowed.

"What a quaint creature you are. Please either take your leave, or sit down. You are tall, and peering up at you makes my neck ache. I am very delicate."

Charlotte was tempted to stay, but she was aware that the general would be waiting for her, and of her duty to him, both as a matter of honor and because she might lose her position and its opportunities if she were to stretch his patience too far.

"Thank you, Mrs. Duff," she said demurely, "but I must return. It has been most pleasant to meet you."

"Come again. You are quite entertaining," Georgiana lay

115

back, the better to survey her frankly. "I don't know what the world's coming to. Give Augusta my thanks. Don't tell her I do not care for the flowers, or that they smell like unlived-in houses."

"Of course not," and Charlotte left her still gazing at the door.

Back in the library Balantyne was waiting for her.

"Georgiana hold you in conversation?" he said, looking at her with a smile, the first she could remember on his face. "Poor old creature. It can't be easy living there with Laetitia. I sometimes think Helena's leaving turned her mind a little."

"Helena?" Charlotte could not place the name, although she thought Emily had mentioned it.

"Laetitia's daughter," Balantyne explained. "Wretched girl eloped with someone about two years ago. Never found out who. Poor Laetitia was quite deranged by it. Never mentioned Helena's name since, pretends she had no children. Husband's been dead for years and she had no one else, so Georgiana came to live with her."

"How very sad." Charlotte saw the waste and her imagination tried to visualize the loneliness, Helena's love—or temptation—all the regret since. She wondered if the marriage was happy. "Has she never written to her mother since?"

"Not so far as I know. Of course Laetitia admired Ross as well, which made it all the harder."

"Who is Ross?"

"Alan Ross. He was in love with Helena. We all thought it was only a matter of time before they married. Shows what nonsense we talk!" He sat down behind the desk again, and she found his eyes on her faintly disturbing. "He has never got over it," he added.

She could think of no expression that was not unbearably trite.

"We so seldom really know what another person feels," she said, picking up the papers again. "There are your uncle's diaries. Do you wish me to number the pages that refer specifically to military matters?"

"What?"

116

She repeated her question, holding up the books for him to see.

"Oh yes, yes, please. You are most helpful—" he hesitated, "Miss Ellison."

She smiled quickly and looked away.

"I'm glad. I assure you I find it very interesting," and immediately she opened the book in her hand and bent her head to read. As soon as it was five o'clock she closed it and bade him good night, and had Max call her a hansom cab. She gave the driver Emily's address, and went clattering through the darkness, news bursting on her lips.

SIX

It was by now rapidly approaching Christmas, there were but two weeks to go, and Augusta decided that the matter of Christina and Max must be resolved. She could not expect the child to spend the holiday season in bed; but before she got up, Max must be out of the house. She had been in touch with her relations in Stirlingshire and a position was arranged for him. Nothing now remained but for him to accept the inevitable, and take his leave with a good grace. Augusta had already made the most discreet inquiries regarding his replacement. It would be difficult to find a man as competent, or even as good-looking, as satisfactory a pair for Percy, the other footman, and footmen came in pairs; but that was of secondary consideration.

With a view to informing him of the imminence of his departure, she sent for Max to wait on her in the morning room. She had not yet told the general anything about it, but there would be time enough for that when it was all over. And since he had been agitating her to get rid of Max for months now, he would no doubt be perfectly satisfied.

Max came in and closed the door silently behind him.

"Yes, my lady?"

"Good morning, Max."

"Good morning, my lady."

"I have concluded my arrangements for your new position in Stirlingshire. You are to go to Lord and Lady Forteslain. She is a cousin of mine, and you will find the situation adequate, although it may not extend your abilities as London does. However, that is a misfortune you will have to make the best of."

"I have been giving the matter some consideration, my

lady." There was a small, complacent smile on his mouth. Augusta wondered how Christina could ever have found him attractive, how she could have wanted to be kissed, to be touched by him. The thought was repellent.

"Indeed?" she said coldly.

"Yes, my lady. I don't think I should care for Stirlingshire; or indeed for any other part of Scotland."

She raised her eyebrows slightly.

"That is unfortunate, but I am not concerned with your likes and dislikes. You will have to learn to make the best of it."

"I think not, my lady. I should prefer to remain in London. In fact Callander Square suits me very well."

"I dare say, but that is not possible. I thought I had already made that clear to you."

"You did state your position, ma'am. But as I said, I have been giving the matter some thought, and an alternative has occurred to me which I greatly prefer."

"It will not be acceptable to me!" She tried to stare him out, but his insolence was insurmountable.

"I regret to be so discourteous, my lady, but that is of no concern to me. As you pointed out so plainly, last time you spoke, there are some things which one is obliged to accept, whether one wishes to, or not."

"There is nothing I am obliged to accept from you, Max. I have told you what I shall do if you do not go to Scotland, and do it graciously. That is an end to the matter."

"If you charge me with theft, my lady, you will regret it," his eyes did not waver.

She stiffened, she could feel the skin tighten across the bones of her face.

"Are you threatening me, Max?"

"If you wish to see it that way, yes, my lady, I am."

"It is an idle threat. There is nothing you can do. I should be believed, and you should not."

He faced her unflinchingly.

"That depends upon what you value, Lady Augusta. Certainly, if I were to say that I had lain with your daughter, the courts would no doubt believe you, and not me, if you were to swear that I was speaking only out of revenge. It would be a lie," he smiled very slightly, a light of wry, superior humor in his heavy face. "But I have no delusions that you would not take your oath on it, even so."

She flushed, feeling the heat in her face, under the sting of his contempt because she was no better than he, and she had permitted him to prove it.

"But," he went on, "I should not claim it was I who had lain with her. I have a friend, not a servant; I'm afraid he is something of a rake—a gambler who has seen better times, but handsome, in a vulgar way, and with no lack of female friends. Most of them are whores, of course, but they find him attractive. Unfortunately," his smile curled a little, "he has a disease." His eyebrows rose, to question if she took his precise meaning.

Augusta shivered with revulsion.

"I should say," Max continued, "that it was he who had seduced Miss Christina; or to be more correct, he would say so. There would be no connection with my misfortune, and it would be uncommon hard for you to disprove, and hardly worth it, I think. The damage would have been done. Men's clubs, and so forth, spread the word; all very discreet, nothing open, nothing for you to deny. And if you charge me with theft, I swear it will happen."

She was frightened, really frightened. There was a power in the man, and a certainty of his own victory. She struggled for something to say. Above all, she would not give in.

"And why should anyone believe that this disgusting friend of yours had ever even seen Christina," she said slowly, "or that she would speak to him, let alone touch him?"

"Because he will be able to describe this house, in detail, her bedroom, even to the decorations on her bed—"

"Which you know!" she said quickly. "He could have got it from some housemaid easily enough. There is nothing to that," she felt a quick resurgence of hope.

His eyes were slow, moist, raking her over.

"She has a mole under her left breast," he said distinctly, "and a scar on her buttock, also the left, as I remember. You will say I also knew that, but I doubt the housemaid does. Do you take my point, my lady?"

It took her the greatest effort of will she could remember

not to shout at him, to let go of her temper, her rage and frustration, and scream, "Get out, out of my sight!" She took a deep breath, and summoned a lifetime of discipline.

"Yes, I take your point," she said quietly, her voice very nearly steady. "You may go."

He turned, then hesitated at the door.

"You will inform your relations in Stirlingshire that I shall not be coming, my lady?"

"I shall. Now go."

He bowed very slightly, still smiling.

"Thank you, my lady."

As soon as the door was closed she gave way. For nearly five minutes she sat and let the shudders of disgust and anger pass through her. To be bested by a servant, a footman with morals of the gutter! She would never forget his hot, familiar eyes on her. To think that Christina had voluntarily lain with this—creature! That she could even now be with his child. It was not to be endured. She must pull herself together. Something must be done. She could not now think how to get rid of Max, but she must at least make absolutely sure that he never touched Christina again. From this hour onward Christina's behavior must be perfect. Max would not use his trump card unless forced, unless he had nothing to lose by it: because he had only the one play. In ruining her he would ruin himself, therefore he would not press Christina if she treated him with total disinterest from now on. And most certainly Augusta intended to see that she did!

She stood up and composed herself. There was no further purpose in Christina's remaining in bed. She was perfectly recovered. She might as well get up and resume her normal life: in fact better that she should, before there was too much speculation as to what condition kept her out of society. If by some disaster she should prove to be with child, Augusta would have to see that she was married as soon as possible, and hope that the birth could be passed off as premature. Fortunately Christina was as dark as Max, so if the child were equally dark there would be no comment. In fact it might be as well if Christina were to be married at the earliest convenience anyway. She obviously had a weakness that required a solution, and there was only one satisfying one.

Her mind began to consider possibilities as she crossed the hall and climbed the stairs. It would have to be someone who could be persuaded to marry at very short notice, and without causing a lot of raised eyebrows: therefore he would have to be someone she knew already, so a courtship could be presumed to have taken place. It was hardly feasible that someone of such devastating charm as to make a whirlwind romance believable would marry other than one of his own desire; and for such a man to cross Christina's path in the next few weeks, and fall in love with her, was expecting too much of fate.

She enumerated the young men of suitable position in her mind, and came up with lamentably few. And among those most owed the Balantynes nothing, nor sought anything from them that would be worth marrying for, without the romantic inclination. Most men married of their wives' or their mothers-in-law's choosing, but preferred to think that it was of their own. In this case such a feat of self-deception might be difficult. Fortunately Christina was engaging enough, pretty, spirited, and of an excellent taste in fashion. And she had a sense of wit, and of enjoyment, which was peculiarly attractive to most men.

By the time she had reached Christina's bedroom door she had whittled the choice down to three, of whom the best seemed to be Alan Ross. Of course everyone knew he had never entirely recovered from his infatuation with Helena Doran, but that also meant he had no attachment to anyone else, and therefore might be agreeable to the arrangement. He could be intractable if he were pressured—he was a man of strong will—but if approached with charm, if Christina exerted herself to attract him, delight him, woo him, he might well, with a tiny added pressure from the general, prove amenable. It was certainly worth trying. There were others who could be bought with military advancement, which of course could be arranged; but they would be far less likely to afford Christina any happiness.

She knocked on the door, and immediately went in. She was startled to find Christina up and in process of dressing. She opened her mouth to be angry at the disobeying of her

123

instructions, then closed it again, realizing she was but spiting her own plans.

"I'm glad you are feeling better," she said instead.

Christina swung round, surprise in her face. She really was a pretty creature, cloud of dark hair, white skin, tilted, wide blue eyes, pert nose, and rounded chin. And her manners were delightful when she chose. Yes, it should not prove an impossible task.

"Mama!"

"I see you have decided to get up. I'm glad, I think it is time."

Christina's surprise at the reaction showed for an instant in her face before she masked it.

"Yes. That Miss—whatever-her-name-is, that Papa has employed, made me realize how much I am missing. And people will begin to talk if I do not appear soon. There is no good giving them cause before it is necessary. Anyhow, I may well not be with child. I feel perfectly well now. I have not felt in the least sick or faint for days." There was a slight edge of challenge to her voice.

"There is no reason why you should," Augusta agreed. "Being with child is a perfectly natural process, not a disease. Women have been doing it since Eve."

"I may not be with child," Christina said firmly.

"No, and on the other hand, you may. It is too early to be certain."

"If I am," Christina raised her head a little higher, deliberately, "I shall go and see Freddie Bolsover."

"You will not. Dr. Meredith will be perfectly adequate to attend you, when the time comes."

"I do not intend to bear Max's child, Mama. I have been giving the matter some thought, while I have been lying here. I shall see Freddie, I have heard he can arrange such things—"

For the first time since she had been a young woman herself, Augusta was quite genuinely shocked, both by her daughter, and by the piece of knowledge that Freddie Bolsover either performed abortions himself, or knew who did.

"You will do nothing of the kind," she said almost softly. "That is a sin which I will not forgive. You can cease to

124

consider it from this moment. I have no wish for any grand-
child of mine to carry the blood of that unspeakable footman;
but you have made your bed, and we must all lie in it—"

"Mama, I will not—you don't seem to understand! I do not
love Max, I never loved him—"

"I had not imagined you did," Augusta said coldly. "I am
equally sure he did not love you either. That is beside the
point. You will not commit murder against your unborn child,
if indeed it exists. You will marry someone who will care for
you in a suitable manner and give your child a name—"

"I will not!" Christina's face flamed. "If you think I am
going to beg some respectable weakling to marry me just to
give my child a father, you are gravely mistaken, Mama. It
would be intolerable! He would make me pay for it the rest
of my life! He would call me a—a whore—and he would
hardly love the child, or give it a home with any—anything
worth—"

"Control yourself, Christina. I have no intention that you
should do anything of the sort. You will marry a man suitable
to your station, and he will have no idea of your condition.
You will say the child, if indeed there is one, is premature.
Under no circumstances whatsoever will you go to Freddie
Bolsover, or anyone else."

Christina's face was twisted with contempt and disbelief.

"And who have you in mind, Mama? Why should anyone
marry me in time to be of any use? And what happens if he
doesn't believe in premature babies?"

"There are several possibilities. Alan Ross suggests himself as the best. And you will marry him straight after Christmas—"

"He doesn't love me either!"

"You will see that he comes to. You can be charming
enough, if you choose. For your own sake, my dear, you had
better choose to charm Alan."

"And if I'm not with child?" Christina's chin rose sharply,
challengingly.

"By the time you are sure you are not, it will be a little
late. Anyway, I think it would be better for you to be married." She took a breath and spoke very levelly. "Christina,
perhaps you do not fully appreciate your position. If you bear

125

a child, without a father for it, you will find that you have no place in society. And don't imagine that you can overcome it. Others have tried, of better birth and greater fortune than you, and all have failed. No man of your own station will marry you, you will become a butt of jokes, decent women will not speak to you. All the places you go now will be closed to you in future. I dislike having to say this to you, but you must understand that it is true."

Christina stared at her.

"Therefore, my dear," Augusta continued, "you will use your considerable charm upon Alan Ross, so that he will be happy to marry you, and you will appear to be in love with him. He is a good man, and will treat you with gentleness, if you permit it."

"And if he doesn't wish to marry me?" There was the first small shrillness of panic in Christina's voice and Augusta felt a stab of pity for her, but there was no time for indulgence now.

"I believe that he will; but if he does not, then I shall find someone else. There are other possibilities. You have an influential father—"

"I couldn't bear him to know about it! Even to guess!"

"Your father?" Augusta was surprised.

"Alan Ross! Or—whoever—"

"Of course not," Augusta said sharply. "I have no intention he should. Now pull yourself together and make yourself your most attractive. We shall hold a series of parties, and no doubt you will be invited elsewhere. The sooner this is accomplished the better. Fortunately you have known Alan for a long time, so there will be no comment when you announce a wedding date."

"How will you persuade Alan of the emergency?"

"Don't worry about it, I shall find a way. In the meantime, of course, you will entirely ignore Max, apart from such civility as is customary toward a servant. If he should prevail upon you for more than that, you will call for assistance and accuse him of familiarity, and he will be dismissed."

"I wish you would dismiss him anyway. I find the very thought of him offensive now."

"I dare say you do. I find it hard to understand how you

ever found it anything else. But unfortunately it is not so easy to bury our mistakes. Max has taken steps to see that I do not, and I have not yet thought of a way round them; but I shall. Now consider your future, and behave with your utmost charm; you have exercised yourself to enchant men well enough in the past. Do not overdo it; Alan, like most men, will wish to believe he has done the choosing and the pursuing himself. Allow him to persist in that belief. And wear pink as often as may be. It becomes you, and men like it."

"Yes, Mama."

"Good. Now compose yourself, and let us direct out efforts to that end."

"Yes, Mama."

The following morning Augusta was late over breakfast, which was most unusual for her. She had slept badly. The whole business with Max had distressed her more than she had realized at the time. Perhaps her mastery of herself was not as perfect as she believed. She was still at the breakfast table at half past nine when Brandy came back for another cup of tea. He sat down opposite her, looking at her closely.

"You look a little bashed this morning, Mother. In fact you look the way I feel after a night at the club."

"Don't be impertinent," she said, but without sharpness. She was extremely fond of her son, indeed she might say with honesty she liked him best of all her family. There was a cheerfulness about him that was gentler then Christina, and warmer than his father. Also he was one of the few people who could make her laugh even when she did not wish to.

Now he was squinting at her thoughtfully.

"Hope you haven't caught Christina's chill."

"That is hardly likely," she said with a shudder.

"I don't suppose you'd take a day in bed," he reached for another piece of toast and started a second breakfast. "That would be too much like admitting frailty. But it might show sense. Give it a thought, Mother." He smiled. "If you like, I'll swear blind you've gone to the races, or shopping!"

"Where on earth should I go to the races, at this time of the year?"

"All right, I'll say you've gone cockfighting, then!" he grinned.

"They'll be more likely to believe it if you left a note saying we'd both gone," she replied, meeting his eyes with a smile, in spite of herself.

He shivered.

"Nonsense. I've no stomach for blood sports."

"And do you think that I have?"

"Certainly. You'd have scared the hell out of Napoleon, if he'd met you on a social occasion."

She sniffed. "Have you just poured yourself the last of the tea?"

"Wouldn't dare. Really, Mother, you do look a bit dragged out. Take a day off. It's a decent day, a bit cold, but quite dry. I'll take you for a drive. We'll get out the best horses!"

She was tempted. There was nothing she would like better than a drive away from Callander Square, with Brandy. She lingered on the idea, savoring it.

"Come on!" he urged. "Crisp air, fast horses, crunch of wheels on a new road. Last of the beech leaves are still red on the trees."

She looked at his smooth, olive-skinned face and saw the child in him now, as twenty years ago she had seen the man in him then. Before she could accept, the door opened and Max came in.

"Inspector Pitt is here again, my lady, from the police. Will you see him?"

The crisp air, the flying hooves, and the laughter collapsed.

"I suppose I have no choice," she pushed her chair back and stood up. "If not now, it will only put him off until later. Put him in the morning room, Max, I'll see him in a few minutes."

Brandy was still eating.

"Is it about the wretched babies still? I don't know why they persist, they'll never find out whose they were, poor little beggars. I suppose they have to try, but it must be a rotten job. Do you want me to see him? He probably only wants permission to question the servants again."

"No, thank you, but I appreciate the offer, my dear. I would love to come driving with you, but I cannot."

"Why not? He's hardly likely to run off with the silver!"

"I cannot leave him," she repeated mechanically. She did not want to have to tell him. "How well do you know Alan Ross, Brandy?"

"What?" His hand with the toast in it dropped in surprise.

"How well do you know Alan Ross? The question is simple enough."

"He's a good fellow. I suppose I know him pretty well. He closed up rather after Helena took off; but he's beginning to come out of it now. Why?"

"I wish him to marry Christina."

He stopped all pretense of eating and put the toast down.

"Your father doesn't know about it yet," she went on. "But I have excellent reasons. If you could do anything to further that end, I should be very pleased. Now I suppose I had better see this policeman again," and she left him still staring after her.

Pitt was waiting for her by the fire, licking its first flames in a still cold grate. She closed the door behind her and stood with her back to it. He looked up, smiling. Did nothing discompose this wretched man? Perhaps he had no sense of what was proper, and thus neither of what was improper? He was enormous and untidy, too many layers of clothes on, and he greeted her with an air of easiness she did not expect, even from her friends.

"Good morning, Lady Augusta," he said cheerfully. "I would be obliged if I could ask you a few questions."

"Me?" She had intended to freeze him, but she was overtaken by surprise. "I know nothing about it, I assure you!"

He moved away from the fire to make room for her, and unreasonably the courtesy irritated her, perhaps because she would have preferred to find fault with him.

"I'm sure you are not aware of knowing anything," he replied, "or you would have told me; but there may be things you have noticed, without at the time realizing their import."

"I doubt it, but still I suppose, if you must—"

"Thank you. It is proving extremely difficult to trace the woman in the affair—"

129

"I'm hardly surprised!"

"No," his mobile face fell into a wry expression, "nor I. We might have better success approaching it from another direction—to find the man."

The thought flashed through her mind that there might be an opportunity to get rid of Max—

She looked up to find his brilliant gray eyes on her face, disconcertingly. She was conscious above all things of his intelligence; it was an unpleasant feeling to her, and quite new. She could not dominate him.

"You have thought of something?" There was a small smile on the corners of his lips.

"No," she denied immediately. Then she decided to qualify it, in case an idea about Max came to her later. "I don't believe so."

"But you are a discerning woman—"

For a moment she was afraid he was going to flatter her.

"—and you have a young and attractive daughter." There was no intent to deceive in his face, which in itself was unusual. Society was conducted on mutually agreed deceits. "You must have formed opinions as to the habits, the inclinations of the men in your circle," he continued, "those who would be suitable for your daughter to associate with, and those who would not; above all, those whose morals were not acceptable to you."

It was a statement she could not reasonably contradict. His conclusion was inescapable.

"Of course," she agreed. "But I would hesitate to pass to the police as suspicions such personal dislikes or misgivings as I may entertain myself. They may be groundless, and I might thus unwittingly cause an injustice," she raised her eyebrows slightly, questioning him in turn, giving him back the onus.

The smile on his mouth flickered upward. She wished he would not look at her so frankly. If Christina had become enamored of this man, she could have understood it a great deal more easily. But then he would very likely have sent her packing! She pulled herself together. The thought was ridiculous—and offensive.

"I will take your advice as merely that, my lady," he said

gently. "Sound advice as to where I might begin. You will agree that I have so far been extremely discreet?"

"I have no idea that you know anything about which to be indiscreet," she said levelly, with a touch of chill.

His smile broadened into a grin.

"Which makes my point perfectly."

"On the contrary," she was terse. "It begs it."

He retreated gracefully, again annoying her.

"I think you are right. Still, the sooner I can finish my investigations, the sooner the matter can either be resolved, or buried as insoluble."

"I take your line of reasoning, Mr. Pitt. What is it that you wish to know from me?"

Before he could reply, the door opened and Brandy came in. Pitt had not seen him before, and she saw a momentary flash of interest cross his face.

"My son, Brandon Balantyne," she said briefly.

Brandy seemed equally curious, to judge from his expression.

"Surely you don't suspect Mother?" he said flippantly. "Or are you consulting her for gossip?"

"You think that would be a good idea?"

"Oh, excellent. She affects to be above it, but in truth she knows everything."

"Brandon, this is not an occasion for levity," she said tartly. "Two children are dead, and someone is responsible."

His humor vanished instantly. He looked at Pitt with an unspoken apology.

"Gossip is most useful," Pitt covered the moment and raised a hand to dismiss it. "You would be surprised how often the solution to a crime lies in some small thing that has been known to the neighborhood from the beginning, they have merely not mentioned it to us because they believed it such common knowledge that we must also have known it."

Brandy relaxed. He made some small remark in reply, and before Pitt could return the conversation to his interrupted questions, Christina came in.

Augusta was annoyed; she knew it was only curiosity that brought her, and the fear that something was happening that

131

she was missing. Being in bed had made her feel that the whole of society was passing her by. Now she was dressed meticulously, her eyes shining, she even had color on her cheeks, as if she were expecting a suitor! She was smiling at Pitt—practicing her technique! Really, had the girl no sense?

"Good morning, Inspector—Pitt?" she hesitated, affecting to be unsure of his name; then came forward, almost as though she were going to offer him her hand. Then she remembered he was a policeman, on a social equal with tradesmen or artisans, and let it fall. It was petty, a little arrogant; without the smile it would merely have been rude.

"Good morning, Miss Balantyne," Pitt bowed very slightly. "I'm happy to see you so obviously recovered. You appear in most perfect health."

"Thank you."

"Perhaps you also can help me. There must be men of your acquaintance whose reputation is less than upright. I imagine you know very well whom you would trust, and whom you could not. Young women discuss among themselves such things, for mutual protection." He turned without warning to Brandy. "Or you, Mr. Balantyne. Have any of your friends become involved with a girl not suitable to marry?"

"Good heavens, dozens, I should think," Brandy was surprised into complete honesty. "But usually one has sense enough not to do it on one's own doorstep!"

Pitt was obliged to smile.

"Quite," he agreed. "What about your servants? That footman of yours looks a lusty fellow." He swiveled till his probing eyes were on Christina.

Augusta could feel the blood drain from her own face, at the same time the rich color heightened in Christina's. The stroke had come out of nowhere, and she had had no defenses ready. Augusta opened her mouth to intercept, and saw Pitt's quick glance at her, wide, waiting; and she bit her tongue. Her very act of speech would betray her, its eagerness, where she should have been indifferent.

"He's merely a footman," Christina said coldly, but there was a small catch in her voice, as if it stuck in her throat. "I have never considered his private life. Perhaps you do not understand, if you have no resident servants of your own,

132

but people of our station do not discuss things with servants. They are here to work, to run the house, that is all that one ever speaks to them about; and even so, usually through the butler. That is what butlers are for. You had better speak to the servants themselves. Those sorts of girls would be a little more in his line, don't you think?"

"Oh, without doubt," Pitt was unaffected by her arrogance. His face was perfectly smooth, his tone warm. "But perhaps not to his taste."

"I have no idea what his tastes might be!" Christina snapped. "It is hardly a matter that interests me."

Pitt grunted, apparently turning the consideration over in his mind. He was still looking at her, and she avoided his eyes.

"How long has he been in Callander Square?" he asked.

"About six years." It was Brandy who replied, his face innocent. Augusta weighed the idea of sending him out, finding some excuse to get rid of him; but seeing Pitt's clever, watchful face, knew it would be a misjudgment, a reinforcement of any suspicion he might be entertaining.

"A good footman?" Pitt inquired.

"Excellent," Brandy answered. "Don't like the fellow, but can't fault him. Believe me, if I could, I'd have thrown him out!"

"Couldn't you throw him out anyway?" Pitt assumed ignorance.

"I suppose so," Brandy was still casual. "Doesn't bother me enough, really. And he seems to satisfy everyone else."

"No complaints from female staff?"

"No, none at all."

"Maids willing? Or does he seek his pleasures elsewhere?"

"Mr. Pitt!" Augusta stepped in at last. "I do not permit fornication in my house, willing or unwilling! Whatever appetites my footmen may have, I assure you they exercise them elsewhere!"

But Pitt was watching Christina. Merciful heaven! Surely he could not possibly know anything? There was no way— was there?

"If you think Max may be responsible, Inspector," she said with as much composure as she could manage, and without looking at Christina, "I would suggest that you look for the woman beyond this house. Perhaps if you resume your questioning in the other establishments in the square?"

"Much easier to ask Max," Brandy offered. "The poor girl will not be likely to admit anything, certainly not now. Press Max a bit, make him squirm. Find out who his lady loves are—"

Augusta gasped, but it was Christina who broke.

"No!" she gulped. "That would be foolish," she said, her tongue fumbling over the words. "And unfair! You have no reason to suppose it has anything to do with Max. I won't have you upsetting our servants. Mother, please!"

"It does seem unwarranted," Augusta chose her words very carefully. "Have you any cause for your suspicions, Inspector? Because if not, I must refuse you permission to harass my staff. Come back with proof, and of course I shall give you every assistance."

Christina took a deep breath and let it out.

The door opened and the general came in. He stopped in surprise.

"Good morning, sir," Pitt said courteously.

"What are you doing here again?" Balantyne asked. "Found out something?"

"He's looking for the man," Brandy answered him. "Thinks it could be Max, and he wants to speak to him."

"Good idea," Balantyne said decisively. "Get it cleared up one way or the other." He leaned over, and before Augusta could stop him, he pulled the bell cord. A moment later Max came in. He must have been standing in the hall.

Pitt's eyes met his, surveyed the dark, sensual face, the immaculate clothes.

"Yes, sir?" Max inquired.

"Any romantic interests, any woman?" Balantyne spoke, abruptly, with all the tact of a heavy cavalry charge. Augusta winced.

Max's face altered only barely.

"I beg your pardon, sir?"

"Aren't I plain enough, man? Have you any romantic attachments? Do you have any lady friends, call them what you will?"

"I have no intention of marrying, sir."

"That is not what I asked, damn it! Don't play the fool with me."

"My most recent romantic attachment has just ended, I fear," Max was smiling under the heavy lids, and he looked almost imperceptibly at Christina.

"Who was she?"

"With the greatest respect, sir that can be of no interest to the police. She is a woman of respectability, of very good family." His voice was rich with his own suppressed amusement.

Augusta could only stand and let disaster come. Perhaps Max himself would protect his own interest, and thus protect Christina. It was her only hope.

Pitt merely waited, letting it play itself out in front of him, watching.

"Good family?" the general said with incredulity.

"Yes, sir."

"Who?"

"I would prefer to protect her, sir. There is no need for her name to be discussed in front of the police. Lady Augusta knows, if you wish to ask her—" He let it hang.

Christina was white-faced, the painted color on her cheeks standing out like a clown's.

"Will that be all, sir?" Max inquired.

Balantyne was staring at Augusta.

Augusta collected herself.

"Yes, thank you, Max. If we require anything, we shall call again."

"Thank you, my lady," he bowed very, very slightly and left, closing the door silently behind him.

"Well?" Balantyne demanded.

"He is quite correct," she replied quickly. "It can be of no possible interest to the police."

Pitt spoke very courteously, softly.

"Why did you not tell me that in the beginning, my lady?"

She felt the cold run through her.

"I beg your pardon?" She played for time, a few seconds to think of an answer.

135

"Why did you not tell me that when the subject was first raised, Lady Augusta?"

"I—I had temporarily forgotten. It is not important."

"Who is this woman—of good family, Lady Augusta?"

"I do not feel free, nor do I wish, to disclose her name."

"Oh, come on, Augusta," Balantyne said exasperatedly. "If she's not involved, Pitt isn't going to do anything to her. You'll be discreet, won't you? Besides, Max's idea of a 'good family' and ours will be quite different things."

"I prefer not to." She could not lie and blame some totally innocent woman—it would be immoral, even if it were practicable.

Pitt turned and looked at Christina, frozen where she stood.

"Miss Balantyne?" he said slowly. "Perhaps you would care to tell me?"

She was speechless.

"Christina?" For the first time there was doubt in the general's voice.

"Never mind," Pitt said quietly. "I shall pursue my investigations elsewhere for a while, and perhaps return here later."

"Yes, by all means," Augusta agreed. She could hear the tension slip out of her voice, and try as she would, she could not control her relief. She understood what he meant—that he knew about Christina and Max, and would seek other ways of discovering whether it was she who had borne the children. But Augusta was sure that it was not. She would have known; Christina had neither the nerve nor the art to have concealed it from her. And now that she had had time to consider it, neither had she the opportunity. She had not spent the appropriate times where such a thing could have been hidden.

She faced Pitt confidently.

"That would be by far the best thing to do."

Pitt looked at her, his curious, penetrating eyes full of knowledge. There was understanding between them. She was not bluffing; she was acknowledging the truth, and he knew it.

"Excellent advice," he bowed very slightly. "Good morning, Lady Augusta, Miss Balantyne, General, Mr. Balantyne."

When he was gone Balantyne turned to Augusta, his face puckered.

"What was all that about, Augusta? What is the man playing at?"

"I've no idea," she lied.

"Don't be ridiculous! You and he understood each other, even I could see that much. What is going on? What has it to do with Max? I require to know."

She considered for a moment. She had forgotten the strength in him, when he chose to interest himself. She remembered how she had loved him twenty years ago. He had been everything that was masculine, clean, powerful; and a little mystical, because it was unknown. The years had brought familiarity, knowledge that his strength was spasmodic, that hers was deeper, more resilient, would rise to meet everything, day by day; the strength that endures wars, not merely battles.

"Christina, you may go," she said quietly. "There is no need to worry about Mr. Pitt, at least for the time being. Address yourself to the problem in hand, and prepare for the dinner engagement this evening. Brandy, you may go also."

"I should prefer to stay, Mother."

"Probably, but you will go, just the same."

"Mother—"

"Brandon," Balantyne said sharply.

In silence Christina and Brandy left.

"Well?" Balantyne asked.

Augusta looked at him incredulously. He still had no idea.

"The girl in question was Christina," she said baldly. "She was having an affair with Max. I thought you might have perceived as much, Mr. Pitt certainly did."

He stared at her.

"You must be mistaken!"

"Don't be fatuous! Do you think I would make a mistake about such a thing?" Her composure slipped at last. She had either to lose her temper, or weep. "Don't look so alarmed. I am taking care of it." There was no need to tell him anything

137

about the possible pregnancy. "I intend to see that she marries as soon as possible, preferably Alan Ross—"

"Does he wish to marry her?"

"Not yet, but he will be made to wish to. That is up to us—"

"Us?"

"Of course, 'us.' The girl cannot do it entirely by herself. I shall tell you when it is time for you to approach him. Perhaps at Christmas."

"Isn't that a little precipitate?" He looked at her narrowly.

"Yes. But it may be advisable."

His face tightened.

"I see. And may I ask why Max is still in the house? Surely she does not entertain ideas about marrying him?"

"Of course not! She has no interest in him, beyond—the—anyway, it is all over. I will get rid of him as soon as I think of a satisfactory method. At the moment the most important thing is to maintain his silence. That can best be done by suffering him to remain here, at least for the present."

"You mean until Christina is married."

"More or less."

"Augusta?"

For the first time she looked at him.

"No," she said simply, answering the question in his mind. "I certainly have made a grave error over Max. I did not judge her well, not know her as I should have: but she had nothing to do with the children in the garden. I should have known that." Peculiarly, she felt ashamed, meeting his eyes like this. It was her job to have known her daughter, and to have seen that this did not happen.

Balantyne said nothing.

"I'm sorry," she felt compelled to say it.

He put his hand on her arm and patted it, then took it away as if he were not quite sure why he had done it.

"What about the police?" he asked.

"I think Pitt and I understand each other," she replied. "He is a very clever man. He knows that I know it was not Christina. That will satisfy him, at least for a considerable time. Although he may well believe that Max might have—other—" she shook herself. "Anyway, Mr. Pitt is not our problem for the immediate future. We must consider Christina and Alan Ross."

"I don't know how you can be—so—" He looked at her with imcomprehension, and something not entirely devoid of distaste.

Surprisingly, it hurt.

"What would you have me do?" she said stiffly. "Weep? Or faint? What help would that be? We must solve the problem now. There will be time enough to indulge our feelings afterward, when she is safely married."

"And if Ross does not wish to marry her?"

"He must be made to wish to. Or else we shall find someone else. You can begin to think of others, just in case."

"Don't you feel anything? Your daughter has lain with a footman, in our own house—"

"What difference does it make where it happened! Of course I feel something—but I do not intend to buckle under it and let a mistake turn into a disaster! Now you had better go back to your papers, that wretched Miss what's-her-name will soon be here. If you wish to be useful, start to think who else would be suitable for Christina, if Ross proves impossible. I am going to make up my social diary for Christina," and before he could argue, she went out. There was much to be done.

Charlotte had been shown straight into the library when she arrived and she went immediately to the letters she had been sorting the previous day. She did not notice that it was a half hour before the general appeared.

"Good morning, Miss Ellison."

"Good morning, General Balantyne," she looked up as she spoke, as courtesy required, and noticed that he stood unusually stiffly, as though conscious of himself and a new awkwardness. She searched in her mind for some cause for it, and could find nothing.

"I apologize for having kept you waiting," he said hastily. "I hope you were not—anxious—?"

She smiled, hoping to put him at ease. "Not at all, thank you. I assumed you must have another call upon your attention, and I continued with the letters."

139

"Police," he sat down.

She felt a hypocrite, knowing that it would have been Pitt, and Balantyne had no knowledge that she was his wife. She was here precisely to observe those things they would not willingly have told the police, and yet she now dreaded it. She liked Balantyne, and would have chosen to retain his regard.

"I suppose they have to pursue it," she said softly. "It cannot be ignored."

"Better if it could," he said, staring ahead of him. "Lot of grief to everyone. But of course you are quite correct, the truth must be uncovered, regardless of the consequences. Trouble is—one discovers so much else. Still," he straightened his shoulders, "we must work. I would be obliged if you would put these in chronological order as well as you can. I'm afraid they are not all dated. Perhaps your history—?" he left it hanging, not wishing to be derogatory about her knowledge.

"Oh, there is an excellent book in that case about Marlborough's compaigns," she replied. "I asked you if I might borrow it two days ago, and you were kind enough to allow me to."

"Oh," he looked taken aback, and she realized that something had indeed upset him more deeply than she had at first understood. "Oh," he repeated foolishly. "I forgot. Of course, you will know—"

She smiled at him.

"If you have other business to take care of, I can quite well work on these by myself," she offered. "You do not need to supervise me, if it is inconvenient."

"You are very considerate, but I have nothing else that I—at least not now. Thank you," and with a faint color in his face he bent to his papers.

Once or twice he spoke to her again, but his remarks were inconsequential, and she let them pass without question, knowing his mind was preoccupied. Had he newly discovered something about Christina? That she feared she was with child? Or something deeper, worse? Compassion forbade her from making any attempt to discover. She would like to have said or done something to comfort him, indeed her instinct

140

was strong to touch him, reduce some of the stiffness out of his body, suffer him to relax. He would be stronger for having given in to himself for a few moments. But of course it would be totally improper. It would produce not the comfort of one creature for another, but embarrassment, misunderstanding, even fear. There were years of icebound convention between them. Instead she affected not to have noticed anything unusual. She could afford him at least privacy, which was second best, but gentler than nothing, and no doubt what he believed he wished for.

It was not long before midday when Max came in to say that Garson Campbell was in the morning room and wished to see General Balantyne, and could he show him in.

"What?"

Max repeated the request. Looking at him, Charlotte found him one of the most offensive men she had seen. There was a curve to his mouth, a wetness that she found repellent, as if he were forever licking his lips, although in truth she had never seen him do so.

"Oh, yes," Balantyne acquiesced. "Send him in. I won't come out, or he'll think I've all day to waste."

Garson Campbell came in a moment later. It was the first time Charlotte had seen him, and she kept perfectly still in the corner, the book on Marlborough held up to her face, hoping that they might not notice her. She peered over the top of it cautiously to look.

Campbell had a clever face, long nose, hard, humorous mouth, and quick eyes. He stamped his feet slightly, perhaps from the cold.

"Morning, Balantyne." He appeared not to have seen Charlotte, and she remained motionless, trusting that the general would have forgotten her also.

"Morning, Campbell."

"Still resurrecting past victories? Well, I suppose they're better than present apathy: so long as we don't think they'll do as a substitute."

"We can hardly learn from history if we choose not to remember it," Balantyne replied a little defensively.

"My dear Balantyne," Campbell sat down, "the day mankind learns to profit from the lessons of history I shall look for the Second Coming. Still, it's a harmless exercise, and I dare say they make good reading. A lot less dangerous than politics. I wish a few of your military colleagues would occupy themselves as innocuously. Why do men presume that because they purchased a commission in the army, and were fortunate enough not to get killed, that they can also purchase a seat at Westminster and survive the infinitely subtler wars of politics?"

"I have no idea," Balantyne said tersely. "I am hardly the person to whom you should address such a question."

"For heaven's sake, it was an observation in passing. I don't expect you to have an answer! I don't expect answers from anyone. The most I ever hope for is that here and there one may find someone who at least acknowledges the question! Have you had the damned police here again?"

Balantyne stiffened.

"Yes. Why?"

"It's about time they gave up. The whole thing's only an academic exercise anyway, matter of public image. They should have satisfied that by now. They'll not find out who did it, and if they've any sense they can never have supposed they might."

"They have to try. It's a very serious crime."

"Some wretched girl had a stillborn child, or killed it straight after. For God's sake, Balantyne, people are dying all over the place. Have you any idea how many paupers' children die in London every year? These probably never knew anything about it. And what sort of a life would they have had? Don't talk a lot of sentimental nonsense. What on earth were you like on the battlefield? Terrified to order the charge, in case someone got hurt?"

"You can hardly compare fighting a war to defend your ideals or your country with murdering babies!" Balantyne's temper was very close to the surface. Charlotte could see the light shine across the tight skin on his cheekbones. It was a stronger face than Campbell's, leaner, cleaner of bone, but there was a softer line to the closing of the lips, a vulnerability. She would like to have faced Campbell herself, driven back his clever cynicism with her own inner steel. She was not afraid of him, because she knew in her heart that to be without optimism, that core of reasonless hope in the spirit rather than the brain, was a fatal flaw, the seed of death.

Campbell sighed with obvious patience.

"It can't be undone, Balantyne. For heaven's sake, let us salvage what is left. I've already put in a few words here and there to get the police to withdraw, call it a good effort, and finish. You have friends, and so has Carlton. See what you can do. I'm sure Carlton will. Poor devil has already uncovered a basket of snakes in his own house. Although if he's surprised, he's the only one. Full-blooded young woman like Euphemia marries a stuffy old bird like that, don't know what else he expected! Still, pity it has to become public. Wasn't necessary, if the police had minded their damned business."

Balantyne's face was white. "It does not have to become public, unless you choose to make it so. Which, I imagine, as a gentleman, you will not!" He was half standing in his chair, as if he would offer some physical threat.

Campbell was more amused then frightened.

"Of course not. We've all got our skeletons. I never met a man yet who had not something he ought to be ashamed of, and certainly a hell of a lot he wanted kept secret. Do sit down, Balantyne. You look ridiculous. Just thought I'd mention it." For the first time he glanced at Charlotte and she dropped her eyes immediately, but not before she had seen the humor in him, and the appreciation. What did he imagine she was here for? She found the blood coming to her face as the obvious thought occurred to her. She hoped the general was too innocent, and too stiff, to have thought of it also.

However, when Campbell was gone he turned to her, his own face flushed.

"Charlotte—I—I—apologize for Campbell. I can only presume he did not at first realize you were here. I—I assure you—"

She forgot her own embarrassment in his.

"Of course not," she smiled. "In truth, I had not thought of it, and knew it to be nothing more than a few unpleasant words. Pray, do not think of it again."

He looked at her closely for a moment, then relaxed gratefully.

"Thank you, er, thank you."

It was an additional week before Augusta finally reached a satisfactory solution to the problem of how to get rid of Max. She had required help, and had had to invent a satisfactory explanation for it before approaching her distant relations and offering to exchange favor for favor. Now it was arranged, and it only remained to inform Max.

It was one week before Christmas. She felt vastly better than she had in the appalling morning Pitt had come. Christina had employed herself excellently, and Alan Ross seemed almost resigned to his fate. Indeed she had seen him only this afternoon escorting Christina out for a drive in his carriage. She had been out in the street herself when they had left. Brandy had been on the pavement, talking to that pretty little governess of the Southerons'. Attractive creature, a little thin, but with a peculiar grace, and such a charming smile: just the person to have charge of children.

She was alone in the house. Brandy had left for his club, the general also; and that young Ellison woman had gone home early. She rang for Max.

He came after a few minutes.

"Yes, my lady?" he was smug as always.

"I have made arrangements for you to take another post, Max—"

"My lady—" He stared woodenly at her.

"In London," she continued, "with Lord Veitch. I have given you an excellent reference, you will be footman and valet when he travels abroad, which he does frequently. He is in London for the season, and goes to the country for the summer, and for the shooting, of course. He very often journeys to Paris, and Vienna. You will travel with him, and he will increase your salary above that which we pay you. An advance, you will agree?"

"Indeed, my lady," he bowed with a slow smile. "I am most grateful. When do I leave?"

"Immediately. Tomorrow morning. Lord Veitch goes to the country for Christmas, and to Paris for the New Year."

"Thank you, my lady," he bowed again, still smiling, and withdrew.

She told Balantyne of it that evening, sitting at her dressing table, her hair loose over her shoulders; her maid had brushed it and been excused.

Balantyne, in dressing gown, stared at her.

"You let the bounder go, to a better position? And what about Bertie Veitch? What has he done to deserve that?"

"He owes me a favor," she replied.

"Augusta!"

"I warned him," she said impatiently. "And I will pay the difference in his salary."

"For how long? And I object to rewarding that—swine—for his vile—"

"He will not profit for long, Brandon. Bertie will take him out of the country, to Paris, and then Vienna. In Vienna he will find some occasion against him, and dismiss him for dishonesty. I dare say Max will not find a Viennese prison to his liking."

Balantyne stared at her, his face white.

"How could you, Augusta? That is dishonest!"

"It is no more than he deserves," she said, a chill inside her as she met his eyes, then looked away. "What would you have had me do, permit him to remain here, blackmailing us? In this house with Christina, and Alan Ross?"

"Of course not! But not this!"

"What then? Had you thought of something?"

He stood silent, tall, straight, his body frozen, simply staring at her.

She stood up and walked over to her bed, her hair falling round her shoulders, feeling appallingly vulnerable, like a new bride in a room with a stranger.

SEVEN

Christmas passed with all the trappings of tradition, the decorations, the dances, the rich food and the heavy wine, the flirtations, the presents, the bells and songs, and even, on occasion, the prayers.

For that week Charlotte did not go to Callander Square but devoted herself to her own home. Last year she had been too new to marriage to feel the warm, easy comfort of complete friendship, of belonging without anxiety or the urgency to please. Now she hung the parlor with lanterns and colored chains, purchased a small tree and decorated it, then busied herself making toffee and fudge, marzipan and mints to give to carol singers, and wrapping small gifts for her family.

On January second the matter of Callander Square obtruded into her life again, and when Pitt departed in the morning to the police station, she finished a rather indifferent effort at housework, and took herself back to the Balantynes' residence to address her attention to learning more about the rest of the square, beginning with the Southerons. After all, if Reggie Southeron really did pester his parlormaids, perhaps not all of them had been as unwilling as Mary Ann professed to be. Indeed, it was by no means certain that Mary Ann herself was paying more than lip service to her indignation, a protest as a matter of form, for her dignity's sake. It would be a good idea to ascertain how long Mary Ann had been in Callander Square, and something about her predecessor.

To this end Charlotte pursued her very natural liking for Jemima Waggoner, and accepted an invitation for luncheon the day after. Accordingly at noon she excused herself from the general in the library, and scurried through the rain to

147

the area entranceway of the Southerons'. She was let in by the scullery maid with giggles, and guided upstairs to the schoolroom where today Jemima was eating alone, since Faith, Patience, and Chastity were dining at the Campbells', in honor of Victoria Campbell's birthday.

Jemima jumped up immediately, her face lighting with a broad smile.

"Oh, Charlotte, do come in. I'm so pleased you were able to accept. General Balantyne did not mind?"

"No, of course not, as long as I am back by about two. After all, he will have to have luncheon himself, and to tell the truth, we are nearly sorted through all the papers, and I think he is not entirely sure what to do next."

"He is rather an intimidating person, isn't he?" It was more an expression of opinion than a question. While she was speaking, Jemima laid a small table with cloth and cutlery, and almost the moment she had finished, one of the maids brought in the tray cook had prepared. It was a surprisingly elaborate meal for luncheon, and Charlotte thought, seeing it, that it probably reflected Reggie Southeron's love of food and comforts.

Charlotte admired the menu, and they fell to discussing food and the general household of the Southerons. Then when the second course was completed and the pudding brought, Jemima returned to the subject of the general.

"Is it confidential?" she asked.

"Oh, I don't think so," Charlotte replied, "In fact I believe the more people who know, and are interested, the better he would be pleased. He is very proud of his family, you know. And I admit, so should I be, if my family had distinguished itself so. There has been a Balantyne in almost every great battle since the time of the Duke of Marlborough."

Jemima similed, looking into the distance, her eyes soft.

"It is a great heritage. It must be quite difficult for a man, born into such a family; so much to live up to. I wonder if young Mr. Balantyne will fight in such battles, and become a general also?"

"Well, there are hardly any wars now," Charlotte replied, but her thoughts were not on military involvements, but involvements of the heart. The look on Jemima's face concerned her. It was not like her own, an impersonal interest, an excitement in the power, the courage, and the pain of all the human beings who had lived and died in wars; she rather feared it had more to do with Brandy Balantyne, to do with a smile, a slender back, and dark head.

Jemima had not yet chosen her words for reply, and seemed somewhat confused.

"I rather hope not," she said, looking at the spoon in her hand. "It is very dreadful to think of the young men who go abroad to fight in battles that have so little to do with us, and then are maimed, or die."

"I wonder how little they really are to do with us," Charlotte said thoughtfully. "We live in the manner we do, with wealth and safety, with sea trade all over the world, with markets for our goods, and exotic things to buy at home, just because we have an empire that covers nearly every corner of the globe. And many see it as our duty," she went on, looking now at Jemima's face, "to spread civilization, Christianity, and good government to the races who do not know of such things."

"I suppose so," Jemima agreed reluctantly. "But it seems a terrible price to pay for it. So many who do not come back. Think of all the wives, and families."

"There is not much that can be purchased without a heavy price, "Charlotte said, thinking back on the few things she knew of real value—of compassion, gratitude, understanding. "What we do not pay for in some way, unfortunately we tend not to regard in its true worth." She smiled to soften the words a little.

Jemima frowned.

"Do you not think sometimes we value a thing merely because we have paid for it?" she asked. "And perhaps paid too much? And so we cling to it, and go on paying?"

Charlotte thought about it for a moment. She had become bound to a thing, committed to it for no better reason than all that she had already sacrificed for it. Perhaps some of her early infatuation for Dominic held some element of such a habit of emotion. But was Jemima thinking about the price of possessions, of war—or about the fear that Brandy Balantyne might fight somewhere, and be killed? She recalled

149

other small fragments of conversation they had had, gentle, frequent mention of the Balantynes.

"Yes," she agreed, bringing herself back to the moment. "Oh yes. Men tend to do that with wars and politics, and perhaps women do so with marriages."

Jemima relaxed with a little rueful sigh.

"Well, for women, where else is there to go? One cannot give up a marriage, however empty it may be; there is nothing to do but work at it. One has no means to leave. Even if one possessed money beforehand, when one marries it becomes the property of one's husband. If one leaves, one goes without anything. And no one in society will help, because divorce is not acceptable. My elder sister—still, that is an unhappy subject, and I am sure you don't wish to hear of it. Tell me more about the work you are doing. You told me that General Balantyne actually saw the charge of the Light Brigade, himself! I pray there may never be such a dreadful, useless waste of lives again. How can the women ever forgive for all those deaths, the losses, and all so unnecessary: a little common sense could have—"

"Common sense is excessively rare," Charlotte interrupted. "I have often seen afterward things which I would permit no one to tell me at the time." She wondered if she should say something about Brandy Balantyne. It was his relationship with Euphemia Carlton that concerned her, of course. If he could have been her lover, he must be a most unprincipled man, and could bring Jemima nothing but pain. One needed only to have been in love once, to have ached in secret and unfulfilled, to see it clearly in others.

She felt the wound now for Jemima.

No, it was better to say nothing. She would have curled with mortification to have had anyone else know how she had felt, in the past. Now of course she loved Pitt, and it hardly mattered. But for Jemima it was the present, and there was no Pitt.

So she talked instead of other things, of teaching history to children, and heard tales of the schoolroom, some that made her laugh. Presently she took her leave and returned to the library, resolved to deal somehow with the matter herself.

She worried about it all evening, till Pitt asked her what absorbed her so, and of course she was unable to answer, since she felt it was an entirely feminine confidence, and he would not understand. She replied that it was a friend whose romance exercised her, and he seemed satisfied not to press further. And indeed, it was true enough.

Much of the night she lay awake, wrestling with her conscience as to whether she should interfere in the matter, or leave it for fear of causing embarrassment. She finally arose still unsatisfied that she was correct, but having reached a decision to approach Brandy Balantyne in a manner which would have annoyed Pitt, had he known, and have horrified her parents. Only Emily might approve, and even she might well consider it socially unwise.

Her opportunity came in the afternoon. Brandy came in from a bitterly cold and wet day to warm himself by the library fire, knowing it to be the best in the house. The general was out on an errand.

Brandy came in cheerfully, rubbing his hands and shivering. He really was a most charming person; she would prefer to have liked him. She had to keep reminding herself that he was careless of feelings, indifferent to hurt, or she would have warmed to him in spite of herself.

"Hello, still working?" he smiled without a trace of condescension. "Do you like that stuff, honestly?"

"Yes, it's extremely interesting." For a moment she was beguiled, and was on the verge of replying with enthusiasm about the glimpses of people coming through the letters, the tendernesses, the vulnerability, the sudden harsh fears and griefs; when she remembered that she had made up her mind to speak to him about Jemima.

"Mr. Balantyne," she said firmly.

He looked a little surprised.

"Yes?"

She stood up.

"I have a matter of some privacy to discuss with you. Do you mind if I close the door?"

"With me?" He did not yet seem embarrassed, as she had feared he might, and then easily refuse to listen.

She pushed the door and heard it catch. She turned to face

151

him. She must hurry, the general might return at any time. It must not be left half done.

"I have formed a considerable regard for Miss Waggoner," she began, trying to conceal her nervousness, hearing her voice go dry. "Because of my friendship for her, I do not wish to see her hurt—"

"Of course not," he agreed. "What makes you think she is in danger of being hurt? She always looks uncommonly well to me."

"Always?" Charlotte said quickly.

"Well, as often as I see her." He frowned. "What is it you fear, Miss Ellison?"

There was no point in prevaricating, and she was not good at it. She wished Emily were here to put it more delicately, to be subtle. She took a deep breath.

"You do, Mr. Balantyne."

His face fell in astonishment. It would be easy to believe he had no idea what she meant.

"I do?" he said incredulously.

She breathed in and out slowly to collect herself.

"I am aware of your relationship with Lady Carlton. If I can prevent it, I shall not let you do the same with Miss Waggoner. And do not say you do not look on servants in such a way. A man who would have an affair with his neighbor's wife does not scruple about governesses." She could not look at him, and felt strangely empty for having said all that was inside her.

"For God's sake don't—I mean—please—" There was such an urgency in his voice that she found herself lifting her eyes to meet his. His concern looked almost genuine. "Look," he held up his hands helplessly, and let them fall again as explanation eluded him, "you don't understand!"

She struggled to remain cold; she wished so much to relent, and like him.

"Is there something more to understand than that you found her attractive, and took advantage of her situation?" she said coolly.

"Yes, there's everything to understand!"

"It is none of my business, but I cannot understand it if I do not know."

152

"And if you don't know, I suppose you will believe the worst, and spread it about." There was a mounting hopelessness in his voice now, and in his face.

"Of course I shall not spread it about," she said crossly. It was a horrible suggestion. "But I wish to make sure you do not hurt Jemima."

"Why should I? Why Jemima?" he fenced.

"Don't be naive! Because she finds you attractive, and does not know that you are—" she could think of no word she wished to employ.

"Very well," he turned away. "Though I doubt you will believe me."

She waited, looking at his dark head against the winter light of the window.

"Robert Carlton is a nice old boy, but pretty remote, detached—"

"That is no excuse—"

"Don't interrupt," he said sharply. "Above all things Euphemia wants a child. She is thirty-six. She has not forever. And if Robert persists in treating her with courtesy and excessive consideration, either because he is abashed by emotion, or because he believes, mistakenly, that it is what she wishes, then she will never have one. She fears that he is uninterested in physical affection, and would find her repellent if he knew she was, so she dares not tell him.

"We have always been friends. I like her; she's a generous woman, with wit and kindness. I saw she was getting more and more distressed about something. She finally confided it to me. Ours was an arrangement of convenience, only until she conceived a child. Now you can believe that or not, as you choose. But it's the truth. And whatever you think of me, for Euphemia's sake—or for Robert Carlton's—don't spread it around." For the first time he turned and looked back at her, his face perfectly serious. "Please?"

It was ridiculous, and yet she did believe him. Without considering, she acknowledged it.

"I believe you. But—do not speak or act without thought toward Miss Waggoner. It can hurt very much to fall in love where you know it cannot be returned."

He looked at her closely, his hazel eyes clouded with a sudden sensitivity to her.

"Oh, not now," she said quickly. "But in the past I have done. He was my sister's husband. I grew out of it, I saw him differently. But it hurt at the time."

He relaxed.

"Please don't speak of Euphemia," he asked again.

She thought of Pitt, the babies in the gardens.

"I promise I shall not speak except in her interest," she said solemnly.

He was not satisfied, sensing evasion in her words.

"What do you mean?"

There was nothing for it but to be honest.

"I was thinking of the police. They know that Euphemia is with child, and that it is yours. They may hold her under some suspicion for the children in the gardens also, you know."

His face went so blank with horror it was impossible to imagine that he had thought of such an eventuality before.

"To tell them the truth," Charlotte said softly, "might be greatly to Euphemia's advantage, do you not think?"

"They wouldn't believe it," his mouth was stiff, still shocked.

"They might."

"How—how did they know of—of the child—about me—any of it?"

"They are quite clever, you know, and they would be looking for such things."

"I suppose so. Mother said she thought that fellow Pitt was clever, and she's usually right. And there are not many people whose intelligence she regards well."

Charlotte did not wish to tell him of her own relationship to Pitt, and she wondered if the warmth of pride that bubbled inside her now was as obvious to him as it felt to her.

"That is all I meant," she said carefully. "Now I think it might be advisable for us to finish this discussion before the general returns, do you not?"

"Oh—yes, yes it would. You won't—?"

"No, of course I won't! I was concerned only for Jemima."

His mouth curved upward in a slight smile.

"You know, I like Jemima. She's a little like you, in some ways. And in other ways, you are a little like Mother—"

Charlotte froze at the thought, although doubtless he intended it as a compliment.

His smile broadened into a grin.

"Don't look so shocked. Mother has more courage than anyone else I know; she'd knock the stuffing out of all the old generals at Father's clubs! And she was quite a beauty too. Only trouble was she could never flirt; didn't know how; had no art of deception."

Charlotte blushed. She had rather charged in, and certainly she had displayed no finesse. Perhaps she was more like Lady Augusta than she would have cared to admit. She looked up at Brandy to say something to excuse herself, make herself appear softer, when the general came in. His face widened in surprise when he saw Brandy.

"Best fire in the house," Brandy said quickly. "You always bragged it was."

"That does not mean I intended you to stand by it all afternoon, distracting Miss Ellison from her work."

"Pity. Can't think of a pleasanter thing to do on a filthy winter afternoon. Do you see the gutters, simply running over with water?"

"Then go and change your boots. I must get on with my work. You would be better if you found yourself something to do."

"Can't write my memoirs yet, I haven't got anything to remember."

Balantyne looked at him with slight suspicion, as if he thought he might be being faintly twitted, but Brandy's face was bland with innocence. He went to the door.

"Good afternoon, Miss Ellison, thank you for permitting me to stand by your fire," and he went out.

"Was he disturbing you?" Balantyne asked a little sharply.

"Not at all," Charlotte replied. "He wasn't here long. I believe I have sorted those Marlborough letters, would you care to look at them?"

* * *

Emily had been several times to Callander Square since her last visit to Charlotte over the matter, and had managed to form quite a friendship with Christina. Therefore she was not surprised when Christina confided in her at the end of the first week in January that she was shortly to be married to Alan Ross.

The confidence itself did not surprise Emily; she had spent their entire acquaintance diligently seeking precisely this. But under any other circumstances, the choice of bridegroom would have surprised her considerably. Alan Ross and Christina Balantyne seemed to her judgment an unnatural partnering. From what she had seen of Ross, he was a serious and rather tense man, possibly even a man of deep feeling: whereas Christina was gay, when she chose, deliciously sophisticated, and essentially shallow. Still, he was of good family, and adequate means, and most important, apparently willing to marry at short notice.

"We are to be married at the end of the month," Christina said, facing Emily in the morning room where they sat by the fire.

"My congratulations," Emily replied, her mind considering the possibility that Christina might know by now whether she was actually with child or not. She was careful not to glance downward to a betraying waistline, but she had admired her gown earlier, to give herself an opportunity to look carefully then. There was certainly no sign of it. But it was early yet. In fact Charlotte was over four months, and still looked quite normal. Of course Charlotte was a bigger person than Christina, and all these things had to be taken into account.

"Thank you," Christina accepted without enthusiasm. "I should like you to be there, if you are able?"

"Of course. It will be charming. Which church do you choose?"

"St. Clement's. It is all arranged."

"I hope you have a good dressmaker? It is so nerve-racking to be let down at the last moment. I can give you names, if you are not already suited?"

"Oh, I am, thank you. Miss Harrison is most reliable."

"I'm so glad." Emily sensed a certain restraint, something

156

beneath the surface that Christina wished to say to someone, and yet could not decide. "You will make a beautiful bride," Emily went on. "Mr. Ross is most fortunate."

"I hope so."

Emily affected to be mildly surprised.

"Have you some doubt? I think you will make him an excellent wife, if you wish to."

Christina's little face hardened.

"I'm not sure that I do wish to. I'm not sure that I wish to give up my freedom."

"Good gracious, girl, there is no need to give up your freedom, or anything else—except money, of course—but even that can be managed properly, with a little forethought."

Christina looked up, staring at her.

"What do you mean? I am marrying a man I am not in love with. What greater sacrifice of freedom can there be than that?"

It was time she was taught a little common sense.

"My dear, very few women marry men they are in love with," Emily said firmly. "And even those who do, frequently find that it was a mistake. The kind of man one falls in love with is usually entertaining, witty, and handsome; but equally often he has no means to support one, is highly unreliable, and as like as not, will in due course fall out of love with you, and in again with someone else. To marry, one requires a man with good character, common sense in business, or else a private income of great proportions; he must be moderately sober and not gamble to excess, and be of gentle manners and acceptable appearance."

"That sounds desperately dull," Christina said sourly. "I don't remember George Ashworth being like that!"

"Possibly not, but then I worked a great deal harder than you were prepared to do. I had not your advantages, so I had to create my own. But Mr. Ross seems pleasantly spoken and courteous; he has means, so I hear; and he is certainly well enough to look at. That is all you can reasonably expect."

"Perhaps, but it is not all that I want!"

"Well, providing you are discreet, you can always fall in love afterward. But in the meantime you would be well advised to make the best of this. You are hardly the sort of

157

person to be happy running off with some penniless romantic, and the sooner you accept that, the sooner you can begin to work on what you have. And make no mistake, my dear, you will have to work on it."

"Work on it? I don't know what you mean. I have done the work; we are to be married before the end of the month. He could not possibly let me down now. It would make his position impossible."

Emily sighed. She had not realized any girl could grow up so ignorant. Whatever had Lady Augusta been thinking of? Or perhaps the Balantynes had enough money and social influence, and Christina sufficient looks, that they had considered it unnecessary. Or it was even possible that Lady Augusta had given all this advice, and Christina was merely too arrogant to have believed it.

"Christina," she said slowly, "if you wish to be happy, you must realize that it depends upon your husband being happy, and upon his being agreeable to your conducting your life in the manner that best pleases you. You must teach him to want what you want, and if possible even to think that it is his idea. If he believes he has suggested a thing, he will never refuse you, even if he changes his mind. You must learn to be courteous to him at all times, or nearly all; never to argue with him, or disobey him, in public, and if you must do it in private, then do it either with a smile, or with tears. Don't waste your time trying to be reasonable, men do not expect it, and it disconcerts them. Always pay attention to your looks; do not be extravagant beyond your means; and see that your servants keep your home properly. Never let there be domestic upsets, men do not like to have the order of things disturbed, above all by quarrels in the household.

"And if you have an admirer, for heaven's sake be discreet; always, whatever it costs you, be discreet. No love affair is worth sacrificing your marriage for. And to be honest, my dear, I cannot see you loving anyone enough to lose your head over; your heart, for a little; or your desires, if you cannot contain yourself, although you would be better if you could; but never forget what scandal does to a woman. Your husband will tolerate all sorts of things, if you treat him well, but not scandal."

She looked at Christina's pretty, rather sulky face.

"And one last thing," she finished. "If he should show undue interest in another woman, affect not to notice it. Whatever you do, never make a scene. Men hate scenes. Jealousy is the most unbecoming of all behavior. Never lose your temper, and be careful how often you weep. It can become most boring, and then when you need it, it no longer works.

"I am surprised your mother has not given you the same advice."

Christina stared at her. "She has, she has done for years. I pay no attention. One's mother is always giving one good advice."

Emily waited, staring back, eyes unflinching. It was a time for reality.

At last Christina's eyes dropped.

"I don't think I really want to be married," she spoke quietly. "It sounds like very hard work."

"Do you have any choice?" Emily was brutal.

Christina's eyes narrowed and her face tightened.

"What do you mean?" she demanded harshly.

Emily assumed innocence.

"That you must make up your mind," she replied blandly, "and whatever you do, you must do it well. We can none of us afford to do anything else. In society everyone knows what everyone else does; it is talked about and never totally forgotten. You will have to live with it all your life, so think before you act. That is all I mean."

Christina took a deep breath, and let it out slowly.

"What a revoltingly practical creature you are. I don't believe you have an ounce of romance in your soul."

"Perhaps not," Emily agreed. "But do not confuse romance with love. I know how to love." She stood up. "I fear your romance is largely an indulgence, and indulgence is selfishness and has to be paid for."

"I do not intend to pay if I do not have to. But I shall remember what you say, whether I follow it or not. You may still attend the wedding, if you wish."

"Thank you," Emily said dryly. "I should be delighted."

Emily decided that with regard to the bodies in the square, Christina was no longer of interest; for one thing, she had not the nerve, the decision, to perform such an act. Lady Augusta most certainly would have had, but then she had also, unless Emily had wildly misjudged her, enough sense never to have permitted such a thing to happen.

Therefore it was time to turn her attention to the other houses. Charlotte had told her that Euphemia Carlton was highly unlikely, although she would not say why, but apparently she had satisfied Pitt. And although Pitt was a peculiar creature, Emily had a great respect for him; purely as a policeman, of course, socially he was impossible. But if he was satisfied regarding Euphemia, then so was she.

So she must look further into the other households, as opportunity could be made. From what Charlotte had learned, Reggie Southeron seemed the most promising, but it might also prove productive to cultivate Sophie Bolsover, and to learn a little more about Helena Doran. She had gone about the time of the death of the first child, just over two years ago. It was possible there was some connection, was it not? Why had she never written? Who was the lover no one had even seen? Had he perhaps loved others also—with different results? The time that the first body had been in the ground, some six months, could it have been longer? Long enough to have been conceived before Helena and her unknown lover disappeared? Could that even be why the child had been killed—a legacy from a love affair that had ended in desertion, and hate? It was certainly a mystery very much worth the solving!

With this in mind she planned to visit Charlotte two days afterward, being obliged to attend to her household on the following morning, a small matter of servants, and be at home to callers in the afternoon. One had certain social obligations to maintain.

However, on the second morning she was free to pursue those things that were really of interest to her.

"Who on earth are you calling on at this hour?" George inquired, still sitting at a late breakfast and flicking through the society pages of the newspaper. He looked very elegant in his silk dressing coat. She thought again how fortunate she was that she had been able to marry a man who could offer her all the social and financial advantages she wished, and whom she could genuinely love. Of course he had many characteristics that, when this fascinating business in Callander Square was over, she would hope to work on. But then if there were nothing to work on, a marriage would quickly become intolerably boring; for a woman, at any rate.

"Charlotte," she replied. "It doesn't matter what time I call on her."

"You've become uncommonly fond of Charlotte lately," he said with a slight frown. "What are you doing, Emily?"

"Doing?" she opened her eyes wide.

"Yes, 'doing,' my dear. You are far too pleased with yourself not to be doing something. I want to know what it is."

She had already foreseen this occasion and had her answer prepared.

"I am introducing Charlotte to a few of my acquaintances, in a range of society that she may enjoy," she said easily; which was true enough, although not for the reason she implied. Charlotte had no interest in Callander Square, except for the purpose of detection. Neither, for that matter, if she were honest, had Emily.

George squinted at her round the paper.

"You surprise me. I didn't think Charlotte gave a fig for any part of society. I would say don't push her into anything she does not wish, just because you enjoy it; only I doubt you would be able to. As I remember Charlotte, she is very unlikely to do anything unless she wishes to herself." He put the paper down. "But in the event she does wish to look at society, why don't you ask her here? We'll give a party and introduce her properly. She's a handsome enough creature, not traditional perhaps, but very handsome."

"Don't be ridiculous," Emily said quickly. "It has nothing to do with her looks, it is her tongue. You can't take Charlotte anywhere, she says whatever comes to her mind. Ask her her opinion of anything, and instead of judging what is appropriate to say, she will tell you what she really thinks. She would not mean to, but she would ruin herself in a month,

161

not to mention us. And of course Pitt is not a gentleman. He is far too intelligent, for a start."

"There is no reason why a gentleman should not be intelligent, Emily," he said somewhat tartly.

"Oh, of course not, my dear," she replied with a smile. "But he should have the good taste not to show it. You know that. It makes other people feel uncomfortable, and it implies effort. One should never appear to make an effort. It is like enthusiasm; have you noticed how ladies are never enthusiastic in public? It makes one look so naive. Still, I suppose there is nothing public to be enthusiastic about. Shall you be in for dinner?"

"We are engaged to dine with Hetty Appleby," he said, fixing her with a penetrating eye. "I presume you had forgotten that?"

"Completely," she admitted. "I must go now, I have a lot to say to Charlotte."

"You could always ask her to dinner here anyway," he called after her. "I rather like Charlotte. She may not be good for society, but I think she might be rather good for me!"

Emily quite naturally found Charlotte at home at that hour of the day and pleased at the excuse to leave her housework, although her home, she would be the first to admit, had fallen into a rather haphazard state since her assistance to General Balantyne began.

"We can discount Christina," Emily said immediately, walking in and pulling off her gloves. "I have looked at her carefully, and I don't believe she would have the nerve."

Charlotte made an effort to conceal a smile, and failed.

"I'm so glad."

"Why? You cannot possibly tell me you like her?"

"Oh no, I don't! But I like the general; and I think I like Brandy too."

"Indeed?" Emily was surprised. "Why do you like Brandy? I told you about Euphemia Carlton!"

"I know you did. Where do you wish to look next? I think Reggie Southeron. He definitely pays considerable attention to his parlormaids. I don't imagine it is a newly acquired habit—"

162

"Certainly not. But as well as that, we should consider the mystery of Helena Doran."

"Why, for goodness' sake? She's been gone for two years."

"I know that," Emily said impatiently. "But what about her lover? Who was he? Was she the only one? Why not court her openly, if he were a man of honor? Why does no one know who he was?"

Charlotte understood immediately.

"You mean he may have courted others, and the babies could have been theirs? Thomas said the times of death were only very approximate." She wrinkled her nose a little. "It depends on the nature of the soil, the wetness, and so forth. It seems horrible to think of human beings like that: but I suppose we must all be buried some time. We are only clay anyway, after the soul has gone. It's foolish how much we love our bodies. I can ask Jemima a little about it."

Emily knew her sister well enough to realize without effort that this last sentence referred back again to Helena Doran's disappearance.

"What is she like, this Jemima?" she inquired.

"Very reliable." Charlotte viewed her as a witness, rightly guessing that Emily was not interested in her qualities of warmth or humor.

"She wouldn't be the one, I suppose." Emily looked at her a little sideways.

"No," Charlotte said firmly. "At least I would say not, if character is anything at all to judge by."

Emily considered for a moment.

"It isn't," she decided. "Still, we'll concentrate on Helena first. There is a mystery there, beyond question. You ask Jemima, and for goodness' sake be a bit more discreet than you usually are. I shall speak to Sophie Bolsover again. She is always only too willing to gossip a little. I must think up what I know to tell her in return."

Having stayed for a little further discussion, and the quite real pleasure of visiting with her sister, Emily took herself home again and prepared to launch her new offensive. First she would call upon Sophie when she might reasonably find her alone; then she would pursue the acquaintance of the last woman in the square whose establishment she believed a possible refuge for secrets, Mariah Campbell.

She was very put out to discover Sophie not at home, and in a considerable pique left her card and gathered her wits to think of something to say to Mariah Campbell, a fit excuse for calling unasked upon someone she had barely met. Any message could perfectly easily be left with servants, therefore she must inquire after something. What?

She was already at the door. It would appear most odd to remain in a stationary carriage, therefore she must alight, and trust to her wits to think of something, should Mariah Campbell be in and able to receive her.

She inquired of the parlormaid, and was courteously received. Yes, Mrs. Campbell was in, and yes, Mrs. Campbell would be happy to receive her. She was shown into the small family parlor where Mariah was sitting with her daughters. Apparently they had not yet resumed lessons after the celebration of Christmas. They both stood and curtseyed as Emily was announced, then retired obediently.

Mariah Campbell was a pleasant-looking woman, not beautiful, but with a distinction about her that was perhaps longer lasting than mere prettiness. She was becomingly dressed, but with no concession to the trimmings of fashion.

"How very civil of you to call," she said, also rising to meet Emily, since Emily was a lady of title, and she was not. She did not pretend any false warmth; they were strangers and both knew it. "I hope I may offer you some refreshment; tea, perhaps?"

"I should be delighted," Emily accepted. She could not possibly give her true reason for having called—curiosity; she must rapidly produce another. "I heard from Lady Anstruther," she sincerely hoped there was no such person, "that you had stayed in Scotland, with the Taits," another invention. "My husband is quite set upon our going too—we have been invited, you know. I have heard that the house is quite impossible! As cold as a tomb, and with servants who can never be found when one wants them, and don't speak English even then. I was hoping you could tell me if that is true. Dear Marjorie does tend to exaggerate, to color a story to make it the more lively!"

164

Mariah looked totally foxed. Quite naturally, she had even less idea what Emily was talking about than Emily herself.

"I'm afraid I have no knowledge," she admitted. "Lady Anstruther—did you say?—must have confused me with someone else. Campbell is a Scots name, it is true, but quite a common one. And I have never been to Scotland myself. I'm so sorry, I cannot be of any guidance to you."

"Oh, never mind," Emily waved her hand to dismiss it before she got too bogged down, and perhaps contradicted herself, having forgotten what she had first said. "I dare say I can persuade George not to go at all. He isn't really very fond of shooting anyway." She had no idea whether it was even the season for shooting; but then with luck Mariah would not know either.

"And of course," Emily continued with a sudden flash of inspiration, "I must be here for the wedding!"

Mariah blinked.

"Wedding?"

"Christina Balantyne and Mr. Ross!" Emily went on with enthusiasm. "I am so very happy that poor Mr. Ross has entirely recovered from Helena Doran's leaving so suddenly. It must have been a great shock for him, poor creature."

"I think it was a shock to everyone," Mariah answered. "At least a surprise. I certainly had no idea."

"Did you not know at least that she had another admirer?" Emily raised her eyebrows at the mystery.

"To tell the truth, I am too busy with my family to have been more than slightly acquainted with Miss Doran; or indeed with most of the families in the square, except for Adelina Southeron, of course, because of her children."

That seemed to close the subject; but Emily was not yet prepared to give up.

"I'm sure if she puts her mind to it, that Christina will make him very content."

"Content?" Mariah's voice showed her understanding, and pity, for such a lukewarm emotion.

But Emily meant what she had said.

"I think so. I think that is all that another person can do for one. I think happiness is something one must achieve for oneself. Do you not?"

Mariah looked at her carefully, but before she could frame a reply, the door opened and Garson Campbell came in. Emily had seen him only once before, and did not care for him greatly.

Apparently he had remembered her.

"Good afternoon, Lady Ashworth," he said. He did not speak to Mariah.

"Good afternoon, Mr. Campbell." Emily profoundly hoped Mariah would not repeat to him the fiction she had invented to explain her visit. "I trust you are well?"

"Well enough," he answered. "How courteous of you to call."

"We were about to have tea," Mariah said quietly. "Do you care to join us?"

"I don't think so," his mouth turned down slightly at the corners. "I doubt I would contribute to your gossip. I prefer something a little more political."

"Than what?" Emily said instantly, before thinking that it might not be in her interest to irritate him.

"I beg your pardon?"

"You prefer something more political than what, Mr. Campbell?"

"I take your point, Lady Ashworth. I have no idea what you were discussing. I was presuming on past experience. I never yet met a woman of good character who had any political sense; only the whores seem to have that kind of acumen."

"Indeed?" Emily raised her eyebrows as high as she could and invested her voice with a trace of humor. "I've never discussed politics with a whore. But I do know Mr. Balfour slightly."

"I apologize, Lady Ashworth," he said with a dry smile. "Were you discussing politics when I interrupted you?"

"Not at all. We were discussing Mr. Ross, and who might have been Helena Doran's mysterious admirer." She watched his face. Men sometimes confided in each other. It was conceivable he might know. His skin darkened, and tightened for a moment across his temples. She felt a thrill of victory. He knew something!

"It is most courteous of you to offer tea," she stood up, "but

I fear I called uninvited, and I would be most distressed to have put you to inconvenience. It has been a great pleasure to have further made your acquaintance, Mrs. Campbell. I hope we shall meet again." Now she wished to be out of this room, away from Garson Campbell before he read too much of her intent. He was a man with whom she did not wish to match wits.

Mariah did not appear surprised.

"I shall look forward to it," she said, reaching at the same time for the bell. "So generous of you to call. I'm sorry I was unable to advise you regarding Scotland."

"Oh, pray don't concern yourself," Emily was already making for the door where she could hear the parlormaid in the hall. "I doubt we shall go anyway, especially if this dismal weather continues."

"It will continue, Lady Ashworth," Campbell said from the center of the room. "It always does, from January right through until March, invariably. I have never known it to do otherwise. And the only difference you will find in Scotland is that it will be worse."

"Then I shall definitely not go," Emily said, almost backing into the maid. "Thank you for your counsel." She left him smiling a little contemptuously at her foolishness, and made her escape into the street. She climbed into the carriage with an air of relief, even though it was cold, and there was a loose spring somewhere, from the feel of it. At least she was spared the necessity of extricating herself from an increasingly impossible conversation. What an unpleasant man! If there was anything more oppressive than stupid people, it was those who felt they knew everything—and disliked everything.

The next time she called upon Sophie Bolsover she found Euphemia and Adelina Southeron there, and consequently could say nothing of Helena Doran and hope to learn answers of value. It was several tedious, desperately impatient days before she felt it suitable to call again.

This time she was more fortunate, although fortune was only partly responsible. She had done a little reconnoitering beforehand, and thus discovered Sophie satisfactorily alone.

"Oh, Sophie, what a pleasure to find you unengaged," she breezed in immediately, making no pretense. "I have such wonderful gossip to tell you. I should have been so disappointed to have been constrained to speak of trivialities."

Sophie brightened instantly. Nothing pleased her more than gossip, except gossip from a lady of title.

"Come in," she urged. "Make yourself comfortable, Emily dear, and do tell me. Is it about Lady Tidmarsh? I have been simply dying to discover whether she really did stay with those fearful Joneses! I can hardly bear the suspense."

This was precisely what Emily had hoped she would ask, for she had taken great pains to provide the answer.

"Of course!" she said triumphantly. "But you must swear not to repeat it!" This added an irresistible spice. Sophie dissembled utterly, her eyes shining with excitement; she almost pulled Emily physically onto the sofa by the fire, curling up immediately like a little cat.

"Tell me!" she pleaded. "Tell me everything!"

Emily obliged, decorating it here and there with detail that might well be true enough, and was certainly no more than harmless color. When she had finished Sophie was ecstatic. It would furnish her with stories to drop hints about and retell to those she wished to impress, one by one, with further swearings to secrecy; and of course, to refuse to tell to those she wished to annoy, with many hints as to how fascinating and exclusive was the information she could not possibly divulge. And it would be only human to imply she knew yet more, which she was bound to keep in the utmost silence. She was beside herself with delight.

Now was the perfect time to ask about Helena Doran. Sophie would tell her everything she knew, or even guessed. Emily made no bones about her interest.

"Oh," Sophie breathed out happily, "of course." Then she frowned. "But it is all a little old now! Are you sure you care?"

"Oh yes," Emily assured her. "I think it is fascinating. Who can he have been?"

Sophie screwed up her face in thought.

"Helena was very pretty, you know, almost a real beauty, one might say; such hair, all the color of winter sunshine, or so poor Mr. Ross used to say. He was quite dreadfully upset, you know?

"I do hope he will be happy with Christina. She is utterly different, as different as could be; to look at, naturally, but in her character as well."

"What was Helena like?" Emily asked innocently.

"Oh," Sophie thought again. "Quiet, not terribly fashionable; of course she did not need to be, she was beautiful enough to get away with dressing plainly. And she didn't need to be witty. She played the piano very well, and she used to sing also. I sometimes wish I could sing. Can you?"

"Not very well. Was she secretive?"

"Quiet, yes; when I come to think of it, she did not have a great many close friends. She was fond of Euphemia Carlton."

"What sort of men did she admire?"

Sophie contorted her face in an effort to remember.

"Men of substance, not just material, but men who had succeeded at something, who were established. In fact, older men. Perhaps because she had had no father for years, poor child. She did admire General Balantyne, I recall. Such a handsome man, don't you think? Such an air of authority about him, and such dignity. If I didn't love Freddie, I would quite care for him myself!"

"Was that why she didn't marry Mr. Ross; because he was not yet of sufficient substance for her, too young?" Emily asked.

"You know, I had not thought of it, but that could be the reason. She admired confidence in a man. Although she did not care for poor Reggie Southeron at all. But then he is so irresponsible! He has not the kind of—what the Romans used to call *gravitas*, so Freddie says. So very masculine, *gravitas*, don't you agree? Really quite exciting!"

"So she would not have run off with a penniless romantic, then? Or someone of unsuitable social class?" Emily asked. Really, the mystery was deepening! This was fascinating, and increasingly incomprehensible.

Sophie's eyes widened with her own surprise.

"No! No, she wouldn't, now that I come to think about it.

Oh my dear, do you suppose he was already married to someone else, and they simply ran off? Oh, how dreadful!"

"Where do you suppose she met him?" Emily pursued. "If they had met at parties and so forth, people would know who he was—and nobody does!"

"Oh, it must have been somewhere secret," Sophie agreed. "Even Laetitia doesn't know who he was. At least she says she doesn't, and why should she lie? Unless, of course, he was somebody simply awful! But I cannot see Helena becoming enamored of someone awful. She was far too proud, and fastidious."

"She was fastidious?"

"Oh very! No, they must quite definitely have met somewhere secretly."

"Well, it must have been close, must it not?" Emily thought aloud. "Or else she would have had to take a carriage, and then the driver at least would know. And one should never trust coachmen, unless one pays them oneself; and even then they may always be better paid by someone else. No, it is good counsel never to trust servants, especially men; they tend to ally with other men."

"Where then?" Sophie asked. "Oh! Why, of course! I know. At least I know precisely what I should do!"

"What? What?" Emily's composure vanished completely.

"Why, the empty house, of course! That house on the opposite side of the square has been empty for years! It belongs to an old lady who will neither sell it nor live in it. I believe she prefers France, or something equally odd. It is quite dreadfully neglected now, but it used to be most attractive, and there is a summer house at the back. Quite the romantic spot to meet. That has to be it! Don't you think I am most clever to have thought of it?"

Emily thought privately that she was quite foolish not to have thought of it immediately, but naturally it would be unkind and impolitic to say so.

"Oh, indeed!" she agreed enthusiastically. "And I am sure beyond doubt that you are right. And one day, I dare say, we shall find out who he was."

"Perhaps if we go and look?" Sophie suggested. "We may

even find some small thing they may have left behind! What do you think?"

Emily had already resolved to do just such a thing the moment the house was mentioned. She did not wish to take Sophie with her, but there seemed no help for it.

"What an excellent idea," she agreed. "The first opportunity it is fine. We will be thought most odd and attract unwelcome attention if we go in this rain. Tomorrow, if it is dry, I shall call for you and we will go together." She fixed Sophie with a frank eye, to let her understand that if she crept in beforehand, Emily would confide no more gossip to her. She saw from Sophie's expression that she grasped the message perfectly.

Emily stood up.

"My dear, this has been the most exciting visit I have paid in months. I shall look forward to our next meeting." She moved to the door and Sophie came with her, forgetting to ring for the parlormaid in her anticipation of tomorrow.

Emily turned at the door.

"Oh, you won't mind if I bring my sister Charlotte, will you? She is a most intelligent creature, and may be of some assistance to us."

Sophie's face fell for a moment, then at the mention of assistance, brightened again.

"No, of course not," she assured. "If she is your sister, no doubt she is most charming."

Emily would have quarreled with that; Charlotte was charming only when she meant it, and she doubted Sophie would bring out the best in her, but that hardly mattered now. She smiled devastatingly at Sophie, and took her leave, her heart singing in triumph.

Her prayers were answered, and the following day was cold and dry. She duly picked Charlotte up from her house before Charlotte had even finished her luncheon, and proceeded at a great pace to Callander Square, explaining her mission to Charlotte on the way, and the necessity for such precipitate speed. She did not entirely trust Sophie not to creep over on her own, and thus discover whatever there might be to find, before Emily and Charlotte got there. She would not have gone in the morning, because it was still rather wet and icebound, but this afternoon she might well think to slip over without Emily, and trust to not being caught at it.

They arrived at Callander Square and alighted from the carriage, bidding the coachman and footman remain where they were. They announced themselves to Sophie, who was ready waiting with her outdoor boots on and a cloak in the footman's hands. Within five minutes they were at the garden entrance to the unoccupied house. It took the weight of the three of them to push it open, so long had it lain shut.

They hesitated on the step.

The garden inside was motionless and cold, trees rimed in frost, path stones overgrown with mosses, and slimy. There were dead leaves on the grass and rotting deep on the flower beds. If there was anything alive, it was asleep till spring.

"A garden shouldn't be like this," Charlotte said quietly. "Somebody must have laid it out carefully once, and people walked and talked to each other here."

"Helena Doran and somebody," Emily said practically. "Let's go in."

Feet soundless on the wet leaves, they moved reluctantly inside, Charlotte pulling the door behind them to hide their presence. They followed the path gingerly, afraid of slipping on the greasy stones. It skirted round the house and then disappeared into grass at the back. The lawn was soggy, and again covered with leaves. Halfway down there was a thatched, wooden summer house, roof collapsing. Obviously a multitude of birds had tweaked and stolen from it over the years.

"There," Emily said triumphantly. "That is where lovers would meet." And she hurried across the squelching grass toward it, her skirts catching in the twigs and leaves. Charlotte caught up with her, but Sophie stepped more gingerly from stone to stone round the remnants of the path.

Charlotte and Emily rounded the corner of the summer house and peered inside. It was very dilapidated, thatch hanging low across the ceiling, several of the seats rotted and fallen through.

172

"Oh dear," Emily said disappointedly. "I wonder if all this could have happened in only two years."

"It wouldn't matter," Charlotte said from behind her. "Don't forget, this is January. In the summer it would all look quite different. The trees would have leaves on them, there might be flowers and birds. It would be more like a secret garden. They wouldn't care if it were a little neglected."

"A little!"

"More to the point," Charlotte stared round, "do you see anything that makes you think it might have been used? She might have dropped a handkerchief, or something, or easily torn a little piece from a dress. There are certainly enough rough pieces around."

They both began to look, and Sophie joined them. After several minutes they satisfied themselves there was nothing to discover, and Charlotte and Emily went out of the other door toward the back of the garden. Sophie remained behind, not having searched thoroughly herself.

Past the bushes Charlotte stopped stark, and Emily bumped into her.

"What's the matter with you?" she demanded crossly, then stared over Charlotte's shoulder, and felt all the warmth drain out of her body.

They were at the side of a small lawn under a great tree. From one of the branches hung a garden swing, and on it, skeletal fingers still round the ropes, were the rag-wisped bones of what had once been a woman. Remnants of her dress hung from the seat of the swing, bleached gray by seasons of rain and sun. Flies and small animals had eaten away her flesh and there was nothing left now but a little dried skin and pale yellow hair, and the fingernails of her hands. Grotesquely, the whalebone stays of her corsets were still whole, though fallen across where her stomach would have been, and on top of them, released from the womb, the tiny, birdlike bones of an unborn child.

"Helena," Charlotte whispered. "Poor Helena."

EIGHT

Reggie Southeron arrived home from his afternoon of card-playing to find Adelina looking tearful and white-faced. It was annoying. He himself was in excellent spirits, having won a handsome sum of money, shared some excellent brandy, rich cigars, and even richer jokes. He had fully intended to keep the same roseate glow all evening, and to discover Adelina in such mind was distinctly dampening. He tried to jolly her out of it; after all, women wept so easily, it was probably nothing of significance.

"Don't you feel very well?" he said cheerfully. "Never mind, it'll pass. Take half a glass of brandy, pick you up no end. I'll join you."

To his surprise she agreed, and a few minutes later they were in the withdrawing room, curtains closed against the night, sharing the warmth of a considerable fire. Suddenly Adelina began weeping again, dabbing a handkerchief to her eyes.

"For goodness' sake, my dear," he said a little sharply. "Pull yourself together! Nothing is helped by sniffling."

She gave him a bleak look and wiped her eyes harder.

"I can only presume that you do not know," she said indignantly.

"I do not," he agreed. "And if it makes you as miserable as you look, I do not wish to. If some sort of calamity has befallen someone, I'm sorry, but since I cannot help, I am happy to remain ignorant of the sordid details."

"It is your duty to know!" she said accusingly.

He started to protest, but she was not to be stemmed.

"Helena Doran has been found!"

"Is that cause for weeping? She ran off. If she now does

not like her circumstance, that is a pity, but hardly our responsibility!"

"Dead!" Adelina let the word fall like a damnation. "She has been dead for two years, sitting there on the swing seat in the garden of the empty house, all by herself, just as if she were alive. She must have been murdered, of course!"

He did not wish to believe it; it was horrible, a rude and ugly disturbance of all that was safe and comfortable, all that he liked.

"Why 'of course'?" he demanded. "She could have died of a heart attack, or a seizure, or something."

"She was with child!"

"You mean they've done a post mortem?" he said in surprise, and some disgust. "Already?"

"She was barely more than a skeleton," she began to weep again. "There were bones. Nellie told me."

"Who is Nellie?" Nobody came to mind.

"The scullery maid. Can't you even remember your own servants' names?"

He was genuinely surprised.

"Why on earth sould I? I don't suppose I've ever seen her. I'm sorry about Helena, but really my dear, it is a most gruesome subject. Let us discuss something else. I'm sure you'll feel better for it." He had a sudden inspiration. "And we don't want to upset the children. They will know if you are distressed. It is hardly something we would wish them to know about." It was actually a ridiculous hope. Chastity at least would discover it in great detail, in fact probably already knew: but it sounded both sympathetic and wise to say so.

Adelina looked at him dubiously, but she did not argue.

Reggie settled down to a pleasant evening by the fire, a good dinner, a little port; and perhaps just a touch more brandy. Helena and her affairs were beyond help now, so there was nothing to be gained for anyone by dwelling on thoroughly unpleasant subjects such as corpses in wet gardens, and murders, and the like.

However, his peace was broken about nine o'clock when the butler brought a new bottle of port, and announced at the same time that Dr. Bolsover had called to see him.

Reggie sat up and opened his eyes.

"Oh well, you might as well send him in," he said reluctantly. He was not really in the mood for conversation, but Freddie was an easy fellow, well mannered, fond of a little civilized conversation, and a good port. "Bring another glass, will you?"

"I have done, sir. I'll ask Dr. Bolsover to join you. Mrs. Southeron is still upstairs."

"Oh good. Yes, thank you. That's all," he reclined again. No need to hitch himself up and be formal for Freddie, thank goodness.

Freddie came in a moment later, elegant in a wine-colored smoking jacket that complemented his fair face.

"Evening, Freddie," Reggie said indolently. "Help yourself to a glass of port. Filthy evening, isn't it? Still, fire's good. Sit down."

Freddie did as he was bidden, and with a glass in his hand, settled in the chair opposite. He sipped slowly, and rolled it round his mouth.

"Miserable business about poor Helena Doran, isn't it?" he said, looking across.

Reggie was annoyed. He did not want to discuss it.

"Miserable," he agreed succinctly. "Still, all over now."

"Oh, hardly," Freddie demurred with a smile.

"She's dead," Reggie slid even deeper into the chair. "Can't be more finished than that."

"It's the end of Helena, poor girl," Freddie agreed. He held up his glass to look at the rich color against the light. "But only the beginning of a lot of other things."

"Such as what?"

"Well, how did she die, for one thing?" Freddie's clear blue eyes fixed on Reggie. "And who killed her? The police are going to want to know that, you know."

"She might have died quite naturally." Reggie found the subject most disagreeable. He wished Freddie would leave it alone. "Anyway, not our business."

"Police all over the place will be our business," Freddie was still looking at him, smiling faintly. Charming fellow, Freddie, but less sensitivity than Reggie would have ex-

177

pected. Rotten subject to bring up in a fellow's house over a good port.

"Not mine," Reggie stretched his legs out. Fire really was excellent, warmed him right through.

"Oh, they'll be onto all of us, asking questions again. Bound to."

"Don't know anything. Can't help. Not a clue who her lover was. Not interested in that kind of thing. Women's business, gossip. Ask the women, if he's any good at his job."

"Pitt?"

"If that's his name."

"No doubt he will. But he'll ask us too," Freddie also sank a little into the deep leather.

"Nothing to tell him," Reggie finished the last of his port and poured some more. The room seemed to glow warmer and redder. "Nothing at all."

There was a moment's silence.

"Suppose it wasn't you?" Freddie said suddenly.

"Me?" Reggie had dismissed the matter and was drifting pleasantly into other things, pretty women, Jemima to be precise. Charming creature, so feminine. "What are you talking about?"

"Helena's lover, of course," Freddie was still faintly smiling. "Wasn't you, was it, old boy?"

"Good God!" Reggie jerked up a full six inches in the chair. "Of course it wasn't!"

"Just thought it might be. You do have rather a taste for that sort of thing, after all."

"Taste for it! What in hell do you mean?" Reggie was offended. It was an ill-bred thing to remark.

"Taste for young women," Freddie did not appear in the least abashed. "Mary Ann, and Dolly, and who knows who else?"

"Mary Ann is a parlormaid!" Reggie said indignantly. "Everyone has a fancy for parlormaids now and then, if they're honest. And Dolly was a long time ago. I prefer not to discuss that. I thought I told you as much."

"Oh, I'm sure you do," Freddie agreed. "Especially now."

"What do you mean, especially now?" Reggie did not care for the turn the conversation was taking. "Why now?"

178

"Well, apparently Helena was pregnant too," Freddie was still looking directly at him, and still smiling. "And then there are the babies in the gardens. If they knew about Mary Ann, and about poor Dolly, they might leap to the very nasty conclusion that they were all connected; don't you think?"

Suddenly the heat of the fire scorched Reggie's legs, and left the inside of him bitterly cold. The thought was appalling, terrifying! His mouth was dry. He stared at Freddie, trying to pretend he did not understand, pretend to himself.

"You do," Freddie's smile was fixed on his face, it seemed to hang in the air in front of Reggie, as if there were nothing else in the room. "You see what I mean?" Freddie pressed the point.

"Yes," Reggie heard his own voice far away. He cleared his throat, and his voice returned louder than he intended. "But they won't, I mean there's no reason why they should hear about any of that. You're the only other person who knows about it, about Dolly, I mean."

"Quite," Freddie reached for the port and poured himself more, still meeting Reggie's eyes over the top. "So it all rather depends on me; doesn't it?"

"Well, for God's sake, you won't say anything! Will you!"

"Oh no," Freddie sipped his port gently. "No, I shouldn't think so, for a moment." He sipped again. "As long as I remember what I've said, and don't contradict myself."

"You won't!"

"Hope not. But rather important, you know. Could do with a small reminder."

"What—what do you mean, Freddie?"

"Reminder," Freddie said easily, "something to keep my memory on the job, something that was always there, something big enough to be important."

Reggie stared at him in cold fascination. The glimmering of understanding was coming into his mind, and it was ugly.

"What did you have in mind, Freddie?" he asked slowly. He would like to have hit him, kicked him, sitting so smugly there in front of the fire. But he knew he could not afford to. The police were too busy, too watchful of anything different just now. The time would come, of course, after all this business was finished, and life went back to the way it had been

179

before: then he would be able to sort Freddie out. The fellow was a bounder.

But in the meantime—

"What do you want, Freddie?" he asked again.

Freddie was still smiling. What a charming fellow he used to think he was! That smile was so frank, so quick to grace his features.

"Got this rotten bill outstanding at my tailor's," Freddie seemed quite unabashed. "Been there rather a long time. Give me a hand with it, old boy. As a favor. Feel that if I actually owned my clothes, instead of that damned stitchin' fellow, I'd be enormously grateful."

"You damn better be!"

"Will, I assure you. Think of you every time I dress."

"How much?"

"Oh, hundred pounds should about do it."

"A hundred pounds!" Reggie was shattered. He did not spend that much on clothes in a year, and he would not have allowed Adelina half of it. Damn it all, he paid maids only twenty pounds a year. "How in God's name did you permit yourself—?"

"Like to dress well, you know." Freddie stood up. He was tall, slim, elegant: indeed he did dress well, far better than Reggie; then of course he had the figure for it, but even so! "Thanks, old boy," he said cheerfully. "Shan't forget it."

"By God, you'd better not!" Reggie could feel anger and panic rising in him. If Freddie did forget, or went back on his word—

"Don't worry," Freddie said easily. "Got an excellent memory, when I choose. Doctor, you know. Doctors never repeat what their patients tell them in confidence. Police can't make them. Perfectly safe." He moved to the door gracefully. "I'll take the hundred now. Tailor chap a bit impatient, you know. Won't take any more orders till I cough up. Miserly wretch."

"Haven't got it now," Reggie replied stiffly. "I'll send the footman round to the bank in the morning. Give it to you by tomorrow."

"Yes, don't forget, Reggie. Good memory could be vital; I'm sure you understand."

Reggie understood perfectly. He would have a footman at

180

the bank door the moment it opened. Damn Freddie. And the worst of it was he would have to go on being civil to the cad; there was no way out of it. If he cut him people would notice, and he must at any cost keep Freddie's good will, at least until the police gave up and left the square.

He sat down again after Freddie had gone. He was glad Adelina had not come back into the room. He wished to be alone. He had had a very considerable shock, and the more he thought about it, the nastier it became. Who would have credited that Freddie could behave in such a way? If a chap was a bit short of ready money, anyone could understand that. But to resort to—well—it amounted to blackmail.

Of course it would all blow over when the police either found out who the wretched girl was, which was unlikely, or gave up, which on the face of it was probably what would happen. Then another very unpleasant thought came to him. What did the police do if they could not solve a case? Did they give up? Or did they put it aside, but always keep it at the back of their minds: someone detailed to keep an ear to it? The possibility was frightening! What if they never gave up, if they kept at it, like an open wound, probing it every time it threatened to close over? That could be very nasty, a permanently ugly rumor never either exposed and lived down, nor yet laid to rest as false.

Good God! What could he do about Freddie then? The man, if he were cad enough, could keep coming back over and over again! A hundred pounds here, a social favor there, or a spot of financial advice under the counter, a gift of this or that— God in heaven, it could be never ending! It was monstrous!

The best thing for Reggie would be if this damned Pitt fellow found out who it was and cleared up the whole wretched business. Then Freddie could say what he liked. It would certainly damage Reggie's reputation for a while, and Adelina would be pretty upset. But then their relationship was not so very close anyway: not a lot to lose, compared with permanent leeching by Freddie! And the very fact that as a doctor and a friend he had broken such a confidence would do Freddie himself a damn sight more damage. Who would trust the fellow after that? No, to tell the police, under pressure, was one thing, there could be a good excuse for that: but to spread it around, merely as gossip, that was unpardonable, and Freddie would be sure to know that.

No, quite definitely, if Pitt found out who it was, Reggie would be safe. He settled down deeper into the chair and stretched his legs out again. This really was an excellent fire. He rang for the footman, gave him instructions about the bank, and ordered more port. He would not have thought the two of them could have got through a whole bottle, but there it was, empty; so they must have. Still, a wretched experience like this called for a little fortification. Natural enough.

Thing was, must see what he could do to help this police fellow to get the matter solved, so everyone knew who was to blame, and thus who was not: and the police took themselves off back to the usual sort of crimes they were really employed to deal with.

He fell asleep, still wondering what he could do to help Pitt.

He woke late the following morning, as was his habit, rose, was dressed by his valet, and took a good breakfast of porridge, bacon, eggs, deviled kidneys, sausage, mushrooms, then several slices of toast, butter, and preserves, then of course a fresh pot of tea. He should have felt a great deal better after it: but he did not. In the gray, pedestrian light of morning, the more he thought about the likelihood of the police discovering the girl to blame, the less likely he considered it to be that they would meet with any success. The fellow Pitt was probably bright enough, he was certainly inquisitive; but where could he find proof? After all, it was all months ago now, even years! Could have been anybody! Some wretched girl even from the neighboring blocks! Did not have to be Callander Square at all! Now had the fools thought of that?

"Don't be an ass! Calm yourself, Reggie. Of course they have. That is probably what they spent their time doing, when they were not here. And they were here quite a small part of the time, considering they quite probably worked from breakfast till dinner, five or six days a week. Yes, of course, they will have asked all over the place." He began to feel better again, and spent a pleasant enough morning going into the city, wandered round the merchant bank of which he was a director, had a long luncheon at his club, and was home again by half past four when it became dark and began to drizzle. The gas lamps in the square were partly obscured by drifting mist and the trees rattled in the rising wind. A filthy night. Glad to have a good fire and a good table to go to.

He greeted the children civilly enough, and of course Adelina, and was relaxing after dinner when there was a knock on the door.

"Come in," he said with some surprise.

Chastity came in, looking very prim and clean.

"What is it, child?" he was a little annoyed. He did not wish to talk.

"Uncle Reggie, Miss Waggoner says I must ask you if I wish to learn mathematics. Please, may I?"

"No. Whatever would you require mathematics for?"

"I would like to learn for the sake of learning," she replied sedately. "You have said to me that it is good to do so."

"They would be of no use to you," he said decisively.

"Neither is painting, but you say I should learn it."

"Painting is an art, that is quite different. Women should become proficient in some art or other: give them something to do when they grow up. Otherwise how will you employ your time?" That was faultless logic. She would have no answer for that. He faced her with satisfaction.

"I shall marry a policeman," she said immediately. "And I shall be poor, so I shall have to keep my own house. It might be very useful to be able to do mathematics. I could deduce things."

"Don't be ridiculous!" he snapped. Really, the child was becoming impossible. "Why ever should you marry a policeman?"

"Because I like them. I like Mr. Pitt. I should like to marry him, only he is already married. He was here again today. He was talking to Mary Ann. I don't think he'll ever find out who killed those babies, you know. He says so himself. It will just remain a mystery for ever and ever and ever. We shall all wonder who it was, and we shall think dreadful things about each other, and no one will ever know. When I grow

183

to be very old, about fifty, I shall tell my grandchildren about it, and I shall say the square is haunted by crying babies who were murdered in olden times; that's now; but it will be olden times by then, and nobody ever knew who did it. And we shall play games as to whom it might have been, and—"

"Stop it!" Reggie said furiously. He could not remember when he had last lost his temper, but this was monstrous. The child was talking nonsense, absurd, ridiculous, and frightening nonsense. She was raising visions of a never-ending bondage, a bloodsucking till he was empty, a fear to stalk him the rest of his life! "Stop it!" he shouted. "That's not true! They'll find out who it was. The police are very clever. They are bound to discover, and probably quite soon." He could still feel his heart bumping, but it was not quite so uncontrolled now.

Chastity looked at him in surprise, but without losing her beastly composure.

"Do you think so, Uncle Reggie? I don't. I think it will be a terrible mystery for ever and ever, and everyone will go around whispering about it. Can I learn mathematics, please?"

"No!"

"But I want to."

"Well, you can't!"

"Why not?" she asked reasonably.

"Because I say so. Now go up to bed. It must be your bedtime."

"It isn't, not for another hour yet."

"Do as you are told, child. Go to bed." He knew he was being completely arbitrary, but then one was not required to explain to children, or even to have an explanation. One could do as one pleased. It was good for children to learn to obey.

Chastity retired as she was told, but there was a look of disappointment in her eyes that was distinctly touched with contempt. The impertinence of it stung him.

He sat staring at the opposite chair, his thoughts going round with gathering momentum, and increasing unpleasantness. What if Chastity were right, and they never did find out who it was? They would go on talking about it—after all,

184

why should they ever stop? Gossip was the lifeblood of women's social round. What was not real or known must be invented! It was appalling, but it was true. Of course other subjects would arise, other scandals, no doubt; but at the slightest reawakening of any suspicions, this one with all its obscene speculation would be resurrected.

And Freddie, Freddie would know that, and thrive on it. Great God, he could be paying him for the rest of his life, being sucked of substance, by a bloody leech—a vampire! This was terrible!

He found himself standing up, without having been aware of rising. He must do something, that was beyond question. But what? His brain was like a cheese, no sense in it. He could not do it alone, that much was sure. He had no ideas. Who could help? Must not let Adelina know, she would blurt it out all over the place. Anyway, she was one of the ones he must keep it from. She would not understand about Mary Ann, still less about Dolly. She would make life intolerable for him. And he valued the comfort, above all else the ease and graciousness of his home. No ugliness or need for the labor of the outside world intruded into it, and he intended to keep it that way, at all costs. And of course for purely practical purposes, he must protect his position at the bank, it was a very lucrative and pleasant situation. He had influence.

But none of that was any use now, and he could see it slipping away from him, and leaving him naked to the chill of life's harsh realities—no succulent foods, no great fires, deep chairs, summer afternoons with strawberries, servants for everything, parties whenever he wished; naked, like a great white animal without its fur or its shell, ready to be shriveled by the first winter blast.

He must get help. Who was the most practical person he knew, the most intelligent? The answer was quick to come to mind, without question, Garson Campbell.

And there was no time to be lost. Anyway, he could not possibly rest until he had done something about it, his mind was in turmoil. He rang for the footman to bring his coat. It was an abysmal night, and he loathed getting wet, but the

185

discomfort inside him was infinitely worse, and growing more acute with each new thought that came to his mind.

He found Campbell in and willing to see him, although in view of the urgency with which he announced himself, he would have been very surprised had he not.

"Well, Reggie, what's the panic?" Campbell said with a slightly caustic smile. "William seemed to think you were in something of a flap."

"My God, Campbell, I've discovered something appalling!" Reggie collapsed into one of the other chairs and gazed up at Campbell with thumping heart. "Simply frightful."

Campbell was unimpressed.

"Oh. I suppose you'll need a glass of port to help you recover." It was an observation, not a question.

Reggie sat up in the seat.

"I'm not joking, Campbell, this is damned serious!"

Campbell swiveled round at the sideboard to face him, perhaps struck by the timbre of his voice.

Reggie could feel panic welling up inside him. What if Campbell would not help?

"I'm being blackmailed!" he blurted out. "For money! At least it's only money at the moment. God knows what it could grow into! Campbell, my whole life could be ruined! He could take everything, like a vampire at my throat, sucking out my life! It's obscene, it's frightful!"

At last Campbell was impressed, his face altered and a hardness, an attentiveness came into his eyes.

"Blackmailed?" he repeated, his hand still holding the port decanter, but absently, forgetting what it was.

"Yes!" Reggie's voice was climbing higher and higher. "A hundred pounds!"

Campbell had control of himself again. His mouth turned down at the corners.

"That's a lot of money."

"You're damned right it is. Campbell, what am I going to do? We've got to stop this sort of thing, before it takes hold."

Campbell's eyebrows rose slightly.

"Why 'we,' Reggie? I agree, blackmail is a nasty thing, but why should I involve myself?"

"Because it's Freddie, you fool!" Reggie lost his temper

186

again; he was badly frightened, their whole manner of life was threatened, and here was Campbell standing with port in his hand and a sneer on his face as if it were merely some minor inconvenience.

"Freddie?" There was steel in Campbell's voice, a quite different tone. His face had stiffened, even his body. "Freddie Bolsover?"

"Yes! Damned Freddie Bolsover. Came to my house as cool as you please, sat in my chair in the library and drank my port, and asked me for a hundred pounds to keep quiet about my fondness for the parlormaid!"

"And you paid him?" Campbell's eyebrows rose and his eyes were full of cynical disbelief, and something that looked like amusement. Although God knew what there was to be amused at!

"Of course I paid him!" Reggie spat out furiously. "What do you think the police would make of it if they knew I had a fondness for parlormaids, with those wretched bodies in the square? They might even think I had something to do with Helena Doran, and so help me God, I never touched the girl! Little harmless fun with a few maids, but never anything really wrong! But can't expect those bounders to know that! They're only working class themselves!"

Campbell looked at him down his long nose.

"Yes, you're in something of a spot, aren't you?" He finished pouring the port at last and handed Reggie one. "Although I shouldn't think anyone could connect you with Helena," he hesitated, "could they?"

"No!"

"Then I don't know why you're so excited. What can Freddie say? That he thinks you had a bit of a toss with your parlormaid? That's hardly damning. And how in hell would he know, anyway? Does he listen to kitchen gossip? You were a fool to pay."

Reggie squirmed in his chair. It was Dolly and her death after the wretched abortion that he was frightened of—Mary Ann was neither here nor there, as Campbell had said. He looked at Campbell now, standing in the middle of the room, broad-shouldered, solid-bellied, a slight sneer on his face. He was clever, Reggie knew that, he had always known it; it

187

was one of those obvious things, inescapable. But dare he trust him? He had to have help from someone. Freddie had to be stopped, otherwise he would rob him of everything that made life of value! Feed off him, like some disgusting animal, take all his comfort, and he could end up a frightened wreck drinking soda water and eating bread and mincemeat. He would sooner be dead!

He did not know how to begin.

Campbell was waiting, staring at him, his eyes still smiling.

"It's rather more than that," Reggie began. "They might think—"

Campbell's mouth twisted at the corners.

"—I mean," Reggie tried again, "other maids, they might—"Damn the man. Why would he not understand?

"—they might think you had something to do with Dolly's death?" Campbell finished for him.

Reggie felt the ice run through him as if his valet had accidentally run him a cold bath.

Campbell was looking at him with a cynical amusement.

"Yes, that could be embarrassing," he said thoughtfully. "Freddie was the doctor called in, wasn't he? Yes, he could probably tell the police precisely what happened. And I suppose he might well feel excused of his usual obligations of silence," he coughed, "under the circumstances. Perhaps you were right to pay, after all."

"God damn it!" Reggie heaved himself out of the chair onto his feet till he stood facing Campbell. "That's no help! What am I going to do?"

Campbell stuck out his lower lip.

"Keep control of yourself, for a start. I agree entirely, old boy. It's bad: very bad. No idea Freddie had it in him."

"He's a complete outsider," Reggie said bitterly. "A bounder."

"Doubtless, but that only means he's the nerve and the wit to do what many others would, if they dared, and had thought of it. Don't be such a hypocrite, Reggie. This is hardly the time to become self-righteous; apart from being a trifle ridiculous, it's of no use."

"Use?" Reggie was flabbergasted. Freddie was a total cad,

188

and here was Campbell talking about it as if it were an everyday occurrence: a problem of logistics rather than an outrage.

"Yes, of course 'use,'" Campbell said a little tartly. "You do want to prevent it continuing indefinitely, I take it? I thought that was why you came?"

"Yes, of course it is! But aren't you shocked? I mean— Freddie!"

"It's years since I've been shocked," Campbell answered, holding his port glass up to the light and examining the color. "I am occasionally surprised; usually pleasantly, when I have expected the worst and it has not happened, when my luck has held longer than I thought likely. But most people who are honest are only so through lack of courage, or lack of imagination. Man is basically a selfish animal. Watch children some time, and you'll see it very quickly. We're all much the same, one hand out to grab what we can, and one eye over our shoulders to see who's looking, and make sure we don't have to pay for it. Freddie's just rather better at it than I gave him credit for."

"Never mind the philosophy, what in hell are we going to do about it?" Reggie demanded. "We can't let him go on!"

"There'll be nothing to go on to," Campbell pointed out. "When the police either find out who is responsible, which I admit is unlikely, or give up, which I dare say they will, in another few weeks, that will be the end of it. After all, they can't waste time indefinitely on some servant girl's mistakes. It's not as if anyone cared or as if discovering anything would make a ha'porth of difference to its happening over and over again into an infinite future precisely the same. Just keep your head. I'll have a word with Freddie, warn him of the several nasty things that could happen to his practice, if he makes a habit of this."

For the first time Reggie felt a spark of hope: sane, rational hope. If Campbell spoke to Freddie, he might realize he could not go on demanding money, that he would make his own position impossible. He would never be frightened of Reggie, but he might well take Campbell more seriously.

"Thank you," he said sincerely. "That will do it; make all

189

the difference. He'll see it will only work once. Yes, excellent. Thank you again."

Campbell pulled a face of incredulousness mixed with amusement, but he said nothing. Reggie left with a firmness to his step. He could see light ahead, comfort again.

Of course General Balantyne also heard about the appalling discovery in the empty garden, and he was deeply shocked by it. He had not known Helena well, but she had been a lovely creature, full of life, gentle, a woman with all her promise ahead of her. To find her in such—the thought of it was too dreadful to frame. Someone had abused and violated her, and even presumably killed her. No one knew a great deal yet, and the police had not so far called. It was to be supposed they would come today.

Meanwhile he would work on his papers. Miss Ellison, although he thought of her as Charlotte now, had done all that she could for the time being, and in truth, he missed her. The library seemed empty without her presence and he found it harder to resume his concentration, as if he were awaiting something.

He had still not settled his mind to work when the police came. It was the same fellow, Pitt. He received him in the library.

"Good morning, Inspector." There was no need to ask what he was here for.

"Good morning, sir." Pitt came in gravely.

"I'm afraid I cannot tell you anything of value," Balantyne said straight away. "I did not know Miss Doran other than to see her occasionally when she visited my wife and daughter. I imagine you will wish to see them. I would appreciate it if you could keep the most distressing facts to yourself. My daughter is about to be married, day after tomorrow, to be precise. Don't want to spoil the—" he stopped; it sounded callous, offensively trite, when another girl was lying alone, a few rag-covered bones in some police mortuary, obscenely eaten by small animals and maggots! It made him faintly sick.

Pitt seemed to read Balantyne's confused thoughts and feelings in his face.

"Of course," he said, without sympathy in his voice; or so it seemed to Balantyne. And why should he have sympathy? Christina was alive and well, on her way to marriage, a life of security and comfort, of social privilege. And if he were honest, she might well feel shock, disgust at Helena's death, and the manner of it, but he would be surprised if she thought of it long, and more so if she wept any tears of pity.

"I'm interested in Helena's life," Pitt continued. "The cause of her death lies in that, not what happened to her body afterward. She was with child, did you know?"

Balantyne felt an added twist of hurt for the double loss.

"Yes, I heard. Unfortunately little remains unpassed from door to door in a square like this."

"Do you know who her lover was?" Pitt asked baldly.

Balantyne was repelled, he winced at the vulgarity of the question. Helena had been a woman of quality, a—he caught Pitt's eyes and realized he was trying to cling to a dream of unreality that was no longer viable. But to think so—of a woman! Damn Pitt for his squalid truths.

"Do you?" Pitt repeated, although it was an unnecessary question. Balantyne's sensitive revulsion had already answered it for him.

"No, of course I don't!" Balantyne turned away.

"It is natural that you should be distressed," Pitt said softly. "You had a high regard for her?"

Balantyne was not sure how to answer, he hesitated awkwardly. He had always found her fair beauty especially clean and gentle; perhaps he had idealized it a little.

Pitt was speaking again at his shoulder.

"I believe she had a considerable admiration for you also."

Balantyne jerked upward with surprise.

Pitt smiled very slightly.

"Women confide in each other, you know. And I have been asking questions about women in this square for quite a long time now."

"Oh," Balantyne looked away again.

"How well did you know her, General Balantyne?" Pitt's voice was quiet, but it put a sudden new and dreadful thought into Balantyne's head. He swung round, feeling the blood hot in his face. He stared at Pitt, trying to see if the suspicion

191

was in his eyes. He found only intelligent interest, waiting, probing.

"Not very," he said clumsily. "I told you—I—I knew her socially, as a neighbor. Not more than that."

Pitt said nothing.

"Not more than that," Balantyne repeated. He started to say something else, to clarify it, so that Pitt would understand, then faltered and fell silent.

"I see." Pitt meant no more than that he had heard him. He asked a few more questions, then sought permission to speak to the women.

He left, and Balantyne stood in the room feeling foolish and considerably shaken. Three, even two months ago, he had been unthinkingly sure of so many things that now lay in ugly and unfamiliar shreds around him. So much of it had to do with women. All the certainties that had provided so much of the security of his life, not materially, but emotionally, lay in his beliefs about women. Now Christina had become involved with that fearful footman, and was going to marry Alan Ross. Thank God that at least had come to a tolerable conclusion. Although Augusta's part in it was something he had not yet come to terms with. Euphemia Carlton was bearing another man's child, which he felt was inexplicable. She had inexcusably betrayed a good man, who loved her. And now poor Helena Doran had been beguiled and used, and murdered. Or had she? Perhaps they would never know the truth of that. The thought of all of it hurt him.

But in some ways the most disturbing of all, the thing in himself he least wished to look at was the warmth with which he regarded Charlotte Ellison, the pleasure he felt in her company, the acuteness with which he could recall to his mind's eye the exact curve of her throat, the rich color of her hair, the way she looked at him, and how deeply she felt all that she did and said, whether it were better said, or not.

It was ridiculous. He did not get disturbed, feel hope or embarrassment, least of all loneliness over a young woman: one who regarded him as nothing more than an employer! Or perhaps a little more? He believed she might have some respect for him, dare he imagine affection? No, of course not. Dismiss the thought. He was making an idiot of himself.

He picked up some paper and began furiously to read, although it was fully five minutes before the words began to create pictures for him, and take on a life separate from the tumult in his mind.

Even at dinner time the conversation passed him by. He would pay for the wedding, naturally, but he left all the arrangements, both social and practical, to Augusta. He would do as he was directed and be as charming as was required of him, but the preparations were out of his grasp.

He did not even really hear the rather unpleasant exchange between Christina and Brandy about the governess next door. As much of it as penetrated his mind seemed to consist of Christina's disparaging her in some way and Brandy's defending her with a vigor that would have drawn a request for explanation from him at any other time. It did trouble the back of his consciousness that perhaps Brandy was developing what seemed to be a family taste for affairs with servants. Of course for a man it was quite different, but it would show considerably more sense if he were to indulge himself a little less close to home.

After dinner he sent for Brandy to see him in the library. The butler brought the port and retired, closing the door behind him.

"Port?" Balantyne offered.

"No, thank you, bit heavy," Brandy shook his head.

"I understand your inclinations," Balantyne began. "Natural enough—"

"Just don't like port a lot," Brandy said easily.

"Not about the port!" Was he deliberately being obtuse? "About Miss whatever-her-name-is, the governess next door. Charming little thing—"

"She's not a 'little thing'!" Brandy said with a sudden flare of anger. "She's a woman, just like Christina, or your Miss Ellison, or anyone else!"

"Hardly like Christina," Balantyne said coldly.

"No, you're right," Brandy snapped. "She doesn't sleep with the footmen!"

Balantyne raised his hand to strike him, outrage knotting his body. Then he saw Brandy's calm face, set hard, unmoving. He let his hand fall. There was truth in the jibe, and he

193

did not wish to quarrel with his son. They were utterly different, and yet he liked Brandy deeply.

"That was unnecessarily unkind," he let his voice drop. "I dare say you have lain where you should not, at some time or other."

To his surprise Brandy blushed deeply.

"I apologize, sir," he said quietly. "It was a filthy thing to say. It's just that I have a high regard for Jemima; not of the sort you supposed. As I suspect you have for Miss Ellison. And I would not insult either of them by making an advance of that nature." He smiled a little bleakly. "I daresay one would get a thick ear if one tried. I certainly feel Miss Ellison capable of it!"

Balantyne grudged it, desperately embarrassed by Brandy's perception. His inside was in turmoil, but he forced a smile in return.

"I dare say," he agreed thickly. "Perhaps we had better discuss something else."

They were not long launched on something less fraught with pitfalls when the footman announced Sir Robert Carlton, and Brandy, with unusual tact, excused himself.

Carlton also declined port, and stood a little awkwardly in the center of the floor. His face showed the fine lines of emotional strain.

"Dreadful thing about the poor Doran child," he said jerkily."Poor creature, poor woman. An appalling thought that she was there all the time, and we had no idea; went about our business."

Balantyne had not thought of it in precisely that light before, and it revolted him: their obliviousness, the immediacy of life and death. They had passed so close to and so unheeding of another creature's extremity. Dear God, did they regularly pass each other like that? Instinctively he met Carlton's eyes. There was something entirely new in them and he could not yet understand what it was.

"About Euphemia—" Carlton said hesitantly.

Balantyne tried to show in his face some of the gentleness he wanted to feel, did feel. He said nothing, thinking it better merely to wait.

"I—" Carlton was stumbling for words. "I didn't understand. I must have seemed—very cold—to her. She wanted a child. I—I didn't know that. I wish—I wish she could have felt she could tell me so. It must have been my fault that she couldn't. I was too—I put her on a pedestal—I didn't realize what a—comfortless thing respect is. She wanted a child— that's all."

"I see." Balantyne did not see at all, but he felt Carlton's need, his groping toward belief that it was understandable, and that he himself understood. "Yes, I see," he repeated.

"I find it," Carlton swallowed. "I find it hard to come to terms with, but in time I shall. I shall consider the child to be mine. Balantyne—you will?" His skin colored deeply. He could not put it into words.

"Of course," Balantyne said immediately. "To do anything else would be monstrous, and quite wrong!"

"Thank you," Carlton's hand was clenched by his side and there was a nervous flick in his temple. "I—I love her very much, you know."

"She's a very fine woman," Balantyne said generously, and he meant it. "And she will love you the more for your understanding."

Carlton looked up quickly.

"Do you think so?" There was a stab of hope in his voice that was painful to hear.

"I'm sure," Balantyne said firmly. "Now are you sure you won't have some port? Very good, you know. Reggie South- eron recommended it, and he may know damn all else, but he does know his palate."

Carlton took a deep breath and let it out slowly.

"Thank you, perhaps I will."

NINE

Reggie Southernon was not visited by Pitt until late the following afternoon. He was just settling into his deep chair to thaw out from the unpleasantness of travel, the hard springs, the drafts, the rain down the neck, when Pitt was announced. He seriously gave thought to the possibility of refusing to see him; but perhaps it would be unwise. It might make him dig the harder into matters preferably left alone: and of course not to see him would be to lose an opportunity to put his own case, defend himself before he was attacked. Damn Freddie Bolsover!

"Send him in," he said a little irritably. "And you'd better put away the good sherry and bring some of that other stuff." Silly to insult him by not offering him any at all, but no need to waste the good.

Pitt came in, untidy as usual, his coat flapping, wet across the shoulders; his face was genial, good-tempered, but his eyes were sharper than Reggie had noticed before.

"Good evening, sir," he said easily. Odd that such a fellow should have so fine a voice, such diction. Ideas above himself, shouldn't wonder; aping his betters.

"Evening," Reggie replied. "I suppose you've come about Helena Doran, poor creature? Can't tell you anything; don't know."

"No, of course not," Pitt agreed civilly. "I'm sure if you had known anything, you would have told us long before we came and sought you out. Still," he smiled suddenly with what would, at another time, have been charm—had he been a social equal, of course! "Still, you might be able to fill in a few blanks."

"Sherry?" Reggie offered, holding up the decanter.

"No, thank you," Pitt declined with a small wave of his hand.

Reggie poured himself some in considerable annoyance. He had got in this wretched kitchen stuff, and now the damned fellow did not want it. He was obliged to stand here like a fool and drink it himself.

"I've told you," he said petulantly. "I don't know anything about Helena Doran."

"Not about her death, perhaps; but you must know something about her life," Pitt said easily. "Maybe more than you realize. I would like your opinions. You're a man of the world, you must have to make judgments about people, as a banker."

Reggie should not have been surprised. Of course the fellow would have found out what he did. It was true, he was a pretty good judge, in the general way of things. Made a mistake about Freddie, though!

"Tell you anything I can, naturally," he mellowed a bit. "Shocking thing; very young, you know."

"And pretty, they say." Pitt raised his eyebrows questioningly.

"Very, in a pale sort of way. A bit fair for my taste, a bit fragile looking, but very nice for those who like that type. Prefer something a bit more robust, myself." Must not let it even cross his mind that Reggie would be the one. Good idea to clear that up right at the outset.

"Not fond of blondes myself," Pitt agreed. "Not the very fair ones. Always look a little cold to me."

Maybe the fellow was not so bad; human, anyway.

"Quite," Reggie agreed. "Nice girl, always civil and conducted herself well, far as I know. Pity. Great pity."

Pitt's bright eyes were still on him.

"Who did admire her, do you know? There must have been some who did."

"Oh, of course," Reggie agreed. Good opportunity, this. "Alan Ross was very much in love with her, at the time. But I suppose you knew that?"

"Alan Ross?"

"Yes. Fellow who just married Christina Balantyne, this morning, in fact."

198

"Oh yes, of course; yes, I had heard he was fond of Helena Doran."

"Damn sight more than fond of her; crazy about her. Terribly upset when she ran off—or I suppose I should say, was murdered." He looked up at Pitt. "I suppose she was murdered?"

"Oh, yes. I'm afraid there is no doubt."

"How can you tell? Thought the body was—well—"

"So it was. But a few rags of the clothes left, and of course the bones. The flesh was eaten away, but the bones were all there. The neck was broken. Must have been very powerful hands to do it so neatly."

Reggie flinched in disgust.

"Yes, nasty, isn't it?" Pitt agreed, although Reggie detected a tone in his voice he could not entirely place. Peculiar fellow. Still, no doubt he served his purpose; and with care, he could serve Reggie's as well.

"Very cut up, he was," Reggie went on. "Quite unhinged the poor chap for a while. Not that I want to suggest—of course—!"

"But it's a possibility," Pitt finished for him.

Reggie assumed an air of reluctance. "Have to admit it," he said slowly.

"Did he ever say anything to you about another man, a lover?"

Reggie screwed up his face in an effort to bring something to mind.

"Can't recall. But my dear fellow, you can't expect me to repeat some casual word, even if I could remember it, that might hang a chap!" he protested.

"Won't hang anybody on a few words," Pitt said softly, smiling again. "And you have a moral duty, after all."

"Oh, quite," Reggie agreed. This was turning out very well: unfortunate about Alan Ross, but then he might very well have killed Helena in a fit of jealousy. It was the most likely explanation, after all!

Pitt was waiting.

"Well—" Reggie hesitated, not through reluctance, but because he had not yet thought of anything suitable to say. "Can't bring back words, of course," he lifted his voice a little

199

at the end, as if to question whether Pitt really wished him to continue; then he hurried on, in case Pitt, by chance, should take it into his mind to stop him. "Just the general meaning. He was very much in love with her. We all thought they would marry, quite soon, in fact. Of course the rest of us had no idea there was another lover. I suppose Ross found out. No idea how. Never said anything to us; but then he wouldn't, would he? Make rather a fool of him, what? Woman you loved taking some other fellow into her bed."

"Yes," Pitt agreed solemnly. "Very painful. A man might react on the spur of the moment."

"Quite," Reggie said quickly. "Quite."

"Then," Pitt said after a moment's thought, "on the other hand, it could have been the lover."

"Lover?" Reggie was taken aback. "Why, for heaven's sake? Would think he had everything his way, what?" He tried to smile, but felt it a bit stiff on his face. "No reason to hurt her, far as I can see."

"She was with child," Pitt reminded him. "The lover's child."

"So?" A dark thought had come into Reggie's mind, a beginning of a very unpleasant fear.

"Would have married her, if he were free to, don't you suppose?" Pitt was staring at him, bright eyes wide.

Reggie's mind whirled. This was stupid. He had never touched the girl. No need whatsoever to be nervous. But there was always Freddie and his damned tongue. If the police ever got to know that Reggie played around a little, they might not understand the difference!

"Perhaps he wasn't suitable, as a husband, I mean," he faced Pitt squarely. "Might have been a tradesman, or something. Couldn't marry a tradesman, could she?" No time to be worrying about Pitt's sensibilities now. Fellow would have to understand there were social distinctions. Must know that anyway; bound to.

But instead of taking offense Pitt merely considered the matter thoughtfully.

"Did she have a liking for tradesmen, then?" he inquired.

"Good God!" Reggie scrambled wildly—what to say? If he said yes, others would give him the lie. Pitt was bound to speak to everyone in the square. Helena had never looked at a tradesman in her life! She was a little over-refined, if anything. Only man, apart from Ross, that Reggie had ever seen her show any admiration for was old Balantyne next door. Liked his bit of pomp and military glamour, no doubt.

"No," he said as calmly as he could, "no, not at all." Yes, that was the answer. "In fact never saw her show any interest in anyone that I can recall," he weighed his words carefully, "except old Balantyne next door. Fine-looking chap, the general. Natural a young girl should be impressed." Let him take it from there. No need to point out that the general was married. Pitt himslef had made the observation about not being free, safe to leave him to infer the rest.

"I see." Pitt looked down at his feet, then up again, quizzically. "No admiration for you, sir?"

"Me?" Reggie looked shocked. "Good gracious, no. Merchant banker, you know. Not nearly as exciting as the army. No glamour in it, what?" He forced a rather sickly smile. "Nothing to appeal to a romantic young girl."

"You think Balantyne might have been the unknown lover?"

"Oh, now I didn't say that!"

"Of course not; you wouldn't: loyalty and so forth," Pitt shook his head. "Very admirable."

Why was the damn fellow smiling inside himself?

"And I take it she was not a type of beauty that especially appealed to you."

"What?"

"I mean you would not have been jealous, or anything of that nature."

"God, no! I mean, pardon; certainly not. Too pale, too bloodless-looking for me. Prefer something a little—I'm a married—" No, that sounded too pompous. He let it die.

"Uncommonly handsome parlormaid you have," Pitt said conversationally. "Couldn't help noticing. Best-looking girl I've seen for a long time."

Reggie felt his face color. Damn the fellow's impertinence. Wasn't driving at something, was he? He looked at the man closely, but there seemed to be nothing beyond innocent appreciation in his eyes.

"Yes," he agreed after a moment. "Pick them for their appearance, you know. Whole point of a parlormaid."

"Is it?" Pitt affected interest. "Somebody else said you had a good eye for a parlormaid."

Reggie froze. Surely Freddie could not have—? He avoided Pitt's eye.

"Freddie Bolsover, was it?"

"Dr. Bolsover?" Pitt seemed not to understand what he meant.

"Yes. Was it Dr. Bolsover who made the remark about me—and—er, parlormaids?" Reggie cleared his throat. "You don't want to take too much notice of anything he says, you know. Young. Got rather an unreliable sense of humor."

Pitt frowned.

"Don't think I quite understand you, sir."

"Makes odd jokes," Reggie explained. "Says things he thinks are funny, doesn't realize people who don't know him could take them seriously."

"What sort of thing? I mean, what would he really mean, and what would be just a joke?"

"Oh," Reggie thought rapidly, mustn't panic. Keep cool. "Anything medical, of course, perfectly serious. But might make a joke about me and parlormaids, just for an example."

"You mean he might say perhaps you had an affair with a parlormaid, or something like that?" Pitt inquired.

Reggie could feel the blood burn in his face, and he turned away.

"That sort of thing," he tried to sound casual, and nearly choked.

"Sure you won't have a sherry? Think I'll have another." He suited the action to the word.

"Dangerous sense of humor," Pitt remarked. "No, thank you," he glanced at the sherry. "I would talk to him about that, if I were you. Could be embarrassing for you, just at the moment."

"Oh, I will," Reggie said immediately. "Yes, must do that. Good advice."

"Surprised you haven't done it already," Pitt went on. "You haven't, I suppose."

"What?" Reggie nearly dropped the decanter.

"Haven't spoken to him already?" Pitt raised his eyebrows.

"Did—did he say I had?" Reggie realized as soon as he had said it that it was a stupid question. "I mean—er—"

"Have you?"

"Well—" What in hell should he say? Damn the man, what did he know? If only Reggie could ascertain how much he already knew, then he could tailor his replies! This fishing round in the darkness was frightful.

Pitt pulled a small face—extraordinary face the fellow had—and looked at his fingernails.

"Normal enough, a bit of admiration for a good-looking maid," Pitt went on thoughtfully. "Lot of men do it. Nothing to remark on. Just could be made to look a bit unfortunate right now." He looked up, his brilliant, penetrating gaze fixed on Reggie. "Hasn't been bothering you—Dr. Bolsover—has he?"

Reggie stared. His brain seemed to melt and freeze again. What should he say? Could he trust Freddie? This was an opportunity to get rid of all of it! Or was it? Just a moment! What if Pitt went to Freddie and charged him? Then Freddie would tell them all about Dolly, and that was quite different! Or did they already know that he had been to the bank and drawn out the hundred pounds? Had he spoken to the footman? Was that the thing? Careful, Reggie, think before you speak. Nearly fell into a trap there.

"Good heavens, no," he forced a sickly smile. "Decent chap, Freddie. Bit of a silly ass at times, that's all. Wouldn't mean any harm."

"Glad to hear that, sir." Pitt's eyes did not move from Reggie's face. "Just thought you might have had a little trouble."

"Er—trouble? What made you think that?" Must find out what he actually knew.

"Talk to all the servants," Pitt said lightly, "in the course of investigations, you know."

Reggie stared fixedly at Pitt's face.

He knew! He knew about the footman and the bank! If he told a lie about what he had done with the hundred pounds, the damn fellow would go and check up on it, and find out! Too easy. Have to invent something else.

203

"Well," he began awkwardly, brain racing. Who should he blame, if not Freddie? Who could not deny it? Who was likely? "Well—to tell you the truth, have had a bit of trouble—not Freddie of course, Freddie's a gentleman. Governess—" yes, that's it, "governess got a bit het up—single woman, no admirers, stuck in a job minding children all day. Got a few wild ideas and put a bit of pressure on. Any other time I'd have sent her packing, but right now, as you say, a bit embarrassing. Paid her. Dare say I shouldn't have, but got to keep the peace, what? You're a married man. Expect you understand. Sooner pay the girl than have her spread gossip all over the place. She won't do it again. Anyway, after you clear up all this business, no need, eh?"

"Oh, no," Pitt pulled a small face. "I take it you don't want to prosecute?"

"Good God, no! Whole purpose of paying up, keep it all quiet. Deny it all, if you go to her: so shall I! Have to, after all. Wife, and all that. Got to consider the children too. Three daughters. Dare say you knew? Actually two of my own, Chastity's my brother's child. Poor fellow was killed. Took her in, naturally."

"Yes, charming child."

"Yes, yes. Well, you understand, don't you? Got to keep it all quiet. Nasty thing if it got out. Very fond of the governess, the girls. And good at her job too," he said hastily. "Very good."

"Quite. Well, thank you, sir, you've been very helpful."

"Good. Good. Get it all cleared up soon, I hope?"

"I hope so too. Good night sir, and thank you."

"Good night; yes, yes, good night."

Charlotte was incensed when she heard about it the following day. She whirled round from the sideboard where she had been standing, to face Pitt in his chair.

"You mean that that dissipated bounder claimed that Jemima was blackmailing him, and you just stood there and let him?" she demanded. "That's dastardly!"

"I could hardly contradict him," Pitt pointed out reasonably. "It seems unlikely, but not by any means impossible."

204

"Of course it's impossible!" Charlotte retorted. "Jemima wouldn't dream of blackmailing anyone."

"Spoken from the heart," Pitt smiled at her with a mixture of affection strongly touched with amusement.

Charlotte was not to be moved. She felt convinced she was right, it was just a matter of thinking of a reason for it.

"All right then!" she looked back at him with determination. "From the head then: do you really think it is worth money to try to keep it secret that he beds the parlormaid? Everyone knows anyway. And Mary Ann hasn't been there all that long," she let a note of real intellectual triumph creep into her voice. "Not long enough to have been the mother of the first baby! There was one before her for a short time; she got married and left, and another before that who died." She faced Pitt with a mounting bubble of excitement inside her. "Everyone knows he behaves badly, I expect even his wife knows, although naturally she would pretend not to—"

He frowned. "Why? Why on earth should she pretend not to know? I would have thought she would be furious, and put a stop to it instantly."

Charlotte sighed patiently. Really, men were very unsophisticated at times!

"I dare say she doesn't wish for his attentions all the time herself," she explained, "and is happy enough for him to take them elsewhere. But if she were forced to know about it, I mean to be seen to know about it, then she would have to complain, be injured, horrified, and so on. Society would require it of her. Also she would look foolish, a deceived wife—a rather humiliating position."

"But she is a deceived wife," Pitt pointed out. "Except, of course, that she doesn't believe the lie, but the offense is the same."

"No, it isn't," she looked at him sideways for a minute. Was he affecting to be ignorant, or did he really not know? Sometimes he teased her appallingly.

He waited in innocence.

"It is not an offense," she continued after a moment, "if she would rather he did it; at least not against her. The offense would be in making a fool of her in public. Everyone knows he does it, and everyone knows she doesn't mind. But

205

if she were forced to acknowledge it, then she would have either to create a scene, which would make her seem ridiculous, or else openly to condone it, which would be immoral."

"How abysmally cynical," he observed. "Where did you learn all that?"

Her face fell.

"Yes, I know. I think it's rather disgusting, but that's what happens. I've learned a lot from Emily. She's very observant, you know; and of course she knows a lot of people of that sort—society, I mean. I would never do that. I should probably have a blazing row."

He smiled broadly.

"I have no doubt at all that you would, my dear."

She looked at him quickly.

He held his hands up in defense.

"Don't worry, we can't afford a parlormaid, and I swear I shall never touch Mrs. Wickes."

Considering Mrs. Wickes was fourteen stone and had a moustache, Charlotte did not feel it a great concession.

"How about Jemima?" she asked.

"He doesn't want to press charges," he replied.

"Of course he doesn't! She isn't guilty!"

"I rather agree with you," he said thoughtfully. "Which raises the question of why he told me about it. Rather a superfluous and dangerous invention, don't you think?"

"I don't care! Jemima wouldn't blackmail him."

"So that leaves the rather interesting question of who did."

Charlotte caught her breath. "Oh!"

"Quite," he stood up in a single movement.

"You're not going to charge her?" She caught at his arm.

"No. But I do have to report it."

"Must you?"

"Of course I must."

"But it would damage her! She will probably not be able to disprove it; maybe not even ever!"

He put his hand on hers for a moment, before removing it gently.

"I know that, my dear. It will be a great pleasure to me if I can ever prove him a liar."

"Oh." She knew there was no point in arguing. If anything

206

were to be done about it quickly, she would have to do it herself.

Accordingly when he had left, she abandoned her housework leaving a note on the door for Mrs. Wickes, and took herself immediately to Callander Square. The only excuse she had was to visit General Balantyne and quickly manufacture some further service, something she had forgotten to tell him previously.

When she arrived at the door and was faced by the footman, she still had not settled on anything satisfactory, but fortunately he did not inquire her business, and merely showed her in to the library. The general was behind his desk, apparently not working, since there was no pen to be seen; he was simply staring at a sea of papers. He looked up with some eagerness when she came in.

"Charlotte, my dear, how very nice to see you!"

She was a little unprepared for such warmth. What an unpredictable man he was. Perhaps he was still feeling the glow of Christina's wedding?

"Good morning, General Balantyne," she replied with the best-judged mixture of formality and feeling she could manage.

"Do come in." He was already standing, coming round the desk toward her. "Sit down by the fire. The day is extremely unpleasant, but I suppose it is all we must expect in January."

It came to her quite naturally to decline, then she remembered that she still had not thought of a reason for coming, and it would at least give her time.

"Thank you, yes, it is very cold. I think it is the wind that makes one feel it so much."

He was still merely looking at her. It made her feel rather uncomfortable.

"One would think all the buildings would be some kind of shelter," she went on, to fill the silence. "But they only seem to funnel it into fiercer blasts."

"You must permit me to have my carriage take you home," he said seriously. "And perhaps you would like something hot to drink now? A dish of tea?"

"Oh no, no, thank you," she said hastily. "I don't wish to put you to any inconvenience. I only came to—" quickly, what

207

on earth could she have come for? "—because—I suddenly remembered that I had—had left out some rather important letters, left them out of the correct sequence. At least I think I have." Did that sound feasible?

"That was most conscientious of you," he said appreciatively. "I haven't found anything out of order."

"Perhaps if I were to check?" she stood up and surveyed the desk. At sight of it the very idea of order became ridiculous. She turned back to him helplessly.

"I've made rather a mess," he announced the obvious. "I really would appreciate your assistance again."

Something in the expression in his face disturbed her, a gentleness in the eyes, a very direct way he had of looking at her. Good heavens! Surely he had not misunderstood her reason for calling again? Her excuse was thin enough, in truth—but not for that reason! She wanted to catch Jemima, and if she called directly at the Southerons' for no other reason, she would arouse suspicion, perhaps let Reggie Southeron know, or suspect, her real intentions. Guilty people, and she was sure he was guilty, were inclined to be highly suspicious. Conscience leaped the bounds of logic and saw accusation even where there was none, let alone where it was the precise purpose, inadequately disguised.

Balantyne was waiting, still watching her.

"Oh," she recalled herself to the urgency of disabusing him. "Well—" she glanced at the heap on the desk, "I should be happy to put that in some order, but I cannot offer more than that, I'm afraid." She smiled, trying to rob her statement of its harshness. "Since I have no maids, I have a rather pressing need to do a little housework. It is really becoming imperative."

"Oh," his face fell. "I'm sorry for having been so inconsiderate. I—of course. I don't wish to take you away from—" he stammered a little, hastily collecting himself. "Yes, I see. But if you would today, I should be most grateful—" he hesitated, and she was almost sure he was wondering whether to offer her payment, and how to do it tactfully. She knew he was embarrassed, and she felt for him. She smiled easily.

"Actually I hate housework, and for one day I can excuse myself to my conscience. I dare say it is most unfeminine of me, but I find the Crimean War infinitely more interesting than the pantry." She moved to the desk, taking her gloves off as she went, keeping her back to him, to give him no opportunity to meet her eyes again, but she was acutely conscious of him standing behind her.

She was not able to excuse herself at lunchtime, and therefore found herself taking her only opportunity to slip next door a little later than she had planned. However, no one saw her but the scullery maid and the cook's assistant, and she was at the schoolroom before they commenced their afternoon lessons.

Jemima was standing at the window, looking down to the square at the front. She turned when Charlotte came in.

"Oh, Charlotte, how good to see you." Her face was alight with pleasure, even excitement; and there was a starry glaze to her eyes. "Are you working for General Balantyne again?"

"Only today," Charlotte said soberly. "I really came because I wished to see you, without drawing attention to myself." There was no point in being evasive. She must tell her the truth about Reggie, and before the children returned.

Jemima seemed to sense no danger, and no urgency.

"I'm sure Mr. Southeron wouldn't mind." She was not looking at Charlotte, but a little beyond her. "I wish you had come for luncheon. You must come tomorrow."

Had she not been listening? Charlotte had said she was only here for one day.

But Jemima had turned back to the window again.

Charlotte crossed the room and stood beside her. She looked down. There was nothing there but the silent, leafless square, rain-sodden, everything in shades of gray and black, even the grass seemed robbed of its green. Wind keened sharply through the areaways and ruffled a few last deadened leaves on the shrubs. There was nothing there to so attract a young woman's attention. Someone must have just passed that way. Charlotte had heard no carriage, and horses' hooves sounded sharply enough, with the rattle of wheels, on the stones. Someone on foot. In this weather? Oh no, not Brandy Balantyne.

"Jemima!"

Jemima turned, her eyes still warm and happy. She looked down suddenly, a faint color climbing her cheek.

"Brandy Balantyne?" Charlotte asked.

"Do you not like him, Charlotte? From something you said last time, I was not sure."

Charlotte had liked him very much, but she dare not say so, yet not lie, and hurt pointlessly.

"I have only met him a few times, and then briefly. If you remember, I was not a social visitor there, only someone employed to help." That was cruel, and she knew it, but Jemima must not be allowed to let dreams grow out of proportion. The more vivid the dream, the more painful the awakening.

The hurt showed immediately in Jemima's face.

"Yes," she said softly. "Yes, I know that. And I know what you are trying to say. You are quite right, of course."

Charlotte wanted to warn her about Reggie Southeron, but that would have meant bringing up the subject of a master who slept with maids, and at this very moment it would seem a crude thing to say, and perhaps totally unjust. It was no parallel, and she did not wish Jemima to think for one moment that she imagined it was. She would have to leave it for another time, a time less open to pain and misunderstanding. All the explanations in the world would not get rid of the impression of a likeness in Jemima's mind, if she were to mention Reggie and parlormaids and blackmail in the same breath with Brandy Balantyne.

"I must return," she said instead. "I merely wanted to see you, and to—to ask you to take great care of yourself. Sometimes people who are frightened will blame others, in investigations like this. I heard about poor Miss Doran. Be most guarded in what you say!"

Jemima looked a little puzzled, but she agreed easily enough, and five minutes later Charlotte was out in the icy street again, hurrying back to the library and the general's papers, feeling unsatisfied with herself, and doubly afraid for Jemima.

* * *

Christina was not away after her wedding for more than a week, possibly because of the tragedies that had happened in the square. It had been considered an unsuitable time for a holiday in celebration; possibly, also, no one had the heart for it: least of all Alan Ross. Even Christina, marrying days after the discovery of Helena's body, could hardly demand of him a honeymoon spirit. Emily, calling upon her barely as soon as was decent, thought privately that she might well consider herself fortunate not to have had the wedding itself postponed. That might truly have been disastrous. Under the circumstances she might be in, even a couple of weeks could make her a liar. Premature birth could be stretched only so far, with a hope of being believed!

She called on Christina with no particular purpose in mind, except that she hoped to learn something further about Helena Doran. They had been much of an age, they were bound to have had a deal in common, attended the same parties, known the same people. She doubted they would have been friends then, and Christina might feel a little bitter about having just married a man whom everyone knew to have loved Helena, at least in the past. But she must know something; and frequently as much truth was spoken in dislike as there ever was in friendship, especially of the dead. Funny how death seemed to obscure all the relevant truths in a sugar coating of decency. Must make detection very difficult.

Alan Ross's house was in an elegant street less than half a mile from Callander Square. It could not claim the same opulence, nor the same fashionable grace, but it was a substantial establishment, and when Emily knocked she was admitted by a smart parlormaid.

Christina seemed quite pleased to see her, although Emily thought she looked a little pale. Honeymoons were very often something of a shock to a woman, but someone who had lain quite happily with a footman should not have encountered many surprises!

"Good afternoon, Emily," Christina said a little formally. "How kind of you to call."

Emily mentally crossed her fingers for lying.

"I wished to welcome you home, and to see how you were,"

211

she said with a tone of concern. "After all, fortune has treated you most unkindly, I feel. It was a most wretched time for that poor girl to be discovered. It could hardly have been worse!"

Christina turned a very cold eye on her.

"Then it was a pity you chose that moment to go looking!"

"My dear," Emily endeavored to look contrite, "how could I have imagined what I would find? I believed, like everyone else, that she had eloped with her lover, and was happily married somewhere—or married, at least. In truth I did not necessarily believe that it would be happy. These romantic things very seldom are."

"So you said before. What on earth were you doing in that deserted garden anyway?"

"Just curiosity, I suppose," Emily said idly, turning to admire the room, which indeed was handsome. "It was a romantic place—"

"A ruined garden, in the middle of winter!" Christina invested her voice with acid disbelief.

"It is not always the middle of winter, it only happens to be so now," Emily said reasonably. "And the garden would have been far less ruined two years ago."

"I fail to see your point," Christina was decidedly cold.

"Why, when Helena met her lover there, of course!" Emily turned back. "What was she like? You must have known her. Was she very beautiful, very fascinating?"

"Not especially," Christina affected some disdain. "She was pretty enough, in a rather anemic way; and she was certainly not witty, in fact I always thought her pleasant, but rather dull."

"Oh dear," Emily allowed her face to fall, although it cost some effort. Actually she was delighted, this was Christina's genuine feeling, revealing as much about herself as about Helena Doran. "What a shame," she continued. "She hardly sounds like the sort of woman to attract a romantic lover, unless he were a very callow sort. Unless, of course, she had hidden depths."

"If she had, then they were very well hidden," Christina snapped. "Nobody I knew ever found them!"

Emily had little compunction about being cruel.

"Not even Mr. Ross?" she inquired.

To her considerable surprise, Christina colored deeply.

"Alan is quite disillusioned about her. He no longer admires her."

"Disillusioned?" Emily pressed the point.

"Well, she was hardly the innocent she pretended to be," Christina said stingingly. "She met some lover in an empty garden, and obviously lay with him, or she would not have been with child! Surely that is enough to disillusion anybody!"

"Then it might become you to be exceedingly discreet yourself," Emily observed. She did not like moral hypocrisy, and she did not particularly like Christina.

Christina's color deepened and she glared at Emily with something akin to hatred. Was it conceivable that at this peculiar point she had actually learned some regard for Alan Ross? It seemed the obvious explanation. She was safely married and had thus acquired the respectability she needed if she were indeed to be pregnant, although that now appeared less and less probable. Unlike Charlotte, she was still wearing gowns with small waists, and her figure betrayed nothing. Yes, perhaps she really had developed an admiration for her husband. It was a bitter thing, but in Emily's opinion, unless Christina were very much to alter her character, the better Mr. Ross were to know her, the less likely was he to return that feeling. Still, that was not something Emily could accomplish for her, nor had she any desire to attempt it.

She remained a little longer, speaking of Helena again but learning little except that Christina heartily disliked her. However, she could not tell whether that dislike predated Christina's regard for Mr. Ross. Half an hour later she took her leave, her mind humming with new and interesting thoughts.

It was the morning after hearing from Emily about this episode, and more importantly about the conclusions she had drawn from it, that Charlotte decided she must go again to see Jemima, and regardless of temporary hurt, must this time convey some warning to her more specific of her danger.

She also wished to see if she could learn something about Reggie Southeron that might tell her who really was blackmailing him; if indeed anyone was. Whatever the facts, for Jemima's safety she must learn the reason behind the accusation.

To see Jemima alone, she must find her before classes began for the morning, which might well be nine o'clock. Therefore it was a little before quarter past eight, and barely light on a leaden, sleet-driven morning when she alighted from the hansom. The driver had mistakenly arrived at the wrong side of the square and refused to go round it because of the danger to his horse's knees on the slimy cobbles where rotting leaves had piled from the night's wind.

Charlotte did not argue. She had no wish that the animal should fall and be injured, not particularly for the cabbie's expense, but for the creature's own sake.

Accordingly she was left to walk, and rather than risk the same difficulty herself, she cut across the garden where there were no stones on which to slip, and where the night frost had hardened the ground to support her weight without sinking into the mud. At night she would not have gone alone, as she carried a memory of Cater Street, which would probably last as long as she lived; but it would be a desperate marauder indeed to be waiting around in this icy gray morning amid the spindly black branches and the falling vegetation.

She moved briskly because the cold bit into her flesh and the sleet on the wind stung her unprotected skin. She was watching where she put her feet, in order not to miss her step and fall over some fallen branch or slip in a patch of gathered slush. It was thus that she did not see the dark mound until she was almost upon it. It was not quite on the path, but close by the side of it, as if it had been on the path and blown from it. Surely no branch could have that mass? A feeling of disaster, a foreknowledge, came to her before she reached it and she stopped.

It was wet clothes: and in among the roots of last year's Michaelmas daisies there was the head, hair dark in the wet, but it would have been fair normally: and the skin was white, as only the cold of death could make it.

She bent down but did not touch him. He was half on his side, one arm crumpled underneath, as if his hand were reaching for the knife that was buried to its hilt in his chest. She had only seen him once that she could recall, but she knew beyond question that it was Freddie Bolsover.

She stood up slowly and began to walk back into the wind again to search for a constable.

TEN

Pitt was called straight away, since anything in Callander Square was considered to be part of his case. Before half past nine he was kneeling on the still icebound earth by the body. A solitary constable stood guard over it. Nothing had been moved. After some protest, Charlotte had been sent home, although Pitt thought it was probably the cold that prevailed over her rather than any sense of obedience.

There was a police doctor with him. After he had stared his fill and the picture was etched on his mind, together they turned Freddie over to look at the wound. The knife was buried right to the hilt, the filigree handle holding no imprint of a hand at all.

Pitt moved the clothes fractionally.

"Single blow," he remarked. "Very clean."

"Could be luck," the doctor said over his shoulder. "Doesn't have to be skill."

"What about strength?" Pitt asked.

"Strength?" The doctor considered for a moment. He reached down and moved the knife experimentally. "No bones cut," he observed. "Clean between the ribs. Nothing but cartilage, and a little muscle; straight to the heart. Average adult could do it quite competently. Too high a wound for a short person. Blow seems to be a downward one, so your murderer was at least five foot six or seven, probably more."

Pitt picked up one of Freddie's hands.

"No gloves," he said, frowning a little. "He must have come out in a hurry, and possibly not expected to be long. Coming to meet someone he knew, I should think." He looked at the nails and knuckles. "Spotless. He can't have made much of a struggle."

"Caught by surprise," the doctor replied. "Only knew for a second before unconsciousness overtook him."

"Surprise," Pitt said slowly. "From the front. That means he knew his murderer, the surprise was that he should strike. Dr. Bolsover considered him safe, a friend."

"Or acquaintance," the doctor added.

"Does one go out to meet a mere acquaintance in the middle of the square, at night?"

"I didn't say he was killed during the night," the doctor shook his head. "Can't tell. This weather, body would freeze in a very short time. Makes time of death a bit difficult."

"Hardly risk murdering someone in the middle of the square in daylight," Pitt said gently. "Too risky. Servants spend too much time near the windows, too big a chance someone would see you walking into the middle of the gardens. After dark, muffled up in scarf with collar up, which would be reasonable enough in this weather, as soon as you're out of the arc of the gaslight you're invisible. Could have gone up the steps to the front door, or into an areaway, off to get a cab—anything."

"Quite," the doctor agreed a little stiffly. "So take it they met after dark. Bit of an odd thing to do, wasn't it? Go to meet someone in the pitch dark in a frozen waste like this? Could fall and break your neck, never mind being stabbed. Hardly see a foot in front of you."

"Raises a lot of questions in the mind, doesn't it?" Pitt stared down at the body again.

The doctor grunted.

"Must have been wishing to discuss something very urgent, and very private indeed."

"Or have an intent to murder," Pitt said softly.

The doctor said nothing.

Pitt climbed to his feet, a little stiff in the bitter cold.

"It occurs to me that I have rather a lot to ask Mr. Reggie Southeron. See to having Bolsover taken to the morgue, will you? You'd better do your post mortem thoroughly, in spite of the obvious. I don't believe there will be anything else, but it's always possible."

The doctor gave him a sour look, and stumped back toward

the constable, slapping his hands together to get the circulation moving again.

Pitt did not want to give Reggie any advance warning this time. He went straight to the front door and when the footman answered, announced that he wished to see Mr. Southeron with all possible speed. He imagined that on a bitter morning like this Reggie would not have risen before nine, and would certainly not have breakfasted and been ready to depart for the city before ten.

He was correct. Reggie was still at the table, and about to expostulate at the footman's unseemly interruption, and to tell him rather sharply that the police could wait, when he glanced past the man's sober figure to see the enormous caped figure of Pitt who had followed him in; precisely to avoid being dismissed in such a fashion.

"Really!" Reggie glared at him. "I appreciate that you have a difficult job to do, but a little unpleasantness in the square does not absolve you from all need to follow the ordinary dictates of good manners. I shall see you when I have finished my breakfast! You may wait until then in the morning room, if you wish."

Pitt eyed the footman, and found to his satisfaction that the man's fear of the police was greater than his fear of his employer. He retreated like water going down a sink, flowing outward with a somewhat circular motion and disappearing down the passage.

"The matter is too urgent to admit of delay," Pitt said firmly. "Dr. Bolsover has been murdered."

Reggie stared at him glassily.

"I beg your pardon?"

"Dr. Bolsover has been murdered," Pitt repeated. "His body was found this morning, at a few minutes after eight o'clock."

"Good God!" Reggie dropped his fork laden with food and it fell with a clatter, upsetting his knife and sliding to the floor, taking bacon and sausage with it. "Good God," he said again. "What a frightful thing."

"Yes," Pitt agreed, watching him closely. Did he really have the wit to act so well? He seemed stupefied with shock. "Murder is always frightful," he went on. "One way and an-

219

other. Of course many people who are murdered rather bring it upon themselves."

"What in blazes do you mean?" Reggie's heavy face flushed scarlet. "I call that damned impertinent! Damned bad taste! Poor old Freddie lying dead somewhere, and you stand there saying he deserved it!"

"No," Pitt corrected carefully. "You leaped to that conclusion. What I said was that some people who are murdered bring it upon themselves; blackmailers, and so on," he leaned a little forward, watching Reggie's face minutely. He saw what he was looking for, the ebb of color, the nervous spasm of muscles.

"Blackmailers?" Reggie repeated hoarsely, his eyes unfocussed like a stuffed doll's.

"Yes," Pitt pulled up a chair and sat down. "Blackmailers rather often get murdered. Victim sees it as his only way out. Blackmailers don't seem to realize when they've reached the critical point. They press too far." He opened his hands wide to express an explosion, an eruption.

Reggie swallowed convulsively, his eyes fixed on Pitt as if mesmerized. He seemed to be unable to speak.

Pitt gambled.

"That is what happened to Dr. Bolsover, isn't it, sir?"

"Dr.—Bolsover—?"

"Yes. He was blackmailing you, wasn't he?"

"No—no! I told you! It—it was Jemima, the governess. I said that to you before."

"So you did: you said that the governess was blackmailing you over the fact that you have had a passing affair with your parlormaid. I wouldn't have thought that was worth paying for, sir, since I knew about it, the servants knew, I would be surprised if the neighbors had not guessed; and I imagine your wife also knows, even if she prefers to pretend that she does not."

"What the hell do you mean?" Reggie tried to look affronted.

"No more than I say, sir: that I find it hard to believe that you would submit to blackmail over something which is a subject of general knowledge, even though it is not mentioned; and which is a little sordid, but not by any means an infrequent offense; and hardly a crime."

"I—I told you—of course it is not a crime! But right now it could be misunderstood! People could think—"

"You mean the police could think—?" Pitt raised his eyebrows sardonically.

A tide of color swept up Reggie's face as he realized his lie was ridiculous. Pitt could almost see his brain racing. Should he catch him now, in panic, or wait till his tongue betrayed him further?

"Er—" Reggie tried to fill in until he invented something, "—well—yes, it does sound—"

"A bit thin," Pitt finished for him. "Suppose you tell me the truth?"

"Er—truth!"

"Yes, sir. Why was Dr. Bolsover really blackmailing you?"

"I—" Reggie seemed frozen.

"If I have to ask others in order to find out, it will be a lot more uncomfortable for you," Pitt pointed out. "If you tell me, providing there is no crime involved, I shall be as discreet as I can. Time is important. We have a murderer somewhere in this square: and he may not be finished yet!"

"Oh God!"

"Why was Dr. Bolsover blackmailing you, Mr. Southeron?"

Reggie gasped and swallowed.

"Another affair I had." His eyes were hot, uncomfortable, searching somewhere over Pitt's shoulder. "Woman was married. Husband important fellow. Could do me a spot of damage, if he found out. You understand?"

Pitt looked at him for a long moment. He was lying.

"How did the governess ever come to know about it?" he asked.

"What?" Reggie's head jerked up. "Oh. Er—"

"You said she was blackmailing you too," Pitt reminded him. "Would you like to amend that now?"

Suddenly Reggie's eyes cleared.

"No! No, she was. Very greedy young woman. That must be why Freddie was killed! Yes, it all fits in, don't you see?" He sat up a little. "They must have quarreled over the money!

She wanted more than her share, he refused, and she killed him. Makes sense: all fits together!"

"How did the governess come to know of this affair of yours? Did you have the woman here?"

"Good God, of course not! What on earth do you think I am?"

"Then how did she know, sir?"

"I don't know! Freddie must have said something!"

"Why on earth should he do that? Why share his spoils unnecessarily? Seems an unlikely thing to do."

"How in hell should I know?" Reggie demanded furiously.

"Perhaps he was having an affair with her, and he told her in a moment of boasting, or something! We'll never know now. Poor swine is dead."

"The governess isn't."

"Well, you can hardly expect her to tell you the truth!" There was a rising note in Reggie's voice that sounded uncommonly like panic.

Pitt gambled again.

"I think it sounds more likely to me, sir, that this woman you had an affair with wasn't the wife of some powerful man at all, but another maid."

Reggie's eyes glinted.

"As you've just pointed out, Inspector; it would hardly be worth anything to me to pay for silence over something as trifling as that!"

"Not if that's all there was to it," Pitt agreed with a small smile, his eyes fixed on Reggie's face unblinkingly. "But what if there were more to it, a child, say?"

Reggie went pasty white. For a moment it occurred to Pitt that he might have a fit.

"One of your parlormaids died, didn't she?" Pitt asked slowly, making each word weigh heavily.

Reggie gagged for breath.

"You didn't murder her, did you, Mr. Southeron?" Pitt asked.

"God! Oh God! No, I didn't. She died. Freddie was with her. We called him in. Had to. That's how he knew."

"What did she die of?"

"I—I don't know!"

222

"Do I have to ask the female staff?" Pitt said softly.

"No!" There was a moment's silence. "No," Reggie said more quietly. "She had an abortion. It went wrong. That's why she died. I didn't know anything about it. I couldn't have saved her. You've got to believe that."

"But it was your child?"

"How do I know?"

Pitt permitted his disgust to show at last.

"You mean you were sharing her with someone else? The footman, perhaps, or the bootboy?" he said harshly.

"How dare you! I'll have you remember your place!"

"Your place, at the moment, Mr. Southeron," Pitt snapped back, "is extremely unpleasant! A parlormaid carrying your child dies in your house from a badly done abortion. You are being blackmailed by your doctor over the affair. Now your doctor is murdered outside your house. What strikes you as the obvious conclusion to draw from that?"

"I—I told you," Reggie fumbled his words and gasped, "the governess! She was with him in it! He must have been sleeping with her, told her! She was the one who came to me for the money! She must have quarreled with him—a case of thieves falling out! That's the obvious answer! Who are you going to believe? Me, who hasn't done anything wrong, or a servant girl who lies and blackmails, and finally kills her lover and accomplice? I ask you!"

Pitt sighed and stood up.

"I shan't believe anyone, Mr. Southeron, until I have more evidence. But I shall remember what you have said, every word of it. Thank you for your time. Good morning, sir."

As soon as he had gone Reggie collapsed. It was appalling! God alone knew where the end of it lay. Scandal! Ruin! He felt ill. The room swam around him and darkened into visions of penury—vague, because he had never actually known it—but none the less frightful for that.

He was still sitting slumped over the table when Adelina came in.

"You look ill," she observed. "Have you eaten too much?"

Her cold unconcern was the last cut to a sore, wounded man.

"Yes, I am ill!" he said angrily. "The police have just been

223

here. Freddie Bolsover has been murdered." He watched her face, satisfied to see the shock in it.

"Murdered!" she sat down sharply. "How dreadful. Whatever for? Was he robbed?"

"I've no idea!" he snapped. "He was just murdered!"

"Poor Sophie," Adelina stared down the table past Reggie into the distance. "She'll be quite utterly lost."

"Never mind about Sophie! What about us? He was murdered, Adelina, don't you understand that? That means someone murdered him, crept out there in the dark and stuck a knife into him, or hit him over the head, or whatever."

"Very unpleasant," she agreed. "People can be very wicked."

"Is that all you can say?" His voice was rising to a shout, out of control. "God damn it, woman, that bounder from the police all but accused me of it!"

She did not seem impressed, far less frightened.

"Why should they do that? You could have no reason for killing Freddie. He was a friend."

"He was a blackmailer!"

"Freddie? Nonsense. Who on earth would he blackmail?"

"He's a doctor, you stupid woman! He could blackmail any of his patients!"

Still she was not apparently moved.

"Doctors are not allowed to tell the things about their patients that are confidential. If they did, they would get no more patients. Freddie would never do that. It would be foolish. And don't call me stupid, Reggie. It's very rude, and there's no need for rudeness. I'm sorry Freddie is dead, but becoming hysterical won't help."

"I don't understand you!" he was angry, frightened, and now utterly bewildered. "You were weeping all over the place about Helena, and here is Freddie dead and you don't seem to care at all!"

"That was different. Helena was carrying a child." Her voice dropped at the memory of it. "That child died before it was ever born. If you were a woman, you would understand that. I look at my own children, and of course I weep. Children are all a woman really has." She looked at him with a sudden harshness. "We carry them, and bear them, bring them into the world, love them, listen to them, advise them, and see that they are married well. All you do is pay the bills, and boast about them if they do something well. I'm sorry Freddie is dead, but I really can't weep about it. I shall be sorry for Sophie of course, because she has no children. And how do you know Freddie was a blackmailer?"

"What?"

"You said Freddie was a blackmailer. How do you know that?"

"Oh," he scrambled for an answer, "someone told me. Confidence, you know, can't tell you about it."

"Don't be fatuous, Reggie. People don't tell you about things like that. He must have been blackmailing you. Was he?"

"Of course not! There's nothing to blackmail me about!"

"Then why do the police think you killed him? It doesn't make sense."

"I don't know!" he yelled. "I didn't damn well ask!"

"I thought it might have been about Dolly."

He froze. She looked like a stranger sitting at the head of the table, monstrous and unknown, inscrutable. She was saying something appalling, and there was no expression on her face except a mild curiosity.

"D-Dolly?" he stuttered.

"I could have forgiven you for sleeping with her, as long as you were discreet," she said, looking directly at him. It seemed as if it was the first time she had ever really looked at him. "But not for killing her child, Reggie; never for that."

"I didn't kill the child!" He was becoming hysterical. He could hear it himself but could do nothing to stop it. "It was an abortion. It went wrong! I didn't do it!"

"Don't lie, Reggie. Of course you did it. You allowed her to seek an abortion in the back streets instead of sending her away to the country to bear the child. She could have stayed there, or you could have had the child adopted. You didn't. I shall not forgive you for that, Reggie; not ever." She stood up again and turned away. "I trust you did not have anything to do with Freddie's death. It would have been extremely stupid of you."

"Stupid! Is that all you can say? Stupid! Do you actually imagine I could have anything to do with killing Freddie?"

"No. I think it would be most unlike you to have done anything so decisive. But I am glad to hear you say it. I hope you are telling the truth."

"Do you doubt me?"

"I don't think I care very much, except for the scandal. If you manage to keep the police out of it, that is all I ask."

He stared at her helplessly. Suddenly he was cold, as if a longworn skin had been ripped from him and left him naked. He watched her go out of the room and felt like a child in the dark.

Having told the police that Jemima was the one who had blackmailed him, and therefore having been unable to go back on it, it seemed the obvious, ideal solution to blame her for Freddie's murder also. Now he must make it stick. He must behave as if he believed it to be the truth. It was inconceivable that a man, knowing such a thing, would keep in his house, tutoring his children, a woman who was a blackmailer and a murderess. The only possible course was to dismiss her immediately.

It was unfortunate, of course. In the circumstances, there would be no one who would take her in, but what else was he to do? Pity he had not taken the opportunity a few minutes ago of telling Adelina—but the thought of Adelina was highly uncomfortable at the moment, better removed from mind. He must find Jemima and tell her she must leave. He need not explain to her precisely why, which would be most embarrassing—he could avoid that very well on the claim that he would not accuse her before the police did, and perhaps jeopardize the justice of her cause. Yes, that sounded excellent. He even felt a flush of rectitude, and rose from the table to set about it immediately.

Charlotte heard of it at midday when Jemima arrived on the doorstep, white-faced, a boxchest on the pavement beside her, a hansom clopping away already reaching the corner of the street. She must have stood on the step for some moments, afraid to knock.

Charlotte answered the door herself, since there was no

one else; one would hardly wish to send Mrs. Wickes, with her hands wet, apron splashed, hair sprouting like a bollard willow.

"Jemima!" She saw the chest. "Whatever has happened? Come in, you look frozen and starved. Can you lift the other end of the box with me? We can't leave it there, or someone may steal it."

Obediently Jemima bent, and a few minutes later they were both inside and Charlotte looked at her more closely.

"What is it?" she said gently. "Has Mr. Southeron accused you of blackmailing him?"

Jemima looked up, shock and a kind of relief in her face that she did not have to break the news herself.

"You know?"

Charlotte was ashamed now for not having warned her, although perhaps it would have done little good. She should have thought of some way for Pitt to prevent Reggie giving tongue to his lies.

"Yes. I meant to tell you when I came the other day." She put out her hands and clasped Jemima's. "I'm so sorry. When I saw how you felt about Brandy Balantyne, I couldn't speak of Reggie and his maids in the same breath, for fear you would think I believed you were no better."

Jemima looked bewildered, but there was no accusation in her eyes.

"How did you know?" she repeated. "Does everyone know except me?" She swallowed hard. "Why, Charlotte? Why should he say such a thing? Certainly he lay with Mary Ann, but everyone knew! I never spoke of it, least of all to him—and asking for money! Why should he say I did?"

"Because someone was blackmailing him, and he did not wish to tell the truth of it," Charlotte replied. "It was easy to blame you, because you are least likely to be able to defend yourself."

"But why should anyone blackmail him over that? It is rather squalid, it is true, and it is an abuse of Mary Ann, and of his wife; but it is not a crime; it would not even be so much of a scandal: not worth paying to avoid, anyway."

"I don't know," Charlotte admitted. "But come and sit down. Let me make you something to drink to warm you. I think I have a little cocoa. We must plan what to do next." She busied herself quickly. They were in the kitchen anyway, it being the warmest room in the house. Charlotte could not afford to burn a fire in the parlor except in the evenings. Mrs. Wickes had finished the floor and gone upstairs to sweep, so they were alone.

"You can sleep in the nursery," Charlotte went on, stirring the cocoa with a wooden spoon to get rid of the lumps. "The bed is a little small, but it will do you for a while. I'm afraid it is all we have—"

"I can't stay here," Jemima said quickly. "Oh, Charlotte, I am grateful, but the police will be looking for me soon. Blackmail is a crime, you know. I cannot bring that disgrace upon you—"

"Oh!" Charlotte turned round in surprise, forgetting Jemima knew so little of her. "Don't worry about that. My husband is a policeman; in fact he is the policeman in charge of this case. He knows you did not blackmail anyone. At least," she corrected herself, "he does not believe you did. Don't worry, he will discover the truth. And Dr. Bolsover has been murdered. Did you know that? I found his body this morning. I was on the way again to warn you about Mr. Southeron when I nearly fell over it. Maybe he was the real black-mailer."

"You—the police—?" Jemima was utterly confused. "But, but you are not married. Are you not Lady Ashworth's sister? At least that is what General Balantyne said. I obtained your address from him this morning. I had to lie. I said I wished to write you a letter." She winced and looked down for a moment. "Before Mr. Southeron should tell anyone about me and I should find no one would open their doors to me. I did not know who else to turn to—" Her eyes brimmed over and she dropped her head to hide her distress.

Charlotte put down the cocoa and went to her, putting her arms round her. For a little while Jemima wept silently; then she pulled herself together, blew her nose hard, excused herself to wash her face, and returned downstairs to take cocoa, now ready, and biscuits. Afterward she faced Charlotte and declared herself ready for battle.

Charlotte smiled back at her.

"Thomas will discover the truth," she said firmly, although she knew that that was not necessarily the case. Sometimes crimes remained unsolved. "And if possible we shall help him," she went on, "to have it done the more quickly. I think I must send a letter to Emily, to acquaint her with the latest events. She may be able to assist us too."

"You are marvelous," Jemima smiled rather weakly. "Are you so used to murders, that they do not frighten you any more?"

"Oh no!" The horror of Cater Street came back to her with all its terror and grief. She felt a quick prickle of tears for Sarah. "Oh no," she said quietly. "They frighten me very much, not just murder, but all the other dark things it stirs in even those who are barely involved in the first crime. It seems so often one crime begets another. People do such strange things to cover guilt. We can become so cruel and so selfish when we are afraid. Murder and investigation reveal to us so many things about each other which we would rather not have known. Believe me, I am frightened by it. But I think I would prefer that it should always frighten me. Not to be frightened would mean that I had lost the understanding of it. But it is my nature to fight, and we shall discover the truth of this yet, whomever it may involve!"

When Pitt arrived home late that evening he was only mildly surprised to see Jemima sitting with Charlotte by the fire. She was both embarrassed and nervous to begin with, but he went to some effort to put her at ease, even though he was appallingly tired, and by the time she retired, she looked as if she might sleep.

After she had gone, he told Charlotte that Reggie had accused her of the murder of Freddie also, and was relieved that Charlotte did not blaze up in temper, nor dissolve in tears, although he had never considered the latter likely.

In the morning he set out again to Callander Square, walking some part of the distance, the better to enable himself to think.

He did not doubt for a moment that Freddie Bolsover had been murdered because he was a blackmailer. He was inclined to think that it was not Reggie Southeron, if only because he lacked the nerve, and had seemed to be totally shocked by the news of the discovery of the body. Surely if he had known anything about it, he would have been prepared with a more plausible story.

But if it was not Reggie, then who were the other suspects? Surely in Callander Square there were enough secrets worth paying to keep!

He would begin with Balantyne.

He found him at home and quite willing to see him. He was shown into the morning room and a moment later the general came in, still looking grave from the news of Freddie's murder the day before.

"Good morning, Inspector. Have you discovered something further about poor Freddie?"

"Yes, quite a lot, sir. None of it very pleasant, I'm afraid."

"I'm sure it wasn't. Wretched business, poor fellow. You said yesterday he was stabbed. Was there something else?"

"Perhaps I didn't explain myself very well. I meant that what I had discovered was about Dr. Bolsover himself, not the murder; although I believe it was the cause."

"Oh?" Balantyne frowned slightly. "What do you mean?. Not something to do with the babies in the square, surely? Always thought Freddie was a pretty sober sort of chap, not given to playing the fool with other women."

"Not directly to do with the babies, but perhaps indirectly. He was a blackmailer."

Balantyne stared at him.

"Blackmailer?" he repeated foolishly. "Whatever makes you think anything—so—vile?"

"One of his victims."

"Must be lying! Fellow who would do something fit to be blackmailed for could well be a liar as well. In fact must be! Or others would know about his crimes."

"Doesn't have to be a crime, sir," Pitt said gently. "Could be something he merely preferred kept private, an indiscretion or misfortune. Perhaps like his daughter having an affair with a footman, and being with child before she was married, or—" he stopped. It was unnecessary to go on, Balantyne's face was scarlet. Pitt waited.

230

"I'd see the fellow in hell before I'd pay him," Balantyne said very quietly. "Believe me!"

"Would you?" Pitt asked, his voice mild, not a challenge, but a soft probing. "Your only daughter, just before her marriage to a most suitable man? Are you sure? Would you not perhaps consider it worth a small expense to protect her?"

Balantyne stared at him, his eyes wavering.

Pitt said nothing.

"I don't know," Balantyne said at last. "Possibly you're right. But it didn't happen. Freddie never came anywhere near me." He looked down at the carpet. "Poor Sophie. I suppose she had no idea. Often wondered how Freddie managed to live so high on the hog. I had some knowledge of the size of his practice. Never occurred to me in the wildest moment—what a wretched business. Do you suppose he knew whose the babies were?"

"Perhaps," Pitt replied. "But I rather doubt it. If he were pressing on that one, I think he might well have been killed a good deal earlier than this. Of course he may have known something without realizing its importance. I don't know, that's why I must question all the people upon whom he may have put pressure."

"Nautrally. Of course you must. Well, I had no idea. I would regret having to do so, but if I could help you, I should."

"Thank you. May I speak with Lady Augusta, please, and then with young Mr. Balantyne?"

Again Balantyne flushed uncomfortably.

"Lady Augusta can tell you nothing, I assure you, she has most certainly never done anything in her life to make blackmail possible! And she is not the manner of woman to be intimidated."

Pitt agreed with this last observation, but if she had done anything, then in all probability it would be the general from whom she wished to keep it secret. He forbore pointing this out; it would only embarrass without serving any purpose.

"All the same, sir, she might be able to help me. I'm sure she is not a woman to gossip, but we are dealing with murder. I need any help I may be able to obtain."

"Yes—yes, I suppose so. Very well." Perhaps he also knew

that the request was only a formality. Pitt could not be refused; he came with official power.

Augusta received him in the withdrawing room, still chilly with a newmade fire.

"Good morning, my lady," Pitt began formally as the footman closed the door behind him.

"Good morning," Augusta replied. She was a handsome woman, and she looked, if anything, a little more relaxed than when he had seen her last. "What can I do for you, Inspector? I have no idea who killed Freddie Bolsover, or why."

"Why is not difficult," Pitt replied, facing her squarely. "He was a blackmailer."

"Indeed?" she raised her eyebrows slightly. "How very unpleasant. I had no idea. I suppose you are quite sure."

"Quite," he waited, wondering what she would say next.

"Then surely his victim is the one who murdered him? You cannot need me to tell you that!"

He smiled very slightly.

"That is to presume he had only one victim, my lady. Why should I presume that?"

She looked at him and the corners of her mouth curled upward very faintly.

"Quite. I should have thought of that myself. When you remark it, it is quite obvious. What is it you imagine I can tell you? I assure you, Freddie Bolsover was not blackmailing me."

"Not over Miss Christina's unfortunate business with the footman?"

She barely flickered.

"It is hardly police business, I would have thought."

"Not at all. Its discovery was incidental. But you haven't answered my question—did Dr. Bolsover not approach you on the matter?"

"Certainly not," she smiled very faintly and looked at him without dislike. "I should not have paid him. I should have found some other way of dealing with him; as I did with Max, who did try it. I have more brain, and more imagination, Inspector, than to resort to violence."

He grinned widely.

"I believe it, my lady. I hope if you think of anything that might help me, however slight, you will let me know, immediately. For heaven's sake, don't deal with this yourself. He has killed once, maybe more than once."

"I give you my word," she said convincingly.

He saw Brandy a little later in the same room.

"What's happened now?" Brandy demanded. "Not someone else dead!"

"No, and I want to see that it does not happen again. I must find out who killed Dr. Bolsover, before he feels threatened again."

"Threatened?" Brandy looked worried.

"Dr. Bolsover was a blackmailer, Mr. Balantyne. That is almost certainly why he was killed."

"Who was he blackmailing, do you know?"

"Mr. Southeron, at least."

"Good—Reggie didn't kill him, surely?"

"You think that unlikely?"

"Well—yes—I do. Somehow Reggie just doesn't seem like—to be honest, I wouldn't think he had the nerve!" Brandy smiled apologetically.

"Nor I," Pitt agreed. "He said it was Jemima Waggoner who killed Dr. Bolsover—"

"What?" All the color blanched from Brandy's face. "Jemima? That's idiotic! Why on earth would Jemima kill anyone?"

"Because she was his partner in blackmail, and she became greedy over the spoils, and they quarreled—"

"He's a liar!" This time there was no mistaking Brandy's emotion, it was rage. "That's your answer! Reggie killed him, and is lying to protect himself. There's the proof of it! If he said Jemima blackmailed him, then he's a liar!" His face was set, angry and defensive.

"One can lie to cover many things, Mr. Balantyne," Pitt said quietly. "Not necessarily murder. Mr. Southeron panics rather easily."

"He's a liar!" Brandy's voice was rising. "You can't believe she— Jemima—" he stopped suddenly, struggling to control himself. He swallowed and began again. "I'm sorry. I feel very strongly about it. I'm sure Jemima is innocent, and I shall find a way to prove it to you."

"I shall be grateful for all help," Pitt smiled. "Did Dr. Bolsover approach you, sir?"

"No. Whatever for?"

"Money, favors, anything?"

"Of course not!"

"I thought you might have been prepared to pay, for example, to protect Lady Carlton."

Brandy flushed deeply.

"How did you know about that?"

Pitt evaded an answer.

"Did he?"

"No. I'm pretty sure he had no idea. It was hardly a thing he would come in contact with. I mean, he might have known she was with child, being a doctor, and so on; but nothing about me. But all that is less important than seeing that Jemima is cleared. Please, Inspector," he hesitated, "please get to the bottom of that."

Pitt smiled very gently.

"You care about her, don't you?"

"I—" Brandy seemed lost. He looked up. "Yes—I—I think I do."

ELEVEN

Pitt also visited Robert Carlton, more to inform him that Freddie had been a blackmailer than with any hope that Carlton might admit to having been a victim himself. He made his questions discreet, almost to the point of nonexistence, as he felt Carlton's cooperation was of more value than any possible involvement he might reluctantly divulge.

He could think of no reason why the Dorans should have attracted Freddie's attention. The whole business of Helena was laid bare for public speculation before Freddie was killed, so he left them to the privacy of their grief.

Lastly he visited the Campbells. He knew of no reason why they should have been put under pressure either, but it was always possible there was some indiscretion as yet unguessed at, although of course they would hardly be likely to tell him. But many small clues were to be found in the most guarded conversations: frequently the very guard itself was an indication of the existence of something to hide.

He saw Mariah first, since Campbell himself was busy in his study writing letters. She was very calm and expressed nothing more than a deep sympathy for Sophie. He learned nothing from her whatsoever, beyond the increasing impression that she was a strong woman who had already surmounted hardships, even griefs, and would bend herself willingly to assist Sophie to endure the shock that was overwhelming her now, and the shame which was doubtless to come.

He was obliged to wait some quarter of an hour before Garson Campbell sent for him to come to his study. He found Campbell standing in front of the fire, feet wide apart, rocking a little backward and forward. He looked angry.

"Well, Pitt, what is it?" he said tersely.

Pitt decided immediately there was no point in trying to be subtle. This was a clever and aggressive man who would see and avoid any attempt at verbal traps laid for him.

"Did you know Dr. Bolsover was a blackmailer?" he asked.

Campbell considered for a moment.

"Yes," he said slowly.

Pitt felt a quickening of excitement.

"How did you know that, sir?"

Campbell's cold gray eyes looked at him with bitter amusement. "Not because he was blackmailing me, Inspector. One of his victims came to me for advice. Naturally I cannot tell you who."

Pitt knew there was no purpose at all in pressing him. Some people he might have been able to coerce, or frighten, or even overcome by power of personality—but not Garson Campbell.

"Can you tell me what advice you gave this person?" he asked instead.

"Yes," Campbell smiled slightly. "I advised them to pay, for the time being. It was an indiscretion, not a crime. The danger of its becoming public and doing any real harm would shortly pass. I also promised to speak to Freddie and warn him that such a trick would not work a second time."

"And did you?"

"Yes."

"And what was Dr. Bolsover's reaction?"

"Not very reliable, I would think, Inspector. A man capable of blackmail would not jib at a little lying."

"Blackmail is a sneaking, underhanded crime, Mr. Campbell. A blackmailer relies on secrecy, and is usually a coward. He might well have been frightened by a more powerful man—which Mr. Southeron is not, but you are."

Campbell's eyebrows went up in amusement.

"So you knew about it?"

"Of course," Pitt allowed himself the luxury of a little arrogance.

"And you have not arrested poor Reggie? He's an awful ass. Panics very easily."

"So I notice," Pitt agreed. "But also something of a coward,

I think. And not, by any means, the only person in Callander Square who might warrant a blackmailer's attentions."

Campbell's face darkened and his big body tensed. It seemed for a moment as if a spasm of pain shot through him.

"I would be very particular what you say, Pitt. You could lay up a great deal of wrath for yourself if you make careless accusations about the people in this square. We all have our foibles, some of them no doubt unpleasant, by your standards, but we do not like them talked about. All men do what they like, as far as they dare. We have the good fortune to dare more than most; we have earned or inherited that position. Find out who killed the babies, by all means, if you must. And look into who stabbed Freddie Bolsover: but have a care for Sophie, and don't go stirring up a lot of scandal just to see what floats to the surface. You won't enhance your career, I promise you. You're a damn sight more likely to finish up back on some beat down by the dockside."

Pitt looked at his face for a moment or two. He did not doubt even for an instant that he meant precisely what he said, and that it was more than a warning.

"Freddie Bolsover was a blackmailer, sir," he answered levelly, "and blackmail feeds on scandal. I can hardly hope to discover who killed him without discovering why."

"If he was a blackmailer, he deserved to die. Perhaps for the happiness of those still in the square, it would be better if you left it at that. I have no scandal to hide, as I imagine you know by now; but there are a good many powerful men who have. For their safety, and my convenience, I would advise you not to press your dirt shoveling too far. We have had the police in Callander Square for a long time now. It is bad for us. It's time you either came to some conclusion, or gave up and left us alone. Has it occurred to you that your persistent poking around may have precipitated these tragedies, that far from doing any good, you are making worse that which was bad enough to begin with?"

"It has happened before that a murderer has committed a second crime to cover a first. That cannot be a reason for leaving him free."

"Oh, for God's sake, man, don't be so damn pious! What have you got? A servant girl who gets herself pregnant and

237

kills her babies—or buries them stillborn—a trollop whose lover tired of her, and a blackmailer! You haven't a devil's chance of finding which servant girl it was now, and who gives a damn anyway? Helena's lover is probably in another country by this time, and since apparently nobody ever even saw him, you've no better chance of hanging him than you have of swinging a noose round the moon. As for Freddie, he amply deserved it. Blackmail is a crime, even by your standards. And who's to say it was anyone in Callander Square? He had patients all over the place. Try some of them. Could be any of them. But don't blame me if they have you thrown out for it!"

Pitt left feeling more depressed than he had felt at any time since the case began. A great deal of what Campbell said was true. It was true that his presence may have precipitated both Freddie's crime and his death. And he seemed no nearer a solution to any of the deaths than he had been on the very first day.

So it was that two days later, when he was called in to his superiors and questioned rather critically about the matter, that but for Charlotte's passionate determination, he would have acceded to their pressure and admitted defeat on all but the death of Freddie Bolsover.

"We appreciate that you've done the best you can, Pitt," Sir George Smithers said irritably. "But you just haven't got anywhere, have you? We're no nearer a conclusion now than we ever were! It was a pretty long shot in the first place."

"And we need you for more important things," Colonel Anstruther added rather more civilly. "Can't waste a good man on a hopeless case."

"What about Dr. Bolsover?" Pitt asked bitingly. "Is he to be marked 'unsolved' as well? Don't you think it's a trifle soon? The public might think we weren't trying!" He was too angry to care if his tone offended them.

"There is no need to be sarcastic, Pitt," Smithers said coldly. "Of course we must make some endeavor with regard to Bolsover, although it does look rather as if the bounder got no more than he deserved. Know Reggie Southeron myself; harmless chap. A bit fond of his pleasures, but no real spite in him."

Pitt snorted at his private thought.

"Somebody stuck a knife into Bolsover," he pointed out.

"Good heavens, man, you don't imagine it was Reggie, do you?"

"No, Sir George, I don't; which is why I need to know who else Bolsover was blackmailing."

"I think that's a dangerous line of inquiry," Smithers shook his head disapprovingly. "'Cause a lot of—er—embarrassment. Better leave it alone and concentrate on the facts, get the doctor to tell you things about the body, lie of the land, find witnesses, and that sort of thing. Get at the truth that way."

"I don't think it can be done, sir," Pitt replied, meeting the man's eyes.

Smithers colored angrily at the insolence, not of the words, but of the stare.

"Then you'll have to admit defeat, won't you! But give it a try; we've got to make some appearance of doing our best."

"Even if we're not?" Pitt's temper gave way.

"Be careful, Pitt," Anstruther warned quietly. "You're sailing perilously close to the wind. Lot of important people in Callander Square. They've taken about as much as they're going to of police noising around in their private lives."

"I take it they've complained?" Pitt asked.

"Yes."

"Who?"

"Several of them, naturally I cannot tell you precisely who, might prejudice you against them, quite unfairly. Now be a good chap, go and look at the facts again. You never know, if you ask all the servants, you may be able to find one who saw something, at least know who was in and who was out; alibis, and all that."

Pitt acquiesced, because there was nothing else he could do. He left feeling angry, and close to defeat. Had it not been for the sure knowledge that Charlotte would warm him, strengthen him, and fight to the last ditch for him, he might well have considered obeying the order in spirit, as well as to the letter.

* * *

Balantyne knew nothing of the pressure that had been put upon Pitt, becuase he was the only man in the square who had not been party to instigating it. When Reggie came to see him, bubbling over with good cheer after his recent reprieve, he had no idea what it was that excited him.

"Damn good thing, what?" Reggie gulped a glass of sherry to which he had helped himself. "Be able to get back to normal soon; and about time. All that wretched business behind us."

"Hardly," Balantyne said a little stiffly. He found Reggie's joviality distasteful. "There is still the matter of four murders, apart from anything else."

"Four murders?" Reggie paled noticeably, but it was not the murders that upset him, it was the "anything else": namely the change in Adelina. The emotional comfort of his home had vanished. He was living with a stange woman he discovered he did not know at all, but who knew him painfully well, and had done so for a long time. It was a very unpleasant feeling indeed.

"Had you forgotten?" Balantyne asked coolly.

"No, no. I just hardly thought of the babies as murders. Probably born dead, what? And who knows what happened with Helena? Can't tell now, poor creature. Could have fallen on something by accident. And really, old fellow, you know, Freddie was no loss. Bounder was a blackmailer. No, far the best thing if the police ask a few questions, see if the servants saw anything; and then if they didn't, mess off and catch pickpockets, or something; anyhow, take themselves away from here."

"I hardly think they'll do that. Murder is a great deal more important than picking pockets," Balantyne said tartly.

"Well, I'm not going to help them any more," Reggie poured himself another sherry from the decanter. "If the fellow comes again I shall refuse to see him. He can talk to the servants, if he wants to. Don't like to seem uncooperative; but I'm not seeing him again myself. Told him all I know, that's an end to it." He swallowed the half glassful and breathed out with a sigh. "Finish!"

Balantyne stared at him.

"Surely you don't imagine one of the servants killed Freddie?" he said with acid disbelief.

"My dear fellow, I really don't care any more. Sooner the police give up and clear out, the better."

"They won't give up, they'll stay here until they find out who it was!"

"The hell they will! Been speaking to a few people, at the club, and what not. That Pitt fellow will be put back on the beat if he doesn't draw his horns in a bit. Just stirring up a whole lot of scandal. Takes pleasure in discomfiting his betters, that's all. All these working class chaps are the same, give them a little power and they run amok. No, don't woryy, old boy, he'll be off soon enough. Just poke around a bit, make it look as if he's trying, then after a decent period, take himself off and look for thieves again."

Balantyne was furious, a blind, incensed outrage boiled up inside him. This was a mockery of the principles he had believed in all his life: honor, dignity, justice for the living and the dead, the civilized order he had fought for and his peers had died for in the Crimea, in India, Africa, and God knew where else.

"Get out of my house, Reggie," he said levelly. "And please do not return. You are no longer welcome here. And as far as the police are concerned, I shall move everything I have, speak to every man in power, to see that they ask every question, investigate every clue until they find out the uttermost truth about everything that has happened in Callander Square, and I don't give a damn whom it hurts. Do you understand me?"

Reggie stared at him, blinking, the sherry glass in his hand.

"Y—you're drunk!" he stammered, although he knew it was not true. "You're insane! Have you any idea what harm it could do?" his voice ended in a squeak.

"Please leave, Reggie. It would make you look ridiculous to have to be thrown out."

Reggie's face darkened to crimson and he hurled the glass into the fire, splintering it into incandescent pieces. He turned on his heel and marched out, slamming the door behind him so hard the pictures teetered on the shelf and a small ornament fell over.

Balantyne stood alone for several minutes, his mind absorbing what he had done. Finally he rang the bell, and when the butler appeared, asked to have the footman fetch his coat as he was going out to see Sir Robert Carlton.

Carlton was at home, and Balantyne found him in the withdrawing room by the fire opposite Euphemia. He had never seen her look so happy, there seemed to be a warmth about her, as if she were somehow in the sunlight. Balantyne wished he had come for any other reason, but the outrage was still hot inside him.

"Good evening, Carlton; evening, Euphemia, you're looking uncommonly well."

"Good evening, Brandon." There was a slight lift of question in her voice.

"I'm sorry, Euphemia, I need to speak to Robert urgently. Will you be so generous as to excuse us?"

Euphemia stood up, a little puzzled, and obligingly left the room.

Carlton frowned, annoyance flickering across his face.

"What is it, Balantyne? It had better be important, or I will find it hard to excuse your manners. You were something less than courteous to my wife."

Balantyne was in no mood for trivialities.

"Did you use your influence to stop the police from investigating any further into the murders in this square?" he demanded.

Carlton faced him squarely, his face quite unperturbed by guilt or reserve.

"Yes, I did. I think they have done enough harm already, and no good can come of continuing to probe into our private lives and our tragedies and mistakes. They have had more than enough time to discover who gave birth to those unfortunate children, and what happened to them. There is no reasonable chance that after all this time they will discover who Helena Doran's lover was, or find him if they did. As for Freddie Bolsover, he may or may not have been a blackmailer, but on the other hand he could perfectly well have been killed by a passing robber. Better for Sophie if we suppose that and leave it alone—"

"Balderdash!" Balantyne shouted. "You know damned well he was killed by someone in this square because he pushed too hard with his blackmail, and this time he caught not some lascivious ass who played around with a maid, but a murderer."

Carlton's face tightened.

"Do you really believe that?"

"Yes, and if you're honest, so do you. I know you're afraid for Euphemia. I'm afraid too. But I'm a damn sight more afraid of what I'll turn into if I try to cover this up—"

"Freddie was a blackmailer," Carlton said less certainly. "Let the wretch lie in peace, for Sophie's sake, if nothing else."

"Stop deceiving yourself, Robert. Whatever he was, his murder cannot be disregarded, swept away because it is ugly and its investigation is inconvenient to us. What the hell do you believe in, man? Have you nothing left but comfort?"

Carlton's head came up sharply, his eyes blazing: but he had no defense. He opened his mouth to speak, but words evaded him. Balantyne did not flinch, and eventually it was Carlton who looked down.

"I'll speak to the Home Secretary tomorrow," he said quietly.

"Good."

"I don't know what good it will do. Campbell and Reggie are pulling pretty hard for it to be closed. Reggie is afraid for himself, of course; but I think Campbell is sorry for Sophie. Pretty frightful for her, poor girl. Mariah's been taking care of her; very capable woman, Mariah; always seems to know what to do in a crisis. But nothing could protect Sophie from the disgrace if this is made public."

"I'm glad there is someone who can keep their head," Balantyne could not resist a last cruelly honest jibe, his anger was still too hot. "I am sorry for Sophie, but the truth cannot be changed. Give my apologies to Euphemia," he said, and then turned and left. When he had spoken to Brandy and Augusta, told them his feelings, he would be drained of anger. Then he could come back, perhaps tomorrow, and make his peace with Carlton. In the future, when he was needed, he would help Sophie.

When he reached his own hallway he was surprised by the footman telling him Miss Ellison had called to see him. He was annoyed, disconcerted. He was far from at his best, and he did not wish her to see him in these circumstances. The footman was staring at him, and his brain could manufacture no excuse.

She was waiting for him in the study. She turned as he came in, and at sight of her face he remembered how much she pleased him, how clear and gentle were the lines of her face, passion without guile. There was nothing sophisticated in her, and it was both restful and exciting to him.

"Charlotte, my dear," he went over toward her, holding out his hands, meaning to take hers, but she held back. "What is it?" She had changed and he was afraid of it; he did not want anything in her to be different.

"General Balantyne," she said a little formally. There was color in her cheeks and she looked uncomfortable, but she did not avoid his eyes. She took a deep breath. "I am afraid I have lied to you. Emily Ashworth is my sister, but I am not unmarried, as I allowed you to believe. Ellison was my maiden name, I am Charlotte Pitt—"

At first the name meant nothing to him, he could see no reason for the deception. Had she imagined he would not employ her if she were married?

"Inspector Pitt is my husband," she said simply. "I came here because I wanted to find out about the babies, and, if they were stillborn, to offer some support to the mother. Now I want to help Jemima. Mr. Southeron has charged that she blackmailed him, and then killed Dr. Bolsover in a quarrel over the money. If Thomas is called off the case and no one ever discovers who did kill Dr. Bolsover, she will have that hanging over her all her life."

"You are married to Pitt," he frowned, "the policeman?"

"Yes. I'm sorry for having deceived you. I never imagined at the time that it could matter. But please, think whatever you like of me, but don't let them prevent Thomas from finding out the truth, at least about Dr. Bolsover. It is wrong to accuse someone, and then leave it unproved. If Jemima had been his social equal, he would not have dared. He only said it because he knew she could neither defend herself, nor attack him in return."

He felt an illusion slip away from him, and a new value take its place. The dream had been fragile, and foolish; he had not named it even to himself. Now the thing in its place was a warm, gentle pain, the kind that becomes a familiar companion in time, part of one's growing.

He sighed very slowly. "I have already been to see Sir Robert Carlton. That is where I was when you came. He will speak to the Home Secretary tomorrow."

The smile started in her eyes and her mouth till it seemed to fill all of her, even to the way she stood, very straight, but with a grace, an ease to the line of her body.

"I am glad," she said quietly. "I apologize for not having known that you would." She gathered her cloak a little closer round her and moved past him.

He let her go, he was too full to speak. The compliment, the trust burned inside him more fiercely than in any sweet moment of youth.

He stood alone for a long time in the room before he finally sent for Brandy.

When Brandy came in he was ready for him.

"I have been this evening to see Robert Carlton," he began straight away. "I persuaded him to speak to the Home Secretary to permit the police to continue to investigate the murders in the square, however long it may be, or however painful, before they discover the truth. Since Freddie Bolsover was a blackmailer, it is highly likely that was the motive for his death. The police will naturally have to pursue that—no, don't interrupt me, Brandon. I am telling you because they will doubtless come to this house again. They are already aware of Christina's folly with Max. If there is anything you have done that would make you vulnerable to pressure, I advise you to tell me now, and then the police. If it has nothing to do with Freddie, I daresay they will be discreet about it."

"They already know," Brandy replied soberly. "It seems they are extremely thorough, in everything except the actual murders! But thank you for the warning." He looked away. "I'm glad you did that. Reggie accused Jemima of having blackmailed him, and then of having killed Freddie over the money. I intend to see him in hell for that."

"How do you know?" Balantyne demanded.

Brandy looked back at him.

"Inspector Pitt told me. I'm sorry about that, Father." Then sensing Balantyne's embarrassment, he spoke quite casually. "Do you want to see Mother? You'd better warn her as well, she does rather tend to take things into her own hands!"

Balantyne winced at the memory of Max. He did not really want to see Augusta tonight. There was a lot he wished to say to her, but not yet. Presently, perhaps, when he better understood himself.

"No, thank you," he replied. "You can tell her, if you don't mind. I don't think it will be necessary to warn her, but it would be a courtesy."

Brandy hesitated a moment, then smiled.

"Right," he turned and went to the door. "Thank you for not exploding over Jemima. I mean to marry her, if she'll have me. I dare say Mother won't be pleased, but she'll accommodate it in time, if you do."

"I didn't say—!" but Brandy was gone, and there was nothing for Balantyne to do but stare at the door after him. Perhaps it was not such a monstrous thought; it was not as if she were a servant, indeed she was not so very unlike Charlotte—but that was another dream he would prefer not to contemplate tonight.

It was after lunch the next day when he saw Alan Ross at his club. Quite naturally, since Alan was both friend and son-in-law, he went over to speak to him.

"Afternoon, Alan, how are you? Christina well?"

"Good afternoon, sir. Yes, in fine health, thank you. And you?"

"Excellent." What a stilted conversation. Why could he not say what he meant? Had he not learned that much at least from Charlotte? "No, that's not true. You heard about Freddie Bolsover?"

Ross frowned.

"Yes. Somebody spoke of blackmail; is that true?"

"Yes, I'm afraid so. There's been a concerted effort round the square to stop the police from investigating it any further, for fear of digging up a lot of scandal, I presume, although of course those are not the motives given. I suppose everyone has something they would prefer not known; something sordid, or foolish, or just acutely private."

Ross made a small face of agreement. Then he looked up as if he had thought of something to say. Balantyne waited, but apparently the words eluded him. They spoke of trivialities for a little while, then Balantyne drew them back to Callander Square, feeling Ross still wished to speak to him.

Again Ross hesitated.

"Is there something you know that I don't?" Balantyne asked quietly, commanding Ross's attention with his eyes.

"No," Ross shook his head, a tiny, rueful smile at the corner of his mouth. "It is something we both know; but I imagine you are not aware of it."

Balantyne was puzzled, but he had as yet no sense of misgiving.

"Then if I already know, why are you having such difficulty finding the words for it?" he asked. "And why the need to speak of it at all?"

For the first time Ross really met his eyes, without veil or deception.

"Because you may otherwise go to some lengths to keep it from me."

Balantyne stared.

"Christina," Ross replied. "I am perfectly aware of her liaison with Max, and the reason for her somewhat precipitate pursuit of me. No, there's no need to look like that. I knew at the time. I don't mind. I loved Helena, and I shall never love anyone else. I have a high regard for you; and, it may surprise you, for Lady Augusta also. I was quite willing to be of use to Christina. I shall never love her, but I shall be a good husband to her; and I intend to see that she is a good wife to me: as good as our feelings, or lack of them, will permit. There is still an honorable way to behave, love or not." He looked down for a moment, then up again. "What I am trying to say is that there is no need to fear my hearing

247

of the affair and treating Christina any differently." The smile warmed his eyes. "Also, I am very fond of Brandy. Although he has tended to avoid me since my engagement. I think perhaps his conscience is affecting him. He was not born for deceit and it sits ill with him."

Balantyne would have defended himself against the implication of his own deceit, but it was true and he had no defense; and also there was no criticism in Ross's face. He had a sudden feeling that Ross was a better man than Christina deserved, a man he both liked and respected himself.

"Thank you," he said warmly. "You could well have let me stew in fear, even betray myself, and have been justified. It is a great kindness that you do not. I hope in time you will learn to forgive us, not only in charity, but in understanding; although I have no right to ask."

"I might well have done the same," Ross brushed it away. "Might yet, if I have children. Join me in a glass of claret?"

"Thank you," Balantyne accepted with real pleasure, and a sense of ease inside himself. "Yes, I will."

When Pitt was called again to Colonel Anstruther's presence he was surprised and relieved to be told that there had been a change of directive from the Home Office, and he was to proceed with his inquiries into all the matters to do with Callander Square. He was surprised, because he had not expected a change of heart, not knowing Charlotte had visited General Balantyne, nor expecting there to have been any results had he been fully conversant with it; and relieved because he had had every intention of pursuing it to the last clue whatever anyone said. Although of course it would have had to be done in roundabout fashion, and largely in his own time, both of which would have been awkward. He did not wish to run the risk of serious demotion for disobedience, and he would very much rather have spent such free time as he had at home with Charlotte, particularly now when she had but four months to go till the birth of their first child.

Therefore it was with a feeling almost of excitement that he ran down the steps and hailed a cab to take him, post haste, back to Callander Square.

Sitting, jolting over the rough paving, he gave his mind to going over, yet again, all that he knew.

He had no doubt in his own mind that Freddie Bolsover had been killed because of his blackmailing; whether or not he had ever actually used the information that had brought about his death, the mere knowledge of it had been fatal to him, the danger of his using it too great for someone to permit. It had been a daring and urgent murder. The murderer had considered his position in imminent peril. What could Freddie have known? Some affair, some illegitimate child? Hardly. With all the other scandals in Callander Square that barely seemed a matter over which to risk murder. Had he known who was the mother, or more likely the father, of the babies buried in the gardens? Certainly not from the beginning, or he would either have used the information sooner, or been killed sooner—

Unless of course he had only just discovered it!

Or there was another possibility—that the murderer had only just discovered that Freddie knew: Freddie had either never intended to use the information, knowing it was too dangerous, or else not understood its meaning. Yes, that made sense. The murderer had killed him so precipitately before he could learn the value of what he knew!

He had arrived at Callander Square and was standing huddled in his coat, collar up, watching the cab clop away into the mist before he realized the last possibility—that it was the knowledge that Freddie had blackmailed Reggie Southeron that had woken the murderer to his own danger! That was the most promising, it gave a precise point at which he could start.

He crossed the square over the muddy gardens, past where the babies had been found, and where Freddie Bolsover had lain; his feet rang hollowly on the road again, the pavement, and up the steps to Reggie Southeron's house.

Since it was a cold and thoroughly unpleasant day Reggie had not troubled to go to the bank, however he sent a message that he would not see the police any further, nor permit the rest of his household to do so.

Pitt replied to the footman that he had authorization from the Home Office, and if Mr. Southeron made it necessary for him to return with a warrant, then he would do so, but in view of the fact that nobody else in the square had yet behaved in such a way—true so far as it went, he had called on no one else—it might prove more embarrassing for Mr. Southeron than for him!

Ten minutes later Reggie appeared, red-faced and extremely angry.

"Who in hell do you think you are, quoting the Home Secretary at me?" he demanded, slamming the door behind him.

"Good morning, sir," Pitt answered courteously. "There is only one thing I would appreciate knowing, and that is, who else did you confide in about Dr. Bolsover's attempts to blackmail you?"

"No one. Hardly the sort of thing you go telling your friends!" Reggie said sharply. "Idiotic question!"

"That's odd, Mr. Campbell told me you mentioned it to him, and asked his advice." Pitt raised his eyebrows.

"Damned fool!" Reggie swore. "Well, daresay I did. Must have, if he says so."

"Who else? It is rather important, sir."

"Why? Why in hell should it matter now?"

"You seem to have forgotten, Mr. Southeron, that there is a murderer still in Callander Square. He has killed once, maybe more. He may kill again, if he feels threatened. Does that not frighten you at all? It could be the next friend you speak to as you walk to your own door, the next muffled figure to bid you good night, then stick a knife into you. Dr. Bolsover was stabbed in the front, by someone he knew and trusted, not twenty yards from his own house. Does that not disturb you? It would me."

"All right!" Reggie's voice rose sharply. "All right! I didn't speak to anyone but Campbell. Carlton is as stuffy as hell, and Balantyne is hardly any better, there's no man in the Doran house, and Housman, the old buzzard at the other end, never speaks to anybody. Campbell's a pretty useful fellow, and not too self-righteous or scared of his own shadow to do anything. I told him. And he stopped it, too!"

"Indeed," Pitt invested it with more meaning than Reggie understood. "Thank you, sir. That may be most helpful."

"I'm damned if I can see how!"

"If it does turn out so, you will know eventually; and if not, it hardly matters," Pitt replied. "Thank you sir. Good morning."

"Morning," Reggie answered with a frown. "Silly ass," he muttered to himself. "Footman will show you out."

Pitt still did not know what he was looking for, but at long last he thought he at least knew where to look.

He knocked at the Campbells' door and asked permission to speak to Mr. Campbell. He was admitted and shown into the morning room where Mariah was writing letters.

"Good morning, ma'am," he said, hiding his surprise.

"Good morning, Mr. Pitt. My husband is engaged at the moment, but he should be able to see you in a short while, if you do not mind waiting."

"Not at all, thank you."

"Would you care for some refreshment?"

"No, thank you. Please do not let me disturb you."

"Did you come to see my husband about the murder of Dr. Bolsover?"

"In part."

Her face was very pale. Perhaps she was not well this morning, or was the strain of comforting Sophie beginning to tell on her?

"Why should my husband know anything about it?" she asked.

There was nothing to be gained by avoiding the truth. She might even inadvertently help him. Possibly she had learned something from Sophie, without knowing its meaning.

"He was the only person in whom Mr. Southeron confided that Dr. Bolsover was blackmailing him," he replied.

"Reggie told Garson?" she said slowly. She looked very white. Pitt was afraid she might faint. Was she indeed ill, or did she know something of her husband that he had not even guessed at?

The answer came instantly.

Helena!

An older man, successful, sure of himself, with dignity, power, not free to marry her—was he the lover? His mind raced over a whole new spectrum of possibilities. But why murder? Was she about to betray him, charge him openly with being the father of her child? Had he panicked and killed her in that deserted garden?

Mariah was watching him. Her face was quite still, eyes clear. She looked like a woman facing execution; but a woman not afraid of death.

"Yes," he replied to her question that seemed hours ago.

"I see," she stood up and gathered her skirts. "Thank you for telling me, Mr. Pitt. I have something to do upstairs. Will you excuse me? My husband will be with you shortly." And without waiting for his reply she walked slowly out of the room, back very straight, head high.

It was another ten minutes before Garson Campbell came in. Pitt had supposed him to be only in another room of the house, but he stamped his feet when he walked, as if he had been out in the cold. Yet he did not rub his hands.

"Well, what is it, Pitt?" he asked, looking him up and down with distaste. "I don't know anything more about Freddie Bolsover that I did before." He stood in front of the fire, feet spread wide apart, rocking a little backward and forward.

Something stirred at the back of Pitt's mind, a man he had seen a long time ago and in some different place, a man who walked stamping his feet, even in the summer, a sick man. The picture of the little bodies in the gardens came back, the swollen head of the deeper one. He remembered Helena's child.

In a shattering instant the answer was there in his brain, as clear and simple as a child's picture.

"Dr. Bolsover knew you had syphilis, didn't he?" he said simply. "When Reggie Southeron told you Freddie had blackmailed him, you realized it was only a matter of time before Freddie also realized the value of what he knew, and tried to blackmail you. You killed him before he could do that. Just as you killed Helena, before her child could be born deformed, like the ones in the square. Or else she discovered your disease, and you could not trust her to keep silent. Not that it matters which it was now."

For an instant indecision wavered in Campbell's eyes, then he saw the certainty of knowledge in Pitt, and his face distorted with rage.

"You bloody smiling hypocrite," he said in a quiet, bitter voice. "I've been tainted, crippled in mind with this disease since I was thirty years old. Fifteen years I've been carrying the beginning of death in me. And there's no quick end, I shall rot from the inside, slowly. The pains will get worse and worse till I'm paralyzed, a filthy vegetable being wheeled round in a chair, for people to whisper and snigger at! And you stand there moralizing, as if you would be any different!

"Yes, you're right! Are you satisfied? Even my own wife looks at me as if I were a leper. She hasn't touched me in over a year. Helena was a whore. When she found out about the disease she became hysterical, and I killed her.

"Freddie was a sniveling little blackmailer. Of course I killed him; it was only a matter of time till he came to me." His hand was behind him, and before Pitt realized what he was doing, he swung round with the paper knife from the desk where Mariah had been writing, the blade swinging in an arc and missing Pitt's chest only when he himself lunged forward, slipped on the edge of the carpet, and fell heavily, hitting Campbell and sending them both crashing into the fireplace.

Pitt scrambled to his feet, ready to strike again—but Campbell lay motionless. At first Pitt suspected a trick, until he saw Campbell's head against the fender, and the small patch of blood.

He went to the door and shouted for the footman, his voice sounding loud and stupidly hysterical.

"Go out and get a police constable," he said as soon as the man appeared. "And a doctor, quickly!"

The man gaped at him without moving.

"Get on with it!" Pitt yelled at him.

The man shot out of the door without even bothering with a coat.

Pitt went back into the morning room and yanked the bellcord out of its socket. He knew there would be a fearful jangling downstairs, but he did not care. With the length of cord he bound Campbell's wrists as tightly as he could, then left him lying on his back, still apparently unconscious, but breathing heavily.

He considered finding Mariah, but decided it would be

253

kinder to have Campbell removed first, especially should he choose to make a scene. It would be distressing enough for her without her being obliged to witness his actual arrest.

He sat down, out of reach of Campbell's legs, in case he recovered and decided to fight again, and waited.

It was some ten minutes before the constable arrived, panting, wet from the fine rain, red in the face. He stared at Pitt, then at Campbell, still on the floor, but regaining consciousness now.

"Doctor's coming, sir," he said with some bewilderment. "What's 'appened?"

"Mr. Campbell is under arrest," Pitt replied. He looked across at the footman who was still standing beyond the constable, in the open doorway. "Call a hansom, and tell the valet to pack some things for Mr. Campbell. When the doctor comes, show him in here." He turned back to the constable. "Mr. Campbell is charged with murder, and he's dangerous. If you have handcuffs, put them on him before you remove my cords! When the doctor has seen him, put him in the cab and take him to the station." He put his hand in his pocket and pulled out his identification, showing it to him. "I'll be along as soon as I've seen Mrs. Campbell. Do you understand?"

The constable jerked to attention.

"Yes, sir! Is 'e the one 'wot done the 'orrible murders o' them babies, sir?"

"I don't know. I don't think so, but he killed Dr. Bolsover, and Miss Doran. Be careful of him."

"Yes, sir, I will that." He glanced down at Campbell with a mixture of awe and disgust.

Pitt went to the door and was across the hall and halfway up the stairs when the doctor arrived. He waited on the landing for five minutes more till he saw the party go out, Campbell still dizzy, stumbling between the constable and the cabbie. Then he continued on upward to find Mariah.

The second floor was tidy and silent. He could not even see a maid. They must all be in the kitchen, or at some outside task.

"Mrs. Campbell?" he said clearly.

There was no answer.

254

He raised his voice and called again.

Still no reply.

He knocked on the first door and tried it. The room was empty. He continued until he came to what was apparently a woman's dressing room. Mariah Campbell was sitting in an easy chair, facing away from him. At first he thought she had fallen asleep, until he walked round and saw her face. It was bleached of all color, and there was a grayness to the eyelids and lips.

On the dressing table there was a small bottle labeled for laudanum, empty, and another clear glass vial that also held nothing now. Beside them was a piece of paper. He picked it up. It was addressed to him.

> Inspector Pitt,
> I imagine you know the truth by now. The sins of the fathers were visited upon the children, but they were my children too, and I could not let them live, rotted by disease, filthy as he was. Better to die while they were still innocent, and knew nothing of it, neither pain.
> Please ask Adelina Southeron to look after my children that yet live. She is a good woman, and will have pity on them.
> May God find mercy for me, and peace.
>
> Mariah Livingstone Campbell

Pitt looked down at her and felt overwhelming pity, and gratitude that she had spared him from having to face her, to be the instrument to begin the long course of public justice against her.

Because he loved Charlotte so deeply, he felt some gentleness toward all women; and was unutterably glad that his own life was not scorched and marred by such tragedy. He thought of Charlotte's face, full of hope for her new child, and prayed that it would be whole, perhaps even that it would be a girl, another stubborn, compassionate, willful creature like Charlotte herself.

He smiled at the thought, and yet in front of this dead woman he also felt like weeping. More than anything else, he desperately wanted to go home.